The Farthest Star

SALLY GLOVER

The Farthest Star

Copyright © 2023 by Sally Glover
Print Edition

ISBN
978-1-7386620-3-6 (ebook)
978-1-7386620-5-0 (paperback)

BOOKS BY SALLY GLOVER

The Farthest Star

Second Chance Rose

CHAPTER 1

Domino

"Does everyone have the agenda in front of them?" My producing partner Trudi's round face loomed large on my computer screen, her big brown eyes slightly magnified by the lenses of her glasses.

Outside, two Mexican fan palms swayed gently in January sunshine, their deep-green, accordion-like fronds fanning in the breeze. Watching their skinny, towering trunks weave back and forth reminded me of the stick figures that flailed around the used car dealerships near the Santa Monica Freeway. I shivered, despite the bright sun. After four years in Los Angeles, I was acclimated to the weather, and temperatures in the upper sixties felt as cold to me now as the low twenties typical of winter in Toronto, where I grew up.

Across the top of my monitor was a row of five small squares, each of which pictured another attendee of our weekly production meeting. My own face was reflected back in one little box, the name Allie Hamilton in small caps across the bottom. A nod to *The Notebook*, I'd used the alias to stay incognito in hotels and online for years, including in the videoconferencing software we were using today.

"Okay, let's proceed," Trudi continued when it was clear the others on the call were distracted by their phones, their cats—really anything other than the business at hand: preproduction on *Shore Thing*. This was the first movie Trudi and I were producing ourselves—and it had to go well if we had any chance of doing others. "Domino, I'll let you start with script details."

I gave the group a bright smile. "As you know, the script was pretty good when we acquired it. But I hired two writers to punch it up and get it ready to pitch. We should have their input by January seventeenth." Trudi nodded back at me, and most of the others bobbed their heads, some with barely a glance at the screen. "Any questions?"

"I need to see it now." Arthur Dagon's gravelly

voice boomed through my speakers. Even on a video call, his face was beet-red, his expression harried. His statement marked the first time I'd seen him actually look at his monitor; the first few minutes of the call he'd spent with his attention elsewhere, on what he obviously considered more important things. Arthur had a reputation for being quick to anger and demanding of talent, but he was one of the best directors in Hollywood, and I knew it was a win to have his interest in my film.

I smiled again, nodding with zeal, hoping it hid my nerves. No matter how many movies I'd acted in or nominations I got, I was still a people-pleaser, and this guy was notoriously hard to please. "I love the enthusiasm, Arthur," I said cheerfully. "Like I said, the script will be ready in a week and a half." I watched in panic as his face grew even redder, like a roasted cherry tomato about to burst. Worst of all, though, he was silent. What did that mean? He could wait a week and a half? He was about to fly into a rage? Or maybe—best-case scenario—his screen was frozen.

The other participants on the call were suddenly hyper-focused, five sets of eyes boring into me. Everyone paid attention when Arthur Dagon blew a fuse.

Trudi came to my defense. "It's a good script, and

we're excited for you all to read it—when it's ready."
She held up a hand when Arthur looked ready to
pounce. I half expected steam to blow from his ears.
"No exceptions. We'd like it finalized before anyone
else sees it." She continued on before he had a chance
to interject. "Moving to budget. Alex, can you give us
an update?"

Alex Falcon was a finance expert who'd copro-
duced my last movie, *Love Letters*. As she began to
break down the funding she'd secured, her hot-pink
glasses perched on the end of her nose, my attention
wavered. There was a reason I did the acting and Alex
the numbers: I sucked at math. Actually, I didn't just
suck at it; it put me to sleep. Which became something
of a joke at school when my tenth-grade teacher
slapped a yardstick across my desk to curb my math-
induced daydreams more than once that year.

A patch of sun glinted off the gold popcorn atop
the MTV Movie Award for Best Kiss I'd won for *Love
Letters*. The award anchored one end of the shelves on
the wall across from my desk. Correction: the award
we'd won—as in me and Harry Roman, my boyfriend
of the past eighteen months. We'd met on set. He was
a handsome pop star–turned–actor with a flop of
brown hair and an impish grin, and I was "that
Canadian actress" who'd made it in Hollywood. Of
course I knew who he was long before we met during

screen tests for *Love Letters*—I'd been to one of his concerts at the big arena back home. But nothing had prepared me for the charm and magnetism he exuded in person.

Other mementos from various projects dotted the shelves of the office in the house I rented near Venice Beach. I'd been reluctant to hang pictures in the house—something about it felt temporary—so several framed movie posters sat propped against the wall. At the edge of my desk was the straw bowler hat I'd worn in *The Muse*.

The sound of Trudi clearing her throat, somewhat pointedly, brought me back to the meeting, where she looked at me expectantly. Alex's expression hinted she was waiting for some kind of answer. The eyes of the three others on the call, including Arthur's, were glazed over. At least I wasn't alone.

"Ah, right." Now it was my turn to clear my throat. "Sorry, could you repeat the question?"

Alex used her pointer finger to push her glasses back on her nose. "That's what we were wondering. Do *you* have any questions?"

"No? No. That was all very clear. Thank you, Alex." I tried to project confidence. "So what's next?"

"Last, and probably most important, we have an update." She took off her glasses and, her fingers clasping one of the arms, spun them around in a circle.

"Emery, you can share the news."

"A little sugar to help the medicine go down, huh." Our casting director grinned, his teeth stark-white against his dark brown skin. "Well, now the money talk is out of the way, I'm excited to share Damon Mann is committed to *Shore Thing*."

Trudi fist-bumped the air. Marc clasped his hands together in excitement. Arthur grunted his approval. Even the normally serious Alex let out a little whoop of joy. "Incredible!" I cried. Hot off the success of the latest Star Force movie, Damon Mann was one of the biggest actors in Hollywood. "Great job, Emery. I knew we'd land the right person once you came on board."

Emery laughed. "That's why you pay me the big bucks." Alex squirmed a little. "Right, Alex?"

A beat of uncomfortable silence followed.

Trudi laughed, too, easing the tension. "We all know you're worth it. Having Damon Mann attached means everyone wins." Marc, our location manager, had picked up his phone and was tapping away furiously. Trudi and I exchanged a loaded glance.

Her eyebrows drew together, her lips pursed thin. "A reminder for everyone—anything we discuss here is strictly confidential. The NDAs you all signed bind you to that." Marc stopped typing immediately, and a loud thud indicated he'd dropped his phone on his desk, his cheeks flushed.

My phone buzzed with an incoming text. I was mindful of Trudi's directive, but I'd been waiting to hear from Harry all morning. I reached to my right and slowly dragged it from the far side of my desk to directly in front of me without taking my eyes from the meeting. I held it up at monitor height and swiped to unlock the screen. Seeing Harry's name, my heart did a little skip. I tapped the messages icon to open it, my eyes darting quickly from the meeting to my phone.

Hey, his text read. **It's been fun hanging out with you.**

I quickly looked back at my monitor, where Marc had started speaking. What a weird way to start a text. As covertly as I could, I tapped a message back, even though three dots hung in the chat, indicating Harry was still typing something. **Aww. I love hanging with you too,** I wrote, followed by the smiling face with three hearts emoji.

But I don't think we're meant to be together.

My heart dropped to my feet, and a whoosh of blood raced through my body, my pulse jumping. I felt my ears burn with embarrassment, and my jaw dropped open as I stared at the phone. Out went any pretense of being immersed in the meeting. I no longer even heard voices, just the steady *thwap, thwap, thwap* of my heart beating against my rib cage. Was I just dumped?

Don't react don't react don't react, I desperately willed before my lizard brain took control of my thoughts. **WTF,** I typed back, fingers flying across the keyboard. **You couldn't tell me this in person? I deserve—**

Midresponse, the message chain disappeared from my phone. Like, disappeared. *No fucking way*, I thought. He deleted me? I felt my shame morph into burning hot anger in the pit of my stomach. How dare he? The past eighteen months of my life were ending with *this*? No way. No fucking way.

"Domino? Domino!"

I was stunned back to attention by Trudi calling my name, concern evident in her pretty round face. *Oh shit.* I drew in a breath and tried to steel my nerves, schooling that wide smile back into place. You know that saying, smile your way to feeling happy? No way was it going to work in this scenario. Fat fucking chance. "Uh huh?"

"Didn't you hear me? Marc is suggesting an island off Washington State to shoot the movie. Of course someone will have to go and—"

"I'll do it." Had I shouted that? It'd seemed extraordinarily loud in my earbuds. From the looks on everyone's faces, it had surprised them, too.

Not a single strand of Marc's silver hair moved as he shook his head. "Oh, that's okay, Domino. You don't have to—"

"I want to."

"But wouldn't you rather I go first before you..."

Marc's words trailed off when he absorbed the hard determination on my face—mixed, I was sure, with the fury I was feeling inside. "Nope, I'll do it. Where is it, again?" I could tell Trudi was desperate to interject, but instead she pinched her lips in a tight line.

"Orcas Island," Marc said. "About eighty-five miles north of Seattle. Heard of Bellingham?"

I nodded. I had cousins who lived in Bellingham. And spoke miserably of it, I remembered.

"Orcas is smack-dab between there and Vancouver Island. You know. You're from Canada, right?"

I nodded again. I didn't know much of Vancouver Island or about things being smack-dab, but I had a general sense: I'd be heading to the edge of nowhere in the Pacific Northwest, where no one knew me or Harry Roman. It sounded perfect.

"When can I leave?"

To her credit, Trudi kept her cool, although her eyebrows shot up so high on her forehead it looked like she'd stuck her finger in a socket. But she simply nodded, as if it was always the plan.

"As soon as possible, really," Marc said. "I'd planned on leaving next week—"

"Perfect," I interjected. "It gives me something to

focus on while we're waiting for the script." And something to think about other than Harry fucking Roman. My heart rate sped up again, and I didn't know which urge was stronger: to scream and cry or to throw my phone at the wall as hard as I could. If there was one thing I knew how to do, though, it was act my way through a stressful situation. "I'll book it as soon as we're done here," I said, voice as steady as I could manage.

Marc's disappointment was obvious in the droop of his shoulders.

"If it feels right, Marc, you can come out and join me, help work with the locals. They probably don't get many shoots there. We'll have to do a lot of groundwork."

He sat up a little straighter. "I'll wait for your go," he said, nodding.

"That's settled then. Thank you, Marc." Trudi ran a hand through her thick brown hair, tucking it behind an ear. "And thank you all for coming this morning. I know everyone's busy." Alex's and Emery's heads bobbed in their little squares on the screen.

"You bet," Emery said.

"Happy to be here," Marc added.

Arthur's square went black. Nice. So far everything I'd heard about Arthur Dagon was proving true: he was an inpatient, gruff, ill-tempered man with the manners of a gorilla. But if it meant the difference between a Rotten or Fresh rating for *Shore Thing* on Rotten Tomatoes, I could overlook his personality defects.

"Thank *you*, Trudi. See you next time."

Just as I readied to hit End to close the meeting, finger hovering above the mouse, Marc spoke up. "Let us know how the location scout goes, yah?"

"Will do!" I said with every ounce of cheer I could muster before I tapped once to exit the call—and enter my new reality as the losing half of one of Hollywood's hottest couples. Correction: *Former* couples.

I headed downstairs in search of... I didn't know what, exactly. Something to dull the pain. Tequila, truthfully. But at ten forty-five on a Tuesday morning, sugar would have to do. I rummaged around the pantry, tossing aside packages of hemp seeds and quinoa, rolled oats and three different types of lentils, growing more frustrated by the second. When I dropped a bag of coconut flour and it burst apart at the seams, I slid to the floor in a cloud of creamy-white dust.

"Fuuuuuuuck!" I shouted at no one. A series of pings in my back pocket only meant one thing: word was out. I rested my elbows on bent knees and, leaning forward, buried my face in my hands. *Ping*

ping, ping. Ping. The influx continued.

Hot tears dripped through my fingers and onto the flour that surrounded me, forming a little puddle of paste on the floor, like the papier-maché we'd used in grade-school art class. Reality was taking hold in the pit of my stomach. I'd lost my boyfriend. I'd taken on the responsibility of finding a location for one of the most important movies of my career. And I'd committed to traveling somewhere I'd never been, by myself, post-breakup.

I let myself wallow until my ass felt numb and the pinging of my phone became more annoying than my self-pity. I lifted my head, smoothed my bangs into place, and wiped the tears and snot from my cheeks with the back of my sleeve. *Ice cream.* I was momentarily buoyed when I remembered burying a half-eaten pint of pistachio ice cream in the freezer last month.

I dusted the flour from my jeans and pushed to stand, surveying the mess around me. It could wait. I had sugar to eat and plans to make.

CHAPTER 2
Forest

Mug in hand, I moved to the bank of windows that looked out on the marina. It was still dark, dreary, and without solace as far as I could see. With hours to go before dawn, fueled by Italian coffee and Fern's optimism, I headed down to the basement to try and figure out why I was intermittently blasted with cold water every time I took a shower.

The steady drip, drip, drip of water hitting the bucket next to my bed was definitely louder at three a.m. than it had been at two. I'd thought about getting up each time the clock on the bedside table turned over a new hour, but what good would that do?

Morning wouldn't come any faster. So instead I tossed and turned, alternating between peering through the dark at the water stain on the ceiling and closing my eyes and counting ten deep breaths, hoping to ease the anxiety that vibrated through me. The inn had forty-three other rooms, but I wasn't about to decamp to any of them. This one and the problems it had were a sign of what was to come if we didn't make changes—soon.

January on Orcas Island was gray and cold and relentlessly rainy. Which meant no tourists—and no guests at the Driftwood Inn. I'd reminded myself eleven times in the past hour that was a blessing in disguise. No guests meant no bad reviews—which were all but guaranteed when you had a leaky roof, a faulty hot-water system, and glitchy Wi-Fi.

As a kid I'd dreamed of taking over the hotel. My parents had put my sister and me to work the minute we were tall enough to see over the desk in the lobby. In its prime, the Driftwood was the jewel of Orcas, a place families returned to year after year to make memories on the beaches, trails, and woods that covered the island. It had seemed like nothing ever went wrong—and nothing ever would. So when Jack and Judy Russo retired to Yuma, Arizona, three years ago, Fern and I jumped at the chance to take over.

But three years of deferred maintenance, so we

could overhaul the old electrical wiring—which we'd thought was a brilliant strategy back then—was turning my dream into a nightmare.

Wind rattled the windows of room 502, which on a good day overlooked Bayview marina and the surrounding San Juan Islands. This time of year, when the clouds were the color of battleships and heavy with rain, you were lucky to see across East Sound to the other side of Orcas. I found myself counting the rhythmic drips as they hit the bucket, hoping it might lull me to sleep.

At 4:25 a.m. I heard the elevator descend, signaling Fern couldn't sleep, either. I threw back the comforter and turned on the bedside lamp, rubbing my tired eyes with the backs of my hands. I reached for the jeans I'd slung over the chair and grabbed a sweater from the closet, figuring we'd keep each other company in our misery.

My sister was behind the bar in the hotel's dining room, pulling espresso shots from the La Marzocco machine we'd splurged on when we took over the Driftwood. The Pacific Northwest had a reputation for good coffee, a tradition we wanted to uphold. Fern was an expert on all things drink-related, and the Italian-made machine was the first change she'd made when we took over.

"One shot or two?" she asked without turning to

look at me. A row of pendant lights illuminated where she stood. Her long blonde hair, usually shiny and neat, hung in a low braid, strands sticking out every which way, glowing around her like a halo.

"Two at least. To start." I pulled out a barstool, its legs scraping the wood floor. On ground level like this, the noise of halyards clanging on the masts of the boats moored at the marina was constant. Through the windows I watched them sway left, then right in near unison, at the mercy of the waves heaving below them. Beams of light from the lamps that lined the docks appeared to flicker as torrents of wind and rain crossed under them.

"So what are we gonna do?" Fern set down a steaming cup on the bar in front of me before reaching for her own and inhaling its rich scent.

I scrubbed a hand over my forehead, pushing through my short brown hair. "Hell if I know. Drink this Americano." I blew cool air across the top of the mug. "I'd say sell that machine, but I think you'd go with it if I did."

Fern laughed. "You don't fool me, brother. I see the look on your face every morning when you take that first sip. Strikes me it's the only thing keeping us going right now." She put down her mug on the bar. "Wind keep you up, too?"

Fern's room was on the fourth floor, below mine

and over one. There was no roof over hers to spring a leak, just the ceiling of the floor above. I debated whether to break the news now or wait until the second cup of coffee. Seeing the shadowed half-moons under her eyes, I decided on the latter. "Mm-hmm," I said instead.

She rustled around on the counter behind the bar until she found what she was looking for. Grasping a rolled-up *Inside Hollywood* magazine, she shuffled around to my side and dragged out the stool next to mine, hiking up her sweatpants before she plonked herself down.

I shook my head, and a "pfffffft" escaped me before I could stop it. I couldn't help it. To my mind there was no bigger waste of time than caring about fake strangers you didn't even know, just because some PR firm made you think you did.

"Oh, come on, Forest. It's five in the morning. The weather is shit. The hotel is empty, and we have so much to do I don't know where to start. Let me escape for a minute, huh?"

Fern hated my disdain for her, as she described it, perfectly reasonable interest in celebrity gossip. But she did have a point. I, too, was desperate for a mental escape from the relentless granite skies and moody blue Pacific in winter. I turned my gaze back outside, caffeine fueling my mind with practical steps we could take to start fixing what we needed to.

Using my hands always calmed me down. When I was a teenager and couldn't concentrate on school to save my life, my dad had taught me to use the tools he kept in the basement: a circular saw, a power drill, a table saw, several types of planes, and many others I'd gradually learned about. Together we'd built console tables for every room at the inn.

Fern flipped over a page and ran her fingers over the image pictured there. "Aren't they dreamy?"

"Huh?"

"I said aren't they *dreamy*." She tapped her pointer finger on the photo, where a woman with long dark hair posed with an impish-looking man in an oversize suit.

"I guess?"

"You don't know who they are, do you?"

I shook my head. Well, the guy looked sort of familiar. But I didn't know where from.

"That's Harry Roman, you idiot. You know, 'Midnight City'?"

That was it. The familiar chorus of the hit pop song Fern named played in my head. "Right."

"And this—" she tapped her finger again, this time on the woman "—is Domino West. I mean, she's lovely. But I think he'd be better off with me."

"Mm-hmm," I humored her, still watching the

boat masts rock left and right like metronomes in a row.

"Seriously, though, what does she have that I don't?" Fern poked my ribs to get my attention.

"Are we really doing this?"

"We're really doing this. Come on, big guy. Let's fantasize. Take your mind off things."

I tipped back my coffee and reached for the magazine, sliding it in front of me on the bar, the light from a pendant lamp above shining brightly off the page. I took in everything I could see of this Domino West person.

"She's tall," I said. "And she has good hair." When Fern tsked beside me, I pushed the magazine back in front of her. "We done here?"

"Wait! Don't you think she's gorgeous?"

I shrugged. "Sure."

"Well, I think you'd look great together."

"What?"

"You know, when Harry realizes he can't live without me, you can swoop in and take Domino."

I rolled my eyes. "Whatever you say." Not that I'd turn down the pretty woman pictured next to Harry Roman, but the odds of me meeting Domino West were about as likely as the Mariners winning the World Series. Besides, didn't Hollywood people have egos the size of elephants and diva demands for everyone within reach?

Fern closed the magazine and stood, loosening the elastic that barely held her braid in place and shaking her long blonde hair loose before she gathered it in a tidy knot high on her head. "All right. If you're not going to play along, time to get to business. Another?" She pointed to the empty mug in front of me.

It would be pitch-black for another few hours; daylight didn't break until well past seven this time of year. Too dark to investigate a leaking roof, and too wet and miserable to go outside. I lifted the mug and held it out to Fern, who moved back behind the bar and began grinding beans that smelled like heaven. "Another double, please."

After she worked her magic on the La Marzocco and served us second cups, she grabbed her laptop from beside the till and took her place next to me again. "When are we calling Mom and Dad?" she said as she flipped open the screen and called up a spread-sheet program.

"Um, never." I set down my mug with a deter-mined thud.

"But they—"

"No buts, Fern. We agreed." Jack and Judy had worked hard for fifty years in this place, day after day, year after year. When Fern and I took over, we pinky swore we'd give them the retirement they deserved.

Which meant not peppering them with questions, leaning on them for advice, or whining down the phone the minute something went wrong. I wanted to prove it to myself, too, that I could handle the business. I'd chosen tree planting over college after high school, and ever since I'd returned after seven years away, I couldn't shake the feeling I was a big lumbering fool who'd inherited a hotel despite my lack of business—or many other—useful skills.

It was a feeling vindicated by my last two relationships. I'd developed a pattern with women, it seemed. They were happy for the first little while, right up until the point when they asked me to change—to let down my guard, to commit to things I wasn't ready for. To be someone else, the way I saw it.

Fern's shoulders slumped, but after heaving a sigh, she nodded her agreement.

"Look, your end of the arrangement has gone pretty well," I told her. "The food last season was great, and your idea to source local ingredients is genius." Fern had taken over managing the kitchen and bar when Jack and Judy left. It'd always been her favorite part of the business. I wasn't surprised when her ideas for the dining room resonated with guests and locals. Last summer she'd brought in Freddy Larsen from Cottle's Fish Market—an island institution—to help her expand the menu, and together they'd created something really special. "It's me who's dragging us down."

She swallowed a sip of coffee, then shook her head. "Uh-uh. We're fifty-fifty here. And what we didn't know, we do now. What's the saying? When you know better, you do better." She slapped a hand on my shoulder. "So what we're gonna do now, brother of mine, is put those big muscles to work and fix what needs fixing. Here—I'll start a list. Just toss things out as you think of them, and we can prioritize them all after."

"Hot-water heater."

Fern nodded and started typing.

"Paint. New chairs in here." I gestured to the dining area behind me, where the chairs and booth seats were upholstered in the same wine-red vinyl our parents had ordered from a wholesaler on the mainland in the 1990s.

"Keep 'em coming."

"The floors need sanding. And we could do with new furniture in some of the rooms."

"And one of those glass washers behind the bar," Fern added.

"A new roof."

Fern stopped typing and whipped her head around to look at me. "What?"

"Unfortunately."

The expression in her gray-blue eyes went from hope to despair. "But...are you sure?"

"There's a bucket collecting rain in my room as we speak."

She put her head in her hands, rubbing her eyes with her fists like she did when we were kids. "Fuuuuuuck."

"I know."

"How are we going to afford that after everything we spent on ripping out wires?"

"I have a bit of savings. We'll manage." I did my best to sound sure, but the hours of staring at the ceiling, counting raindrops, had allowed doubt to creep in.

"Well, that's our first priority." She inserted a new cell at the top of the spreadsheet and typed in *Roof*. I had to hand it to her; she'd taken it better than I'd expected.

"Cool. We're just waiting on Mother Nature to cooperate so I can get up there and take a look."

"You're *not* doing it yourself." She said it like there was no room for debate.

"Why wouldn't I?"

"Forest, have you ever even *been* on a roof?"

I got up from the bar, collected our mugs, and walked around to the sink. "I got it. Relax." She rolled her eyes but knew it was pointless to argue. She was familiar with my pattern: see what I can do myself first—with help from YouTube—before calling in help. "What else?" I gestured to the laptop.

"We need the Wi-Fi fixed so I can stop wasting money buying this—" she lifted up the magazine we'd been looking at "—and just read it online." She thought for a minute, her eyebrows furrowing. "You know what we really need?"

I moved to the end of the bar to stretch by gripping the edges and folding at the waist, then leaning straight back with my weight in my heels. "What?" My voice was muffled by the hood of my sweatshirt falling forward.

"A social media person. Someone who can help bring our marketing efforts into this century."

"Sounds expensive."

"Maybe. But it's how people advertise these days."

Standing upright, I twisted left, right, left, right, vertebrae clicking with each rotation. "Put it on the list, I guess." Social media was the last thing I thought we should spend money on, but I obliged my sister with a shrug.

"We need a big splash—a huge splash. Something to put us on the map." Her feet clad in thick, slouchy socks, Fern wrapped her ankles around the legs of the barstool, her fingers poised on the keyboard while she looked straight ahead, eyes unfocused, deep in thought.

I cleared my throat. "I'm not sure *splash* is the right word given our current situation."

She flapped hand. She never appreciated my stupid sense of humor when she was really concentrating.

"What about a contest of some kind?"

"Like a meat draw?" Our parents had done meat draws in the off-season to lure locals to the hotel's dining room.

"Ha!" she burst. "No, silly. Like on Instagram. I'll reach out to some influencers—"

"Some what now?"

"Ugh! You're so frustrating sometimes, you know that?" She clapped her laptop shut and got to her feet, hiking up her sweatpants. "Never mind. Leave it to me."

I'd always preferred being outside and didn't understand the appeal of social media. Now it felt too late to learn, even if I wanted to. But I trusted Fern's judgment—and I knew my old friend Rocky Black had used social media to help him win the mayoral race in Bayview last spring. "Whatever you say."

"Meat draw!" she repeated and laughed as she walked out of the dining room. I could still hear her cackling in the lobby while she waited for the elevator.

CHAPTER 3

Domino

I spent the first two days after The Text at home, with my phone turned off once I'd let Trudi and my parents know I was fine, just taking some time for myself. It was kind of blissful, in truth. Not the being-broken-up-with part, but the clean break from social media and the gossip cycle and responsibility in general. It brought my nervous system to a state of calm I hadn't experienced since before moving to LA.

I binged TV and movies—including *The Notebook* twice, didn't wash my hair, ate pasta and bread and whatever else I felt like, and cleaned the house to sparkling, beginning with the mess of flour in the pantry. It wasn't all R and R, though. My emotions took sharp dives and extreme curves no roller-coaster could achieve. I was embarrassed, humiliated, and mortified about what had happened and how, but when I let down the walls of my ego and allowed myself to really *feel*, a singular truth came into sharp focus: I'd never loved Harry.

He wasn't The One, I realized. I'd let myself get caught up in the spectacle of it all. It had been fun to be the darling of every red carpet, to hitch my booster to Harry's rocket on its ascent into the universe. But something felt right about falling away from his shuttle and coming back to earth. I'd lost sight of *me* in all the chaos, and I needed to reconnect. It was too easy to believe I was who the media said I was rather than the down-to-earth Canadian with goals and dreams that weren't worth compromising for.

The kitchen in my Venice Beach rental had cantilevered double doors that led out to a flat cedar deck, beyond which the swimming pool sat covered for the winter months. The garden was mostly dormant beyond blooms of pink and creamy-white camellias anchored in dark glossy leaves. It was warmer today, enough that I let fresh air and light stream into the room. Cold glass of white wine in hand, I settled at the kitchen table in leggings and a baggy sweater, my hair in a long braid over my shoulder, bangs falling in wisps around my face. Time to face reality—and by reality, I meant the never-ending churn of the Hollywood rumor mill. I booted up my phone for the first time since Tuesday night and watched in horror as my inbox filled with Google Alerts.

"Domino's Heartbreak," read the first one, followed by "Domino's Shock!," "It's Over!," "Split! Why Harry Left Her"...and on and on until the last one loaded: "DUMPED!"

Not a single news outlet had contacted me for comment. That I knew of. It was possible my agent, Deidre Dunbow, had shielded me, but still it felt strange to see myself spoken about in the third person. It was like I had an avatar out there that looked identical but had a whole other life. I finally understood—deep in my bones—why some stars took umbrage with the press: it was the loss of control that was so hard to stomach.

I closed out of my email and started in on the text messages that had piled up in the past few days. Some I could save until later to respond. I checked in with my mom and sister Saylor in Toronto, recoiling at the pictures my mom had sent of the two feet of snow that'd fallen this week. There was also a message from Marc, asking if I'd booked my trip yet. **Tonight,** I replied. **Just dealing with a couple of things.** Of course he'd know all about it; everyone would.

Notably absent from my messages was any contact from Harry. I debated calling him to ask... I didn't know what, really. *Why* seemed obvious—because he didn't love me either. Did we need to belabor what was probably hard for both of us?

I texted Trudi and made arrangements for lunch with her the next day. **I'll let TBA know,** she responded, referencing the Bright Agency. I sighed. That would mean paparazzi for sure, but I had to face it sooner or later.

I opened my laptop and typed "Orcas Island" into the browser. Like Marc had described, it was less than a hundred miles north of Seattle. Accessible by boat, ferry, or float plane, Google said it had a population of 5,387. Compared to LA or even Toronto, it was the size of a thimble. But the pictures online looked nice, kind of rugged and picturesque, and reminded me of a family trip we'd taken to Vancouver one summer in middle school—only more quaint and without the mountains and tall buildings. But it didn't matter whether I liked it. What mattered was whether it was right for the movie.

I booked a nonstop flight from LAX to SeaTac. In summer months float planes were an option, but in January I'd have to rely on the Washington State ferry system or a chartered flight to get to Orcas. I'd figure that part out tomorrow. For now, I turned my attention to accommodations.

The island was populated with bed-and-breakfasts and Airbnbs, but I decided I was better off in a hotel to get an idea of whether it could be home base not just for me but for the wider cast and crew of *Shore Thing*. The Driftwood Inn, a century-old hotel on the harbor in the town of Bayview, looked to be the only place with enough rooms to hold us. The hotel's website was from the MySpace era, but the rooms were a decent size and the price was right. Its booking system didn't exactly instill confidence, so I picked up the phone and dialed the reservations number.

After five rings I was about ready to give up when the call was answered. "Hello," said a deep, gruff voice.

"Uh, hi. Have I got the right number?"

"Depends who you're looking for."

"The Driftwood Inn?"

"Yep."

"O—kay," I said, doubt growing in my belly like a ball of dough rising. This was about the weirdest hospitality approach I'd experienced. "Could I book a room, please?"

"Hang on." I heard a thud as the man put down the receiver, followed by the sound of shuffling pages. "When are you looking to book?" His voice came online again.

"Sunday, please."

The man cleared his throat. "*This* Sunday? You sure?"

I was growing more unsure by the second. "Mm-hmm?" It went up as a question.

"We've only got... Well, we've only got the second floor available."

"That's fine."

"Name?"

"Allie Hamilton."

"Allie Hamilton," he repeated. "Number?"

I rattled off my phone number and provided the credit card number Alex had given me for expenses.

"See you Sunday."

This guy was something. "Don't you want to know how many nights?"

He cleared his throat again. "How many nights?"

"I don't know yet, actually. Could be a week, maybe longer—"

"I'll put you down as open-ended."

He must not be the usual desk clerk. "Maybe you'd like to put me through to your front desk?"

Four seconds of silence followed. "This is the front desk."

"Oh, okay. I'm sorry, it's just that—"

"See you Sunday." A click indicated he'd ended the call.

Jesus. If everyone there was as surly as this guy, Orcas Island was a bad idea. I wondered if Marc had done any research or just flung out the first place that'd come to mind.

Can't we just use Catalina? I texted Trudi, referring to one of California's channel islands southwest of LA, where Natalie Wood mysteriously drowned in 1981 and Marilyn Monroe had lived for several months in the 1940s.

Too expensive!

I exhaled a long breath, knowing she was right. Flight and accommodations booked, I turned my mind to the next week. I had two days to ready myself for a trip to the middle of nowhere.

The next morning, the LA sun dependably bright, I finally washed my hair, then dried and flat-ironed it until it was smooth and shiny. Years of doing my own makeup for indie films in Toronto had taught me how to best highlight my features: intense blue eyes, a small but pointed nose, prominent cheekbones, and full lips. At the door to the walk-in closet in the master bedroom, I surveyed the racks, which stylist Luna Chavez had lined with designer and vintage pieces, organized by type: dresses and suits on the left side; denim, jackets, sweaters, and workout wear on the other. In the center an enormous island held wide drawers filled with shoes, bags, and jewelry. I knew just what to wear for my meeting with Trudi and the dozen photographers likely lying in wait. Casual but cool, sophisticated but sexy. Your basic eat-your-heart-out-Harry-Roman ensemble: a lush green knit dress, red velvet Gucci purse, and black leather jacket.

At the front door, I closed my eyes, willed confidence to replace the nervous energy zinging through me, and held my head high. Minutes later I was on the road, driving northwest on Route 2 toward Wilshire Boulevard. The iconic striped awnings of the Beverly Wilshire beckoned me to the valet stand, where a line of paparazzi blurred into a sea of black hoodies, their cameras already pointed at the hybrid Porsche Cayenne Deidre had insisted I lease. The black lenses of my sunglasses did little to dull the blinding camera flashes as I pulled to a stop. While the valet and a hotel security guard came around and opened the door for me, I waved, remembering what Deidre always said: smile like you mean it.

"Domino, how does it feel?" one paparazzo yelled.

"Over here!" shouted another.

"You look gorgeous! This way, Domino!"

"Domino, why'd he do it?" Cameras clicked and whirred amid their calls as I made the short walk to the hotel entrance, guided by the security guard. I turned back and flashed a big smile before passing through the door the guard held open.

Inside, I looked around the lobby and mentally pinched myself. Amid the hustle of trying to make it in this impossible business and getting caught up in the tabloid press, it was easy to lose perspective. Here I was, standing where Julia Roberts stood with Richard Gere in *Pretty Woman*, on my way to meet my producing partner on a big-budget movie. My life was pretty charmed, with or without Harry Roman.

Forest

"Got a call from Rose Hardy," Fern said the next afternoon as we sat down to lunch in the Driftwood's dining room. We ate here every day to give the skeleton staff we kept on year-round something to do other than twiddle their thumbs and worry about their jobs. George, the head chef, had prepared scrambled eggs for me, with chevre, toast, and pesto made with nettle from Rose's farm in Winslow.

"Yah?" I layered a thick piece of sourdough toast with a spread of pesto and a slice of the tangy cheese.

"She's trying to plan her crops this year," Fern said between bites. "Wants us to commit to some sort of monthly minimum." Knowing how much work we had to do to get the Driftwood ready for full capacity, it was going to be hard to predict what we'd want and when.

I hemmed and hawed, trying to come up with a plan that could satisfy everyone. Around us, the dining room was empty except for one booth of women who met here every Friday. Wet rain gear was slung over a chair next to them, likely Angela Fletcher's riding clothes. A fixture in Bayview, Angela was a mystery writer who cycled year-round and kept her finger on the pulse of everything—and everyone.

A fire crackled in the big stone fireplace at the far end of the room, where Fern's friend Bluebell, who worked with us as a server, sat with her legs curled under her on one of two big leather chairs, her attention buried in her phone. Outside the wind had eased but the rain continued, casting the marina in somber shades of gray.

"Come on, Forest. We'll be ready."

I turned to look at my sister, her eyes gleaming despite the gloom outside, her blonde hair pulled up in a high ponytail. "We have to be."

"That's more like it. Okay, I'll make plans with George." Fern bit into a pear-and-roast-beef sandwich. "Think it'll be dry enough this weekend we can take a look at the roof?" she said once she'd swallowed.

"Hope so." I finished my toast. "Oh, 204 is booked for tomorrow."

"How many guests?"

"Just one. Said she's not sure how long she'll be here." I pushed away my plate and stood. "Anyway, I'll get back to the basement. Think I know what the problem is—a heat exchanger."

"Whatever that is," Fern replied with a shrug. "I'll get 204 ready."

Thankfully the water for the second floor was fed by a different heat exchanger, so the guest in 204 wouldn't be blasted with cold water every time she took a shower, but the sooner I got the problem solved, the better. We could only go so long operating with a patchwork of available rooms.

An hour and a half later, sweat beading my forehead despite the chill in the basement, I heard the stairwell door slam shut. "Forest?" Fern called into the cavernous mechanical room.

"Over here." I put my tools down on the little bench I'd pulled alongside the heat exchanger and wiped my forehead with the back of my sleeve.

"Allie Hamilton?" Fern stood in front of me, arms crossed.

"Pardon?"

"Allie Hamilton. That's not a real person."

"What are you talking about?"

"Allie Hamilton. Ring any bells?"

This cryptic conversation was making an already frustrating afternoon even more so. I racked my brain. It was just a name. Nothing was unusual or familiar.

Fern stomped her foot. "Ugh! Don't you know anything? Allie Hamilton—that's the name of Rachel McAdams's character in *The Notebook*."

"O—kay?" I'd heard of the movie—and the actress—but I didn't see any significance to it.

"So it can't be real. The reservation. Something's up."

"Listen, I'm sure you're right—"

"See? So you do know."

"No, I'm sure you're right that's the name of some character in a movie. But it's a coincidence."

She stood quietly, brow creased, as if calculating something. "Hmph" was all she said.

I gestured around the basement. "Fern, I'm in the middle of—"

She held up a hand. "Right. I'm out of here. But mark my words, Forest. Allie Hamilton isn't who she says she is."

CHAPTER 4

Domino

After forty-eight hours of being tracked by paparazzi, I was more than ready to leave Los Angeles. The media always took sides when a celebrity couple split, and since Harry's star was infinitely brighter than mine, I was taking the brunt of the blame in the press. The barrage of insulting headlines continued, along with endless dissections of my every expression in the candid photos the media had been spewing since I became newly single. Harry, meanwhile, was getting more love than ever.

I packed on Saturday night, surprisingly relieved to be free of the need for Luna's styling services for the near future. I appreciated the designer clothes and bags, but I couldn't wait for a week of comfort in clothes of my own choosing. In the early years of my career, when I was making the trip from Toronto to LA regularly, I'd mastered the art of traveling light. I left the fancy luggage Luna usually insisted I travel with in the back of a closet and dug out my old carry-on bag. I reveled in the Tetris game of fitting everything I needed neatly into the small, lightweight suitcase.

The car service picked me up before the sun on Sunday morning. I hid behind my biggest sunglasses anyway, since a few photographers were camped outside my front gate even at this hour. I promptly removed them once we drove away and the cries of "Domino!" faded behind. Hollywood could be a prison of your own making if you let it. I had no knowledge of where I was going beyond the rugged depiction presented by Google Images, but I had high hopes I'd have a chance to get grounded and remind myself who I was and what was important to me.

Traveling on the studio's dime meant I was using the private terminal on the far side of LAX, away from photographers. I was ushered to my own suite with two bathrooms, a big-screen TV, a daybed, staff, and all the kale chips and 85-percent cacao bars I could eat. There was Veuve Clicquot champagne, which I was tempted to indulge in just because it was there. At one end of the suite was a pocket-size gallery filled with photos from Tracy Johnson, a series of olive-green hummingbirds in magnificent, close-up detail. As my boarding time neared, I completed security screening in the terminal before being driven, like a head of state, across the tarmac to the plane in a black BMW 7 series sedan. The whole experience made me feel underdressed and overappreciated.

A few passengers around me in business class seemed startled to see me but nodded and smiled. One woman thought she'd covertly take my photo despite me holding up my hand and asking her not to. She was clutching her phone at too awkward an angle to be checking Instagram or email. Once we were in the air, though, everyone settled in and kept to themselves, and it was a relatively peaceful flight despite a few bumps of turbulence.

When the captain announced preparation for descent, I peered through the window, hoping for a glimpse of Seattle, but all I could see was drab gray. Wisps of cloud blew past the plane as rain splattered the window. Eventually we were below the cloud layer, and in the distance I could see the stem of the city's iconic Space Needle reaching up for the sky, its UFO-like cap obscured by fog.

It'd been a while since I'd traveled solo. I was excited to navigate my way around without a tail of security or photographers. Before disembarking I pulled on a long black wool coat, wrapped a pink scarf around me, and tucked my hair into a newsboy cap. I hailed a cab north to Pike Place Market, where I planned to catch the Seattle Clipper to Orcas Island. It was cool to see the iconic, towering neon letters that spelled PUBLIC MARKET at the entrance, familiar from *Sleepless in Seattle* and *Frasier* and so many other TV shows and movies.

With an hour to spare before the ferry departed, I wandered the historic market, listening to the good-natured shouts of fishmongers tossing whole salmon across the stands, the hum of vendors and customers exchanging goods, and seagulls squawking in the background like grandmothers wailing at a funeral. During a break in the rain I stood in line at the first Starbucks—almost the first, I learned. The original store opened a block north in 1971 but moved to its Pike Place location in 1975. Just like any other tourist, I took photos of everything I saw. I sent a shot of the original Starbucks mermaid logo to my mom.

My cap, scarf, and coat not only kept me warm in the damp chill of the Pacific Northwest but also meant I stayed mostly incognito—either that or people in Seattle were more polite than tourists in Hollywood. Even a single hour of normalcy before boarding the

Clipper was more relaxing than any SoulCycle class or meditation room in LA.

The Clipper was fairly empty—surprising for a weekend, I thought, but I soon learned why. The January seas were less than smooth, and the pastries and fruit I'd bought at the market for the journey remained untouched in the tote bag next to me. I kept my eyes on the horizon, which helped ease the nausea. The journey would take about four hours as we voyaged up Puget Sound toward Orcas Island.

The land and seascapes here were so unlike the Pacific Ocean views I'd come to know in Southern California. Gone were the mile-wide sandy beaches, supplanted with rocky outcroppings marked with enormous red cedars and Douglas firs. Out here, in what seemed like wilderness to me, they stood like majestic giants, keepers of the land and witness to centuries of change. Even from a distance like this, they grounded me in a way no palm tree or jacaranda could. Maybe it was proximity to Canada and a sense that home was near. Even the dreary skies and constant rain seemed to encourage the quiet state of mind I'd felt since landing in Seattle.

The ferry stopped first at San Juan Island, the largest of the archipelago, where more than half the ship's fifty or so passengers disembarked, replaced by eleven new ones in hooded rain jackets in primary colors that reminded me of a box of crayons. Water beaded off their coats like sweat off a cold glass. With my cap in place and my head held low, I made myself invisible as they took their seats or wandered around the boat. At least I thought I did.

A pretty young Asian woman in a tangerine-orange raincoat cautiously approached, her expression a mix of nerves and hope. I smiled.

"Excuse me? I don't mean to bother you," she said, her voice shaky. "But are you…?"

I nodded, then put a finger to my lips. "Hi." I motioned her to sit. "What's your name?"

She put a hand to her chest and looked around, as if doubting it was her I was talking to. I nodded again. She sat on the very edge of a seat across from me. "Me? I'm Song." She got tongue-tied then, just blushed and stared.

"What a lovely name. Are you from around here?"

She relaxed a little. "Anacortes, on the mainland. But that's boring! What are *you* doing here?"

"I'm here for work. I'll be staying in Bayview for a week or so. Got any tips for me while I'm there?"

"On Orcas Island?" Song thought for a moment, looking through the windows to the ferry terminal we were quickly approaching. Rain dripped down the outside of the glass in long rivulets. "I wouldn't say it's the most interesting place. Especially not this time of year. Summer is great. But in winter? Deadsville. Whatever you can do to stay dry is my recommendation," she said, smiling.

I laughed. "Got it, Song. Guess I need to trade this in for a rain jacket like everyone here wears, hey?" I gestured to my wool coat. The ferry slowed as we pulled alongside the terminal, then eased to a stop, the boat gently rocking as the crew secured the gangplank. My new friend jumped to her feet when I stood to gather my tote and wheelie suitcase. "Nice to meet you." I winked and ducked my head back down as I followed the short line of people disembarking. It didn't take long until I was on terra firma, following the signs that indicated the terminal exit.

Out on the sidewalk, I took a moment to look around and get my bearings. With rain sheeting down the way it was, I was about to be soaked. I weighed my options. I could see the town of Bayview from here; it looked like a ten-minute walk, max. My fellow passengers had quickly scattered, leaving me alone, gazing down the hill to the sweet little village, lined with colorful storefronts and a gray clapboard building pitched over a marina packed with boats.

"Fuck it," I said aloud to myself. "You're Canadian. This is nothing compared to Ontario in January." I grabbed the handle of my suitcase and started the walk, thankful I was wearing comfortable—if already wet—sneakers in place of the designer shoes Luna usually put me in.

Not a single car passed by on my way into town. Song was right: Deadsville. But Deadsville was just what I wanted, I reminded myself. No people meant no one to stare at me and no cameras stalking every move. It was me and only me for the next week.

The gray clapboard building loomed larger the closer I got, until I was able to read the sign that hung above a set of double doors: Driftwood Inn. It was shaped like an oversize Victorian beach cottage with a generous wraparound porch, steeply pitched gables, and white-painted iron railings. It looked more like it belonged on Martha's Vineyard than it did on this little island in the Pacific. Under the cover of the porch, I took off the sopping-wet newsboy and let my hair fall loose, finger-combing my bangs into place before I tugged open the doors and stepped inside.

The lobby was unlike any other I'd been in. An impossibly high ceiling was suspended by thick wooden beams, and old hardwood floors cast a warm, inviting glow around the room. A big stone fireplace sat dark to one side, and a beautiful red-patterned rug ran the length of a long desk. Concern flashed through me when I realized I'd been standing there for ten minutes and hadn't seen a soul.

I didn't see a bell to ring anywhere. "Hello?" I called loudly.

"Shit," I heard a woman mutter, followed by, "Hi! Be right there!" The voice had come from what looked to be a dining room off the side of the lobby. It was dark in there. I'd expected the hotel to be quiet, but I was beginning to wonder if I was the only guest.

Within moments a curvy blonde woman appeared, shuffling papers in her hands and stepping quickly behind the desk. Her hair bounced in a high ponytail as she walked. "I'm so sorry, I—" Her jaw dropped open when she finally looked up at me. "I—" She put a hand to her mouth and swallowed on a gulp. "You're Domino West," she said in disbelief. "What are *you* doing here?" She shook her head, flustered. "I'm so sorry. I don't mean it that way. It's just—I didn't know... Let's see here." She looked down at the desk and ran her finger through the columns of a guestbook.

I smiled. "It's okay. I'm the one who should be sorry. Here. That's me." I pointed to the only name entered under today's date. "Allie Hamilton," we both said at the same time.

"*You're* Allie Hamilton? So I was right." She tsked, staring at me. "Wait until I tell Forest," she said under her breath as she returned her attention to the book in front of her.

"Who?"

The blonde woman turned her back abruptly, then

whirled around to face me again, holding out a hand to shake mine. "You know what? Let's start this all over. I'm Fern Russo. Welcome to the Driftwood Inn." Her slate-blue gaze was sincere.

"Domino." I clasped her hand, and we each gave two short, firm shakes before releasing. "Nice to meet you, Fern. What a beautiful place."

Pink colored Fern's cheeks. "Oh gosh, thanks so much. I—we—are thrilled to have you stay with us. Let's get you sorted. I imagine you had a long journey."

I nodded gratefully.

"Clipper?" she asked, tilting her chin in the direction I'd just walked from.

I passed Fern my ID, and as she wrote a few things down, I said, "Yep. Started this morning before the sun came up in LA and now I'm here—in this torrential downpour."

She handed back my passport, along with a key card, a menu, and the hotel's Wi-Fi password. "Oh, this?" She shrugged. "It's nothing. Just January in the Pacific Northwest. Gotta embrace it—and get a good raincoat. Can I show you to your room?" She came around the desk and grabbed the handle of my suitcase.

"Sure."

"Please, *please* let us know if there's anything we

can do to make your stay more comfortable." Fern wheeled my suitcase toward an elevator at the back of the lobby, again framed by thick wooden beams. A giant taxidermy deer glowered down at us from above the elevator door. Catching me staring at it, Fern said, "Our great-grandfather hung that there. We don't have the heart to remove it. He kind of grows on you, you know?"

I didn't really know, but I smiled anyway. Fern was charming.

A ding signaled the elevator door was about to open. "If we'd known it was you, I would've done a lot more—"

I held up a hand. "No need for special treatment." Fern's face fell slightly. "I have to tell you I'm looking forward to a week of just...being normal," I confided.

"I bet, after what you've been through." Fern's eyes went wide, and she quickly backpedaled. "I mean, what I imagine you've been through. I read about...you know." Pink tinged her cheeks again but this time from embarrassment, not pride. She made a motion of zipping her lips shut. "Anyway. You've come to the right place. We're about as normal—and average—as you can get here." She let out a little giggle. "I'm really selling the place, aren't I?"

The elevator dinged at the second floor, and the door opened again. I followed Fern down a brightly lit hallway carpeted in deep green. Whether it was the West Coast vibe or the emptiness, this place was already having an effect on me. I couldn't explain it. I just felt...relaxed. We stopped in front of room 204.

"Here we are," Fern said. "Again, please let us know if you need anything. Anything at all." She touched her hands together in front of her in a prayer sign.

"Thank you, I will." We both stood there, smiling awkwardly, until Fern hopped from one foot to the other and realized it was her cue to exit.

The room was plain, pleasant, and surprisingly modern. Crisp white sheets covered the king-size bed pushed against an exposed brick wall on one side of the room, with windows on the other that looked out at the marina. A flat-screen TV was mounted over a teak bureau in the same warm wood tones as the floors. I hefted my little suitcase onto the rack in the closet, figuring I'd empty it later, then moved to the windows to see the town of Bayview. In front, boats bobbed in their slips at the marina, where the docks were slick and dark with rain. To the west a row of storefronts and restaurants ringed the harbor. The clouds hung low and gray in the sky, shrouding any view beyond.

Tomorrow I would begin the work of assessing Orcas Island for *Shore Thing*. The rest of today, though, I planned to make that big comfortable bed my own, devour the fruit I'd bought at Pike Place, and see if the fresh West Coast air would inspire sleep.

Forest

The deluge of rain continued for most of Sunday. To shake free of the cabin fever setting in, I decided a wet run was better than no run at all. Around four o'clock I cut two armholes and a spot for my head into a big black garbage bag and threw it over my jogging pants and a sweatshirt. I had a proper rain jacket, but it was bulky, and the zipper scratched against my neck when I ran.

I jogged down Water Street with the sidewalks practically to myself. I passed by Grind House, where the windows were steamy from brewing coffee, and waved at Ginger Kidd behind the counter. A little farther along, the staff at Isola, the Italian restaurant run by River Black, were readying for dinner service.

When you grew up in a town of 3,500, more than half the population of the island, you pretty much knew everyone, and everyone knew you. When I was a kid I'd dreamed of leaving, believing I was meant for big-city life, but a couple of trips south to California and east to New York City during my tree-planting years had showed me how lucky I was to live among the pristine beaches and wild open spaces on Orcas. As I pounded off the main street and wound through Sombrio Park, Coltrane's *A Love Supreme* in my headphones, the weight that'd hung over me for the past few days began to lift. Fern and I had a lot of work to do to get ready for spring and summer. But what was better than putting time and effort into something—someplace—you loved? I'd come to learn my purpose in life was to protect the magic of this special island for its future inhabitants.

My hair was soaked, the rain streamed down my face, and I loved it. It felt like freedom.

It was dark by the time I rounded the seawall and jogged back along Water Street toward the Driftwood, where the porch lights shone like beacons against the black sky. A golden glow beamed through the windows of the dining room, where our Sunday regulars were gathered for their weekly dinner. Recently George had taken to serving a traditional English spread each week, reflecting his Yorkshire heritage.

I climbed the front steps and brushed off as much rain from my garbage-bag poncho as I could. My sweatpants were soaked from the thighs down, the light gray cotton now a dark charcoal. Hearing my feet squelch in my waterlogged sneakers, I bent down to unfasten the laces, stepping onto the huge doormat outside the entrance in wet sports socks, dripping shoes in hand.

Light poured out as I opened the big double doors, and I was immediately enveloped in warmth. Slicking the hair back from my face with my free hand, I made my way toward the elevator at the back of the lobby as quickly as I could, watching to make sure I didn't leave a trail of puddles someone could easily slip on.

"I will. Yep, starting tomorrow." I heard the woman's voice before I saw her. "No, in a hotel. It's the only place I could find that would accommodate all of us." I stopped where I was, interested in what she might say next. "Oh, it's...all right. I mean, what did I expect for an island in the boonies?" She laughed. "Yeah, right... It's no Four Seasons, that's for sure... Okay, gotta go. Talk soon... Okay, bye."

A split second later I was face to face with the woman I'd heard belittle my family business—and my beloved island. She was tall and slim, with long, shiny brown hair, dressed in faded jeans and a black sweatshirt.

"Were you eavesdropping on me?" She put her hands to her hips, tapping the sole of her white sneaker impatiently. Her blue eyes shot determined sparks below her bangs.

"I—No, of course not. Excuse me." I sidestepped to get around this self-important woman, who could only be the new guest in 204. Amy something? The name didn't come to mind.

"I think you were." She whirled around, her stare following me. When I stopped to respond, she pointed to the puddle that had formed on the floor where I'd stood listening to her call. *Busted.*

"I'm soaked, and I'd like to get out of these wet clothes." I gestured to the garbage bag, my drenched pants, and the dripping sneakers I held. "Excuse me." I stalked forward, relieved when I pressed the elevator button and the door opened right away. I stepped in and turned to press the number five as the door slid closed, but not before I received another indignant look from...

Allie Hamilton, I remembered.

CHAPTER 5

Domino

When you'd spent a week with every move documented by photographers, it was even more unnerving to be eavesdropped on. From where I'd been sitting in the lobby on an upright chair tucked to the side of the big desk, I'd heard the lobby doors swing open and felt a sweep of cold air around my ankles. At first I'd noticed what sounded like plastic crinkling, but it had stopped abruptly. Right around the time I'd started describing the hotel to Trudi.

I stood to confront the interloper and was struck by the odd sight in front of me. A tall, handsome guy with gray-blue eyes, dark wet hair slicked back, and rain beading down what looked to be a garbage bag. Who did he think he was, Bradley Cooper in *Silver Linings Playbook*? Handsome or not, I would not have my privacy invaded after the week I'd just had.

When he denied my accusation, the gruffness in his voice was unmistakable. The reservation-taker. The Driftwood Inn's concept of hospitality was getting more bizarre by the minute. Fern was light and bubbly and polite, where this guy came across as downright rude.

"I'm soaked, and I'd like to get out of these wet clothes," he said before he walked away from me, leaving a little puddle on the floor where he'd stood. His words twirled around in my mind as a vision of a very fit, very wet, very naked version of Mr. Grump flashed through me. Only the sound of the elevator door gliding closed snapped me out of the thought. I fanned my face with my hand to quell the mixture of anger and attraction sizzling in my veins. I shook my head clear, dropped my phone in my pocket, and entered the dining room.

I hadn't eaten since the fruit I'd brought from Seattle, and my stomach was making noises to prove it. A bar was tucked along the left side of the room, behind which Fern motioned for me to take one of the counter-height stools opposite where she stood. "Dom—" she started but quickly slapped a hand over her mouth. "I mean, Allie, come join me here." She made a point to glance around and check if anyone had heard her, but the hum of diners enjoying their meals carried on uninterrupted. Despite the high ceilings that continued from the lobby, the space was made cozy by the glow of wood floors and a fire roaring in a massive fireplace at the far end. A server with a mop of curly brown hair ran plates of food out from the kitchen.

"Drink?" Fern asked.

I pulled out my phone and placed it facedown on the bar, leaning forward on my elbows. "You read my mind."

Fern dug her hands deep in the pockets of the apron tied around her waist. "We're serving traditional English roast tonight, so how about a glass of house red?"

At my nod, she poured from a bottle and set the glass in front me.

"This is a pinot noir from Alloro Vineyard on the mainland," she said. "We try to do all our sourcing as close to home as possible." Fern beamed as she described where the ingredients for tonight's meal came from: beef from Sweetgrass Farm on nearby Lopez Island and vegetables from Big Oak and Morning Glory farms here on Orcas.

I sipped the wine as I waited for dinner, impressed

with its savory, fruity notes. Who knew the Pacific Northwest had wineries? I hadn't considered American wines much beyond the Napa and Sonoma valleys, but I saw now that was an oversight. Fern got busy filling drink orders and working at a laptop behind the bar, giving me space to take in my surroundings. The view of the marina outside was similar to the one from my room upstairs, but from here it was made prettier by the glinting of boat lights bobbing up and down, reflected in the dark ocean like stars twinkling in the sky. A half dozen of the dining room's tables were occupied with happy-looking groups, their cheeks glowing from good company and candlelight. Much like the lobby, the floors were worn but gorgeous, the decor simple and tasteful. Along one wall was a row of booths with upholstered red bench seats. The votive candles on each table were accented with sprigs of evergreen and chunky pine cones.

Roast beef was far from my usual fare, but I enjoyed every bite. I sighed with pleasure around a mouthful of Brussels sprout flavored with Dijon and something sweet—honey, maybe. Creamy squash sautéed with onions and garnished with parsley and roasted pecans paired beautifully with the rich, savory beef. And the Yorkshire puddings were light, crisp, and filled with air bubbles the perfect size to hold gravy. If tonight's meal was any indication of the food

I'd be eating for the week, things were looking up.

As I laid my knife and fork on an empty plate and leaned against the back of the barstool, Fern slid over from where she was working. "Everything okay?" She smiled, surveying the clean plate.

I laughed. "I haven't had a dinner like that in a long time. A decade, even. Eating habits are...different where I live."

"You never did say why you're here." Fern clapped a palm to her forehead. "That came out wrong. It's just—We don't see a lot of movie stars on Orcas island. Especially not in the middle of winter."

If I had any hope of determining whether Orcas Island was right for *Shore Thing*—not to mention if it could accommodate a full cast and crew for several months—I needed help from the locals. Now was as good a time as any to plant the seed. "I'm scouting locations for my next movie."

Fern jumped in excitement, her eyes lighting up. "Ohmygod!" she said, then covered her mouth again. "Oops, sorry. I mean, ohmygod." She whispered the words this time, reaching to collect my plate. "Is it a secret?" Her gaze darted around furtively.

"Not really." I waved a hand to calm her nerves. "Besides, people seem pretty chill here."

"They do?" Fern considered this a moment. "I never think of us that way. But then people who come here always talk about island time," she said. "I always thought it was a joke, but maybe I'm on it, too." Her blue eyes sparkled.

"Island time?"

"I think it just means none of us is in a hurry—you know, everything moves nice and slow here." She shrugged. "I mean, what *is* the rush? I never understood that about city living."

I laughed again. Having lived in big cities my whole life, I'd had the opposite experience. We really were always hustling to get somewhere, finding where we fit in. In LA, even though I lived near the beach, I rarely went just for the sake of it. I was always too busy, with too much to do and not enough time to do it. "Maybe I'll soak in some of that energy while I'm here." I fought the urge to busy myself even now, resisting the pull to pick up my phone.

"What's the movie about? Or is *that* a secret?"

I shook my head. "Nope, not especially. Besides, I'll need your help to figure out a few things." Fern nodded eagerly. "It's about a marine archaeologist who lives on an island—that's where Orcas comes in. His friend posts an ad online to find him a date." I pointed at myself. "That's me. But my character is a marine archaeologist, too—one who's secretly searching for the same buried treasure he is."

"Cool! Orcas would be *per*fect." Fern's smile

stretched wide before being replaced by a look of confusion. "Wait. How come you're the location scout? Is that what actresses do?"

"Absolutely not. But I'm producing this movie. Coproducing, actually."

The curly-haired server approached the end of the bar and tapped an order into the computer system. "Two gin and tonics, please," she called to Fern. I watched, impressed, as Fern expertly poured shots into highball glasses from a bottle with an Orcas Island Distillery label and topped it with tonic water from a can with another cool logo I couldn't quite read from where I sat. She finished the glasses with a sprig of greenery with flat, needlelike leaves. "Juniper," she said, seeing my curiosity. Tray perfectly balanced in one hand, the server spun off to deliver the drinks.

I indicated the can she'd poured from, and Fern held it out in front of me. "Sparkmouth Cucumber Mint Tonic," I read aloud. "Should have ordered the G&T."

"The tonic's local, too. More or less—it's from a brewery on Vancouver Island. Can I make you one?"

Why not? The company was good, the mood was pleasant, and I had nowhere to be in a hurry. Might as well get on island time.

Once she'd placed the crisp-looking cocktail in

front of me, she said, "Actor, producer, location scout—you're a triple threat. No wonder you're a big movie star, and I'm slinging drinks at the family hotel."

"This is your family's place?"

"Me and my brother, yep. We grew up here. Our parents ran it before they retired to Arizona. Now it's our turn." She paused for a beat, then added, "We're still figuring out what we want to change and what to keep the same. I revamped the menus to work with local producers—that's my passion."

"If dinner tonight is any clue, you're doing a great job," I assured her. I thought about what it would be like to live and work in the same place you grew up and shuddered, feeling a wave of claustrophobia. "Is it hard to work with your family?"

"Nah, we do okay. My brother is..." Her forehead wrinkled as she chose her words. "He takes a little while to warm up to people. But since I'm the opposite, we make a good team."

I considered telling Fern about my reservation-making experience, but whatever slight I'd felt at the time had been made up for in spades by Fern's warm hospitality since I arrived this afternoon. They'd figure it out.

"So tell me about your location scout. How can I help?"

"My producing partner, Trudi, and I are the only ones who've seen the script since she bought it. We have a real location manager, who'll join me if I like what I see. My job is to soak in the vibe of the place, see if I think it matches the aesthetic of the writer's vision and its description in the script."

Fern was listening attentively.

"In terms of distance, it's about as good as it gets. Not too far from LA, so it would work for transporting the cast, crew, equipment—and whatever else we need." I turned over my phone and called up one of the lists I'd made in the Notes app. "Much of the movie takes place on—and in—the water. We'll be bringing in a team of divers. And we're looking for a calm, deep bay. Our location manager's notes are specific about East Sound fitting that bill."

The curly-haired server appeared with another order. I smiled and waved to her, and she waved back. Fern signaled for me to keep talking while she made cocktails.

"And we need a home base—somewhere where the full cast and crew can camp out for, I don't know, maybe two months? That's why I booked here. You're the largest hotel on the island, right?"

"One of only two. Your choice is limited. But we've got lots of rooms, and I'd love to work with you any way I can. I'm sure my brother would, too. When do you start production? A couple years out?"

"Oh god, no. We're looking at this summer."

Fern stood stock-still, her back to me on the other side of the bar.

"Would that work for you?"

She seemed to take a deep breath, then faced me with a forced smile. "Absolutely." She didn't make direct eye contact, though, just turned back to lift the drinks she'd made onto the end of the bar for the server to pick up.

I finished the gin and tonic, and we spoke more about what was involved in scouting a location—going through the script to determine every place I needed to find for the film, compiling a list of locations, seeking permission from property and business owners, finding a boat we could rent, a production headquarters preferably near the hotel, and a dive team who could shoot the underwater scenes—all within budget. Fern was genuinely interested in the process, although her enthusiasm had decidedly cooled since I mentioned our schedule. Which was moderately concerning, but I'd only just arrived. I still had plenty to do to figure out if Orcas Island was going to work.

Forest

I'd grown used to the sound of drops hitting the bucket since the leak started last week. But sleep had become my foe, a demon I battled every night while I stared at the ceiling, my brain consumed with all the work we needed to do on the hotel. When Monday morning dawned bleak and overcast but somewhat dry, I leaped from bed, anxious to get up on the roof before it started raining again.

It was bitingly cold, I discovered as I stood on the balcony, with a wind blowing off the water that turned my knuckles to ice. I'd bundled up with long johns under my jeans and a thick wool shirt over the fisherman's sweater I wore most days in winter. With a rope around my waist secured to the vent pipe closest to where I thought the leak was, I ventured up the steep climb, my boots slippery on the wet shingles. Surveying the roof, I determined roughly the area I needed to replace, taking a few photos with my phone.

I crouched to my knees, then sat on the shingles, facing East Sound, so I could shimmy back down rather than attempt to walk. It was like hiking; the journey up was easy. The climb down was the scary part. Something about forward momentum and the fear of my feet slipping out from under me was terrifying.

A flash of pink on the docks drew my attention. A woman in a long black coat with a scarf the color of magnolias stood with her back to me, her long dark hair whipping around in the wind. Our new hotel guest. *What the hell is she doing out there?* It had to be as bitterly cold by the water as it was on the roof. She turned to the east, so I could see her face in profile. Her eyes were closed against the wind, and she just stood like that, unmoving.

My hands numb, my fingers clenched, I shimmied to the edge of the roof and jumped down to the little balcony, my boots hitting the surface with a thump. I looked out at the marina again. The woman—Allie, was it?—stared directly at me, her mouth slightly open. She raised her hand in a wave as our eyes caught.

I nodded in return, then began untying the rope around my waist. I left the other end tied to the vent. I'd be back up here as soon as I had what I needed to do the repairs.

Even from a distance, Allie Hamilton's beauty was undeniable. Something about her was familiar, but I couldn't place what. Maybe it was the perfect symmetry of her features playing a trick on me. Or had I met her somewhere before? I couldn't figure out why she was here—in the middle of January—alone, wandering listlessly around the Bayview marina like a boat drifting out to sea.

Inside, I went down to the dining room for coffee. Fern sat on a barstool, laptop and an empty cup in front of her.

"You're way ahead of me," I said as I swung around the end of the bar.

She moved to stand. "Want me to make you a—"

"I got it." I stood in front of the espresso machine.

"Don't forget to fill it to slightly heaping." She watched me add coffee grounds to the basket.

I rolled my eyes. "I think I can manage. Your machine will survive."

"Hmph." Fern watched me carefully. I knew she was more worried I'd do something to her precious La Marzocco than she was about how my coffee turned out.

"Went up on the roof this morning."

"And we're ready to call a roofer, right?" she said, typing away, focused on the screen now I'd finished making an Americano.

I chuckled. "Just the opposite. As soon as I get to the building supply store in Anacortes, I can fix it."

She leveled a cold blue stare at me. "Just when are we going to be able to do that?"

"I'll go this week—tomorrow."

Fern adamantly shook her head. "Uh-uh. No, you don't—not until the heat exchanger's fixed."

I folded my arms over my chest. "Who made you boss? We're equally in charge here. If it works for me to go to the mainland tomorrow, then that's when I'm gonna go." Intending to take it with me—somewhere, anywhere away from my sister—I uncrossed my arms and wrapped a hand around the mug of coffee I'd made. But I let go quickly. I hadn't added milk yet, and the hot liquid had heated the ceramic cup to scalding. I shook my hand, willing away the sharp pain of it. "For fuck's sake," I muttered.

There was that gray-blue stare again, but this time cast with concern. "You okay?" When I grunted, Fern went on. "In case you've forgotten, we have a guest now. A *paying* guest. One who could really change things for us if we play things right. I'm not taking any chances with—"

I held up a hand to stop her. "What do you mean, change things?"

"Uh, Earth to Forest. Room 204? You booked her in, remember?"

"So?"

"So you know what I'm talking about. This could be amazing for us—"

"Fern, what are you on about?" I interrupted her again in exasperation. "As far as I can tell the woman in 204 is here to mope around and feel sorry for herself. Just this morning I saw her standing on the edge of the docks, face against the wind, eyes closed. Talk about depressing."

"You can't be serious."

My sister was making things more infuriating by the minute. "Do I look like I'm joking?" I snapped, more frustrated than a bull trapped in a pen.

Fern slammed shut her laptop and hopped to her feet, then walked determinedly in my direction. But she pushed past me behind the bar, shuffling around at the end where she kept paper receipts and invoices, her forehead creased with her own frustration. She found what she was looking for and waved it at me. "See?"

It was a magazine rolled into a tube. "Your point?"

She slapped it on the bar in front of us, her ponytail flicking just so as she began flipping the pages until she stopped, pointed her finger, and tapped it at something on the page. I leaned forward to see what it was.

It was the same photo she'd shown me the day before. Harry Roman and a tall woman with long dark hair. Realization tingled across my scalp. That's why the woman on the docks seemed familiar. She was the woman in the photo.

I leaned back on the edge of the counter. "Harry

Roman's girlfriend is staying in 204?"

"Ex-girlfriend," Fern corrected.

"Why?"

"Well, according to *Inside Hollywood*, he left her. But we don't know the details yet."

I huffed out a breath. "No, Einstein. Why is she here?"

"Oh!" Unsurprisingly, Fern was disappointed in my disinterest in celebrities. "She's here to find a location. For her next movie."

Domino West, I read her name in the caption under the photo. "Who's Allie Hamilton, then?"

Fern filled a water glass and stepped back around the bar to her stool, a smug look on her face. "Told you it was a fake name, remember?" She sat down and set the glass on a coaster in front of her, then leaned forward on her elbows. "Anyway. Now you understand, right? This is—could be—a big deal for us. One I intend to use to our advantage."

I shrugged. "I don't see what that has to do with when I get building supplies."

"Let's start with fixing what might actually influence the movie star staying on the second floor for the next week. She won't be going up to the fifth floor, right? But she will be expecting hot water. And working Wi-Fi. And whatever information we can give her about the island and why it's the perfect place to shoot a movie."

"Hmph." I didn't give a fig about movie stars or Hollywood celebrities or who they were dating, but I knew as well as my sister we didn't need any bad reviews—and certainly no bad publicity.

"Besides, it's supposed to rain tomorrow—right through till Sunday." She sighed. "This time of year—it gets to me every time. I need more coffee." She got up again and came back behind the bar, nudging me out of the way. I sat on her barstool and slid her computer to the side.

An idea dawned so simple I was kicking myself for the sleepless nights. "I'll get a tarp today."

A flash of pink caught my peripheral vision. I looked to the left to see Domino West approaching, her cheeks and the end of her nose rosy from the cold, her coat and scarf bundled around her. "Uh, Fern..."

"Like hell you will," Fern argued, back still turned.

"Fern, I—"

"No, I mean it, Forest. A tarp will just make it obvious something's wrong. If we have any hope of pulling this off, we have to pretend we're a well-oiled machine rather than an old—"

"Fern." I said it firmly this time, and this time she turned around.

And stopped talking the minute she saw Domino, mouth dropping open in a perfect O.

CHAPTER 6

Domino

"I'm sorry, am I...interrupting something?" Fern and the man from the lobby last night stared at me, slack-jawed, four gray-blue eyes wide. Now they were next to each other, it was clear they were siblings, so similar Fern's brother could be her dark-haired twin. A tarp? If this guy's crankiness was strike one against Orcas Island and this hotel being a good fit for *Shore Thing*, whatever required a tarp was strike two.

Fern quickly recovered, the round O replaced with a smile. "Domino! Good morning. Hope you slept well?" She placed a steaming mug that smelled like heaven on the bar in front of her. "Can I interest you in coffee? You look like you could use something warm. It's cold out there this morning, isn't it? At least the rain stopped. Have you been out exploring?"

Her rambling was an obvious attempt to change the subject, but whatever they'd been discussing was hardly my business. I played along. "Yes! Wonderful. Thank you."

Fern gestured at a fancy-looking espresso machine behind her. "Cappuccino? Americano? What's your preference?"

"A latte? But just half the caffeine, please."

"Half-caf latte coming right up." She twirled around to face the machine, reaching for the espresso basket to load with coffee grounds.

"What kind of milk do you have?"

I caught Fern's brother rolling his eyes.

"I don't think we've met—formally. I'm Domino." I stepped forward, drew my hands out of my pockets, and held one out to him.

"I know who you are," he said bluntly, but he stood to grasp my hand in his. It was warm and strong around my cold fingers. He let go just as quickly as he'd grabbed it, but I felt the sensation of his grip long afterward, like aftershocks from an earthquake. *What was that?*

He remained standing but looked away, his gray-blue eyes trained on Fern behind the bar. In his green fisherman's sweater, not the garbage bag he'd been wearing like a cloak last night, it was obvious this was a man who took care of himself. In appearance, he was the opposite of Harry Roman. He was around six three, I guessed, with thick, dark hair that was short at the sides and a little longer, and messier, on top. He radiated strong and rugged and capable—of what, I wasn't sure. Building things. Chopping wood. Fixing motors. Protecting people. None of which I needed while I was here on Orcas Island.

Mr. Tall, Dark, and Rugged still hadn't told me his name. But Fern had mentioned it, hadn't she? Something nature-themed.

"What would you like?" Fern's voice brought my attention to her. She'd turned toward me, a carton of full-fat milk in one hand and a box of almond milk in the other.

"Almond milk is great, thank you."

Fern raised her voice so it could be heard above the hum of the steamer wand. "Now it's stopped raining, will you be out looking at locations today?" she practically shouted. "If you need any help at all, or even a guide, Forest and I are happy to help. Aren't we, Forest?" She glared over her shoulder at her brother.

Forest shrugged. It was clear playing tour guide to the likes of me was the last thing he was interested in.

He sat back down on the barstool and pulled out his phone.

"Oh, that won't be necessary. I've equipped myself with this—" I raised my own phone and waved it in front of me "—and a long list of places to see on the island. I can't wait to get started. I'm going to Winslow first." I named a small town on the other side of Orcas. "With a beach stop on the way. Moonstone Beach, is it called? All I need is for you to point me in the direction of the closest car rental place."

"You're out of luck there." Forest's reply was the only indication he was paying attention.

"I'm sorry?"

Fern held a huge mug in one hand, and in the other was a jug of steamed milk. I watched as she carefully tilted the mug forward and poured a thick stream in the center of the espresso. As it neared the brim of the cup, she dropped the pitcher low and tilted it to pour faster, now bringing the mug to an even level and artfully wiggling the pitcher back and forth to create a beautiful tulip pattern. "He's right," she said. "All the rental places—all two of them—are closed in January."

She put the coffee on the bar in front of where I stood. I was still cocooned in my long coat and pink scarf and growing warmer by the minute. With my hands wrapped around the hot drink, my fingers finally began to regain feeling, the numbness wearing off in pins and needles. "Oh, okay. I'll just use Uber then. Having a driver who knows their way around will save me time, anyway."

Forest eyed me sideways, shaking his head. "No luck there, either. You're a long way from California now." And then he went right back to staring at his phone.

"Oh! I didn't realize... Well, I'm happy to take the bus," I said. It'd been years since I'd been on public transit. I sort of liked the idea, actually. I took a long sip of latte, which was so good I closed my eyes, savoring it. "Wow! This is unbelievably good. I don't think I've had coffee this good. At least not in America."

Fern thumped a hand to her chest, beaming with pride. "That's the nicest thing anyone's said to me in ages. Isn't that nice, Forest?"

"Sure," her brother all but grunted, still focused on his phone.

"You have good coffee in Canada?" she asked.

"Ah—no. Well, it's fine. Same as here, more or less? But your coffee's as good as some I had in France this year."

Fern's expression lit up. "You mean Cannes?" I nodded, smiling. "I *loved* the dress you wore for the *Love Letters* premiere. Is it as glamorous and exciting as it looks?" She leaned forward, setting her elbows on the bar and folding her hands under her chin, a dreamy look in her eyes.

"Thank you! I can't take credit for the dress. My stylist does all the hard work."

"Luna Chavez, right?" Her cheeks reddened. "I'm sorry. I'm gushing, aren't I."

"Not at all. She'll be thrilled to hear people appreciate what she does. I'll pass it along. Mind if I sit?" I gestured to the stool next to Forest, who shrugged his response. That seemed to be his go-to response for everything. I unwrapped my scarf and shrugged out of my coat, laying them both on another stool before sliding out the seat and perching on it to enjoy the magnificent coffee Fern had made. She was still looking at me expectantly. "Oh! Right. Cannes is incredible. That was my first time going, and I think I was more excited to be there than just about anyone."

"The stars, the dresses—it all looks so…French," Fern said.

"Doesn't it? It's a picturesque little place, and it's so festive. All the shops and restaurants decorate for it, almost like it's Christmas. And I got to meet Lea Duvall! It was amazing and such an honor to be invited."

"You love her, too?"

"I'm such a fan. I was so nervous my whole body

was shaking." I took another long, satisfying drink of coffee, enjoying the heat of the mug in my hand. Next to me Forest was typing away on his phone. My paranoia kicked in. Was he writing down what he heard? It wouldn't be the first time someone tried to sell me out.

Seeing my concern, Fern laid a hand on my wrist. "Don't worry about him. I'd bet he's never heard of Lea Duvall—or Cannes. Anyway, I can't believe you get nervous meeting people when you're so talented and famous yourself!"

"Are you kidding? I *love* meeting my idols. Besides, I'm from Canada. We're polite, we're shy, and we feel inferior by nature—at least I do. I still don't feel like I belong in LA. It's bizarre. Growing up I always thought we were the same as Americans, but being immersed in such an American industry showed me just how different we are."

"Forest spent some time up in BC when he was tree planting. What do you think, Forest, do you agree?"

When Forest lifted his gaze to mine, it felt like he was staring directly into my soul. I'd never had quite the same feeling before. It was as if he held one half of a magnet and I was the other. I was drawn to this quiet, slightly intimidating man, and I wasn't sure why. "I never met a Canadian I didn't like." His voice was deep and resonant. Then he returned his attention to his phone.

After a moment of quiet, during which Fern watched me finish the last sip of coffee, I pushed off the barstool. "Thank you both. For the coffee and company. I should go while it's not raining. Can I get the bus near here?" I reached for my coat and fished around in the pockets to find my phone.

Before I could find it, though, Forest spoke up. "We have a hotel car you can use." Again, his slate-blue gaze was intense.

"Great idea!" Fern said, clearing away the mugs. She gathered them in a bus tray and walked out from behind the bar and through a swinging door into what I assumed was the kitchen.

Forest cleared his throat. "It's not really a car. It's a jeep. You can drive, can't you? Or do you get driven everywhere?" He looked me up and down.

"Of course I can drive. If I can conquer LA—and Toronto in winter—you can trust me with your jeep."

Forest nodded once, then stood next to me. I felt dwarfed by his size. I was no shrinking violet at five seven, but his presence was larger than life. Something about him felt...safe, even though I hardly knew him, and he seemed at best disinterested in me or my reason for being here. "I'll get the key." He strode past me toward the lobby.

Fern returned then, arm in arm with the server who'd been here last night, the one with the big brown curls. "Domino, this is my friend Bluebell," she said.

Bluebell looked like she could hardly contain herself. "Can I give you a hug?" She clasped her hands in front of her, her face eager.

I held out my arms. "Always happy to meet a fellow hugger." She squeezed me firmly, then held me at arm's length. "Boy, you're even prettier in person."

I felt my cheeks burn as we pulled apart. "Oh, that's such a nice thing to say. Thank you." Compliments about my looks always made me uncomfortable. "Wait a minute. Bluebell? And Fern and Forest?" I shook my head and laughed. "*Three* plant names can't be an accident."

The two women exchanged a smile. "It's not," Bluebell said. "A bunch of us around here are named for flowers."

"Not all of us," Fern cut in. "Me and Forest— neither of us has a flower name. But as the story goes, our parents and a lot of our friends' parents got together and decided to name any daughters they had after the wildflowers on Orcas Island."

"That's so cool," I said.

"Some chose botanical names for their sons, too. Besides Forest, there's Rocky and River..." Fern thought for a moment. "I think that's it for boys."

"You forgot Ash." I heard Forest's voice behind me. And felt his presence. The air felt warmer when he was near, I was learning. "Jeep's out back. Follow me." He turned on his heel and headed for the swinging door Fern had disappeared behind earlier.

I grabbed my scarf and coat and quickly moved to follow him. "Sorry to run out on you," I called over my shoulder to the women. "Nice to meet you, Bluebell!"

"Nice to meet *you!*" she shouted in reply.

"Good luck today!" Fern added just as I pushed through the door and it swung shut behind me. When my eyes adjusted to the dim light in the kitchen, I saw Forest's imposing figure across the room by a door to the outside.

"This way," he called. I followed him into the gray light of Bayview.

Forest

"*This* is your hotel car?" Domino asked as we neared the ocean-blue Jeep Wrangler hybrid parked behind the Driftwood. She'd rewrapped her scarf around neck, casting her cheeks in a pink glow.

I shrugged as I came to a stop in front of it, my hands deep in my pockets. I'd come out without a coat or gloves, and the wind was still bitterly cold. "Yep."

Her breath came out in short puffs in the frigid air. I caught myself staring at her lips while her attention was on the jeep. They were impossibly soft-looking, just plump enough to be so damn sexy without any effort. Botox, likely. Or—wait, maybe that was something else. I made a mental note to ask Fern what famous people did to their faces. Domino pursed those rose-colored lips and turned my way.

"It's not exactly...what I was expecting." Her eyebrows rose high enough they disappeared under her shiny bangs.

I laughed. I realized that was the thing with superstars—they didn't get there by accident. This woman was as charming as she was beautiful, and even I wasn't immune to her appeal. "Got me there," I told her. "Fern was against it, but since I paid for it, I got my way. Besides, it goes with the territory." I clicked the key fob to unlock the doors and handed it to her.

"How do you mean?" She pulled a hand from her coat pocket, grabbed the fob, and slid it back in.

"Orcas Island isn't a conventional place—it likely won't be what you're expecting either." I wrapped my arms around myself in an attempt to stop shivering.

"Good luck today." I bowed my head before returning to the warmth of the hotel, leaving Domino staring after me, a little bewildered.

Once in the kitchen, I stood far enough from the window inlaid in the door I didn't think she could see me, watching as she pulled open the driver's-side door and climbed in. She shook her head once, then adjusted the seat and mirrors before starting the engine. I stayed there as she drove off, the tail lights growing smaller and twinkling red as she went.

I didn't give a shit about fame, I reminded myself. As far as I was concerned, we were all equals on this planet, and we should all work together to look after it. I was happier wandering in the woods with friends or paddling in the ocean than I was stuck in front of a TV or movie screen. No matter how charming she was, this woman wasn't going to get any special treatment from me—any more than anyone else we hosted at the Driftwood Inn.

Still, something deep within me stirred when I thought about her. *It's just her looks*. I left the kitchen and headed for the basement. *Don't be thrown off by the pretty, shiny actress*. She was probably even acting just now. No one was *that* famous and *that* nice.

I spent a couple of hours working on the heat exchanger. I'd looked up the problem on YouTube this morning while Fern was gushing to Domino about

France and clothes and whatever else. Confident I'd fixed it, and Fern could cross at least one thing off our list, I wiped my forehead with the bandanna I'd been using to keep my hands dry while I worked, then gathered my tools and tossed them, along with the bandanna, into my dad's old toolbox that sat propped open on the bench next to where I'd been working.

Dad had that toolbox for as long as I could remember. He didn't like to spend money on frivolous things, but he always chose quality over everything else when it came to his tools. I'd tried to convince him to take it with him to Arizona, but he'd just clapped me on the shoulder and said, "You'll thank me later, son."

He wasn't wrong.

Ready for fresh air, I went upstairs to grab a jacket and wool beanie. I waved to Fern as I passed the dining room on the way through the lobby. She tipped an imaginary hat my way before she returned her attention to Bluebell.

Outside, the air was still crisp, but the wind had died down, and the sound of the boat halyards jangling in the marina had quieted. The haunting cries of seagulls accompanied me down Water Street, where the lights in the shop windows were bright and inviting. I walked to the end of the strip, anchored by the run-down Surf Motel, where the water met the

edge of Sombrio Park, then turned back, smiling at
Juniper Eliot as she walked determinedly away from
Grind House. What was bothering her?

A dark gray Toyota truck rolled by slowly. This
was the second time it'd passed me, I realized. Must be
looking for someone inside, I thought, although I
didn't recognize the vehicle. From this angle I couldn't
see the driver.

A bell above the door jingled as I entered
Bayview's locally owned coffee shop, the smell of
warm pastries filling my nostrils.

"Hey, Forest." Leo Wolff greeted me from a table
near the front. That explained Juniper's expression.
The Eliots and the Wolffs had a feud that went back
as long as anyone around here could remember. Leo
and Juniper—and Ginger, the owner of the café—were
all around the same age as me and Fern and Bluebell.
We all went to school together at Orcas Island High,
and most of us had stayed on the island—or gone
away and returned, like I had. Something about the
place just did that to you. Pulled you back into its
warm embrace, with its wide open spaces, fresh Pacific
air, and glorious old trees. It was hard to explain to
outsiders, but you felt it in your bones. It was home.

"Hey, man," I called in reply as I took my place in
line. Ginger stood behind the counter, welcoming
customers with her trademark good nature and

copper-red hair. In a way we'd lived parallel lives, Ginger and me. She, too, had left the island after high school—although her pursuits were far more impressive and ambitious than mine. Where I hiked around the mountains of British Columbia planting seedlings, she'd been at Stanford in northern California, studying science. Or was it physics? Afterward she'd worked in Silicon Valley for a few years but gave up big money— so rumor said—to return to Orcas, around the same time I did. She'd been here running Grind House ever since.

"Hey, Forest! The usual?" She welcomed me with the same big smile she gave everyone. Thing was, she meant it. I had to hand it to Ginger; she always seemed...content.

"You read my mind." I pulled my hat off, running my fingers through my hair to try to smooth it into place.

"Here." Ginger reached across the counter and patted the side of my head. Her eyebrows drew together, and she suppressed a giggle. It must not have behaved in the way she'd hoped. "Can't say I didn't try." She grabbed an enormous doughnut from the display case with a pair of tongs. It landed on a plate with a thunk. "Coffee'll be up in a minute," she said as she slid the plate toward me.

I took a seat at the window, where a bar was lined

with counter-height leather stools. Julian Cooper, a teenager who worked part-time for Ginger, delivered my coffee, and soon I was tucking into the doorstop of a doughnut in front of me. I could never resist Grind House's classic old-fashioned doughnuts—which meant I had to ration how often I came to the coffee shop. I bit into its cakelike texture, enjoying the hint of nutmeg and the richness of buttermilk. It was a perfect doughnut, as far as I was concerned—thick, delicious, and not too sweet with a firm, almost crunchy shell coated in vanilla glaze.

I looked up at the sound of the doorbell. I didn't recognize the man who'd walked in, which was unusual this time of year. In January, February, and even March, the island was quiet and mostly free of tourists, which gave the locals a chance to catch their breath and take some time to relax. This guy definitely wasn't a local. Instead of the pull-on leather boots most of us wore in winter, he had on red-and-white Air Jordans against otherwise all-dark clothing, including an LA Dodgers ball cap covered by the hood of a black sweatshirt. He carried a big, heavy-looking backpack.

I watched with interest as he scanned the room, looking for but not finding someone in particular.

"Hi there. Can I get you anything?" Ginger called. I swiveled around to observe their interaction.

"I, uh... No, thanks." He turned away from the counter, facing the door again. But something crossed his face—an idea, and he spun back around to Ginger. "I'll take a coffee after all," he told her. "To go."

After paying, the man shuffled to the side of the coffee bar to wait for his drink. This guy rubbed me the wrong way. He rested his elbow on the bar and leaned on it. "Anything exciting going on around here?" he asked Julian.

Julian glanced up from the espresso machine, lifting his shoulders. "Not really, dude."

"Cool," he said, acting more cool than he was, especially in Julian's eyes. "See you around, man." He grabbed the cup Julian placed on the bar, scanned the room one more time, and walked past me on his way out. He'd been so preoccupied with looking for...I didn't know who, he hadn't even noticed me staring at him.

My attention went to Poppy Willoughby, who came through the door held open by the stranger. Seeing me by the window, she pulled out the stool next to mine. Another island kid around the same age as me, Poppy was a writer who often worked from one of the tables at Grind House. "Hey, Forest. I haven't seen you in a minute." She set down a laptop she had hugged to her chest and took off the black leather jacket she was wearing, slinging it on the bar in front of her. Registering my surprise, she said, "Stopped raining, right?"

She whirled around on the stool and waited to catch Ginger's attention. "Julian's already on it," Ginger called.

"So I was texting with Fern this morning." Poppy spun back to face me dead-on. *Shit.* Fern must've told her about our guest.

I crossed my arms. "You can't print that." Poppy wrote a regular column about island life for the *Bayview Chronicle.* I didn't particularly care about Domino's privacy, but I *did* care about protecting all our guests' right to privacy—movie stars or no.

Julian appeared behind us, coffee in hand. Once he'd set it in front of Poppy and retreated, she rested a hand on my shoulder. "I know that. I would never." Her shoulder-length dark hair framed big green eyes that held a characteristic deadpan expression. "What I *would* like to do, though, is a proper interview with her. Something high profile." She drew the mug up for a sip, then held the cup aloft, looking out the window at the darkening sky. "Could be a game changer."

This was the second time someone had suggested Domino's presence here was a life-changing opportunity. It didn't sit right with me. She was here only a week, and she didn't owe us anything. "She'll be gone in a few days."

"But I thought she was shooting a movie here," Poppy said immediately. Clearly she was as enamored as Fern was with the idea of it all.

"Doubt it. Look around. Doesn't look like movie material to me."

Poppy watched me for a minute, then laughed. "Come on, you old grump. You know what it's like here come May. It's paradise. Best place on earth. Of course she's gonna make her movie here."

Visions of the leaky roof and scuffed floors at the inn played in my mind, but I didn't mention them to Poppy. The last thing we needed right now was to be featured in one of her upcoming columns. Changing the topic was the safest bet. "What're you working on now?" I gestured to the laptop on the counter.

"Couple things, actually." Her face lit up as she described two profiles she was working on: one on Juniper Eliot, who'd recently launched a business building passive houses, and the other on Mayor Rocky Black. "Oh! And I'm writing a script."

"A movie script?"

Poppy took another drink of coffee. "Started this morning," she said. "Hey, if the biggest actress in Hollywood comes knocking on your door, you gotta be ready." She winked when she saw me shift uncomfortably.

This woman was delusional if nothing else, but I

kept that thought to myself. "Sounds like you're busy. I'll get out of your way." I tugged the wool hat from my pocket and slid it on before I picked up my jacket.

She stood, too, and leaned over to kiss my right cheek. "Bye, Forest. Say hi to Fern."

Poppy had known me long enough to push past my grouchiness, a trait I appreciated—especially when it led to kissed cheeks. "Take care." I waved to Ginger and Julian. It was a good thing Orcas was filled with cheerful, positive people—to counterbalance the petulance that followed me everywhere I went.

CHAPTER 7

Domino

My day of exploration turned out to be fun. Grateful for a vehicle that easily handled the hills and gravel roads that wound across the horseshoe-shaped island, I could see Forest's point in insisting on something like a jeep. Despite the pewter skies of January, the drive made it obvious I was in a pretty special place. Outside town, Orcas was rustic and rural, an emerald paradise of fields and forests.

My first stop was Winslow, a farming community about twenty-five minutes from Bayview. At its center sat a big old post-and-beam building surrounded by rolling green hills and massively tall trees. Some were evergreen—redwoods of some type, I suspected from the cinnamon-hued bark. Others had shed their leaves for winter, their branches reaching for the sky like thick, twisted tentacles. I stopped in the gravel parking area next to the building and got out to look around. A few posters were tacked to a notice board with GRANGE HALL in large letters across the top.

Wide double doors were covered by a porch overhang. "Winslow Farmers Market," I read aloud, then skimmed the dates listed. I cupped my hands around my eyes and peered through the windows, the glass wavy with age. Wooden tables were spaced in neat rows across an enormous open room. It might be old, but someone took good care of this building.

It had potential as a production headquarters. It was big and open with plenty of parking. But was it too far from the main town? I stuck a pin in that thought to return to later.

The sound of an engine drew my attention. I turned to see a dark gray truck stopped at the entrance to the grounds. It was far enough away I couldn't make out any details in the gloomy day, but after a minute of sitting in one spot, the driver revved the engine and reversed quickly, gravel spitting under its tires before it sped down the road.

Was I trespassing? I didn't think so. Maybe they were looking for someone.

My next stop was Cottle's Fish Market. I guided the jeep slowly down Larsen Road, its sloping hill punctuated by a weathered old building perched on the end of a pier. With the view obscured by fog, it sat suspended over the edge of the water. Old orange-and-yellow fishing buoys hung against cedar shingles, and a sign pointed around the side of the building to the entrance, which faced the water.

The quiet outside, interrupted only by seagulls' wails and the high-pitched, piping call of another bird, belied the cheerful interior, where an older man with the cragged skin of a fisherman worked in the kitchen, a younger man by his side. A woman with long gray hair stood behind a small counter, taking orders from the two parties ahead of me and calling them behind her to the cooks. I looked around the space as I waited, taking in the cooler of freshly caught fish, where pink salmon fillets were lined up next to ribbed-shell clams on ice, their rust-colored ridges curved like rippled sand. A lively-looking woman with short auburn hair waved from her table.

"Were you waving at me?" I asked, glancing behind to check if someone else was there.

When she smiled, it was with her whole face. "Yes! Yes, I was. I saw you were by yourself. Would you like to join me?" She gestured to her table, where a bicycle helmet occupied the spot opposite her.

I was surprised by her openness, but I didn't get the impression she recognized me. She looked older than my mom, which might explain why. "Oh, that's lovely. I'll just—" I pointed at the order counter.

"Of course, dear. Go on. I'll clear my things so you can sit."

The line had cleared. I scanned the chalkboard menu behind the woman at the till. It all looked good, but I hadn't had fish and chips since that family trip to Vancouver in high school. "Halibut and chips, please," I told the woman as I unbuttoned my coat.

"One piece or two?" She wasn't inputting my order in a computer or even holding a pad and pen. She just waited patiently for me to dig my purse out of my pocket.

"Two," I said without hesitation. While I was here for the week, I planned to take in as much of the place as I could—including the food. The woman turned to the duo in the kitchen and repeated my order. There really was no need for a fancy computer system. This crew had it down.

"I haven't seen you here before. Friend of Angela's?" she asked as I handed her cash.

"Who?"

"Angela." She indicated the auburn-haired woman.

Yet another person who didn't seem to know—or

care—who I was. This was heaven. "Oh! No. Not yet, anyway. She asked me to join her. I'm here from Los—California," I said. The vaguer the better, I figured.

"Welcome. I'm Mary." I refused to take any change, just pointed to the tip jar. "And that's Louis, and that's our son, Freddy," she said of the men in the back.

"Domino. You work with your family—how wonderful." That made two family businesses I'd encountered here in as many days. Maybe that was the norm in small towns.

"I reckon you're right," Mary said, then leaned forward and added, "Most days." She placed her hands on her hips and laughed. "Freddy will bring out your food when it's ready."

As I made the short walk to Angela's table, I heard low murmurings from the two groups who'd been in line in front of me, now seated on the right-hand side of the small restaurant. Looking at one, then the other, it was obvious they recognized me. I brushed my hair in front of my shoulders and finger-combed my bangs. Hiding behind my hair was a defense mechanism I'd adopted when I started dating Harry. I knew it was ridiculous to think it worked, but somehow it made me feel less...visible.

Angela watched with interest as she gestured to the

seat across from her. I was grateful now for the company. Eating alone was a different prospect when you weren't anonymous. "You're causing a stir. Am I missing something?" Her eyes were wide with interest, her mouth slightly open.

I shrugged out of my coat and hung it, along with my scarf, over the back of the chair before I pulled it out to sit. "Oh, it's nothing really. I think they recognize me is all."

"Oh yes?" She tilted her head to one side, even more interested.

I smiled at the two groups, then focused on Angela, hoping now they'd turn their attention elsewhere. At least no one pulled out their phone. "I'm an actor. Domino." I held out a hand, which she took in hers and held, searching my face. "Maybe you've seen *Love Letters*? Or *The Muse*?"

Freddy approached the table holding an oval plate lined with red-and-white-checkered paper. Angela let go. "I'm sorry, dear. I don't think I have."

"All the better," I told her, ogling the food in front of me—golden chunks of fried halibut, bright-green peas, and thick, chunky fries. A slice of lemon was curled around the edge of a little pot of tartar sauce. "Angela, is it?"

"Yes, that's right. Angela Fletcher. Thank you for joining me. I love talking to younger people. Tell me, are you in any whodunits?"

"Whodunits?"

"Murder mysteries. You know, your movies." Angela rested her elbows on the table, crossing her arms over each other. Somehow I didn't mind her watching me eat. The fish batter was crunchy and hot, and the halibut inside melted in my mouth. Sure, you *could* get fish and chips in LA, but it wasn't anything it was known for. Mexican? Absolutely. British fare? I avoided it any day of the week.

"Not yet. I'd like to, though. That's your favorite?"

"Oh, yes. I'm a writer—I write mysteries. Maybe you've heard of me?"

I looked up from my plate to see her eyes twinkling. "I'm not sure. Angela...?"

"Fletcher. I've got quite a following, too, you know."

The name wasn't familiar, but I didn't read a lot of mysteries. "Have you written many books?"

"Fifty-four. Fifty-five, actually. I've almost finished the last. I'm published in seventeen countries."

I just about spat out the french fry I'd bitten into, slathered in tangy tartar sauce and ketchup. "Now I'm the one who's sorry," I said. "Fifty-five? That's incredible. How on earth do you come up with all your ideas?"

"Oh, it's not that hard. I cycle all over the island, keep my eyes open, observe everything. I bet I know more about what's going on with some folks than their families do. But mine is not the job to judge. I see what I see, absorb it, then, over time, stories just...come."

"Wow." I listened as she talked more about her process, devouring both pieces of halibut and nearly all the fries. I saved the last few and battled with my fork to catch a mouthful of peas. "But you write fiction?"

Angela reached into a pannier pack next to her and pulled out a notepad, which she flipped through in front of me. Pages and pages were filled with neat handwriting. "Fiction, yes. Inspired by real events and people, who most of the time don't even realize it." A smirk lit up those round green eyes again. "My next book is a real-life murder mystery, though—my first."

"Someone was killed here?" A pang of worry shot through me that the quiet little island I'd landed on had a dark underbelly.

"A long time ago, yes." Phew. "It was the start of a decades-long family feud."

"It's unsolved? Oh, thank you," I told Freddy as he cleared my plate.

"It's been a cold case for as long as I can remember. I doubt a detective has touched it in years." She held her head a bit higher. "I think I may have stumbled onto something," she said proudly.

I loved this woman, I decided. She had to be nearing eighty, but she had the spirit—and work ethic, apparently—of someone fifty years younger. I hoped I was like her at that age. And she was disarmingly friendly. I could see how she might just hold the secrets of the whole island behind those big green eyes.

I could've talked to Angela for hours, but I needed to get back on the road to see the other spots I'd flagged before it got dark. Cottle's was quaint and charming, and there was no question it embodied the coastal ambience embedded in the script for *Shore Thing*. I could easily see it as a good date spot for the main characters. "I'm so glad I met you." I reached across the table and took Angela's hand in mine. She gave me a squeeze.

"Likewise, Domino. I'll see you around." I didn't doubt it for a second.

"I would love that." We let go, and I dug in my coat pocket for my phone. I had a vague idea where Moonstone Beach was, but Google Maps didn't give exact directions. Angela would know. "Moonstone Beach?" I stood, slipping into my coat and fastening the buttons.

"One of my favorites. Now, it's a little off the beaten track." At my nod, she continued, "When you get to the top of Larsen, turn left on Ellison. Drive about ten or eleven miles, and you'll come to a three-way stop. You must've come through it on your way here."

"I followed the sign for Winslow."

"That's it. Instead of turning left back to Bayview, take the right onto the gravel road. Follow it until it ends, and you're there."

Wrapping my scarf around my neck, I dropped the phone in my pocket and thanked her before heading for the door. "Bye, Domino," Mary called from behind the counter. Freddy and Louis stood next to her, all three of them grinning like Cheshire cats. Freddy shrugged, a blush creeping up his cheeks. He'd recognized me after all.

"You're our first movie star," Louis said, his wrinkles turning rightside up as he smiled.

I touched a hand to my chest. "The pleasure was all mine," I said. I meant it. To the right, the two tables of people were smiling as well. Angela beamed. There was something magical about this little island and its inhabitants. Maybe it was living at the edge of the world. Maybe it was all that fresh Pacific air. Or maybe all small towns were this way. Whatever the reason, I was here for it.

Moonstone Beach only added to the allure of the place. Despite the dreary cold, the slow crashing and swelling of the surf hitting the beach caught me in its rhythm as the wind whipped my hair around like the blades of a helicopter. Healing was the only word to describe the feeling it all gave me—the waves, the ever-present cries of seabirds, the layer of marine mist hanging in the salty air. Harry Roman couldn't have felt farther away from this moment. And I was slowly beginning to feel closer to myself. I don't know how long I stayed there, gazing out at the blue-green water tipped with froths of white, but when the daylight began to fade, I took in one last deep breath, hoping to hold on to the feeling of strength that'd washed over me here.

On the road back to Bayview, I turned over in my mind the things I needed to figure out before my weekly production meeting. I needed to find a boat—and someone to drive it. And then there was catering. Could the Driftwood handle the needs of a full cast and crew? At the intersection of Ellison and Water Street, I made a left. Parked behind the hotel, with the hum of the engine switched off, I heard my phone buzz with incoming texts. I hadn't looked at it since before I left Cottle's. My heart dropped, and panic shot through me. Was something wrong?

But when I fished the phone from my pocket, my heart fell even further. Message after message filled the screen: **Are you ok? Who took those pictures? They're not**

that bad, really! I scrolled and scrolled, ignoring the images people had sent, until I landed on the last one, from Trudi. **Call me.** I had eighteen missed calls.

Dread trickled through me like a spider crawling over my skin. I closed my eyes, willing serenity, before I started tapping the pictures to open them. The first was of me on the docks this morning, arms folded over my chest, eyes closed against the wind. The next was outside Grange Hall, my gaze narrowed at something in the distance, lips in an upside-down U. I knew I'd been staring at that truck, but in the photo I looked full of despair and anger. Deirdre had forwarded a few memes already circulating the internet crowning me the new "Sad Affleck."

Hot shame burned my cheeks. Could this be any more humiliating? The very public breakup was bad enough. Now I was "Depressed Domino." This stuff never happened to Julia Roberts. How had I gone from Hollywood sweetheart to the object of pity and ridicule—practically overnight?

The only way to stop the onslaught of texts was to shut off my phone. Everyone could wait. Determination took the place of shame as two intentions crystallized in my mind: find the bottom of a bottle of tequila—and figure out which local had sold me out.

Forest

I returned from Grind House as the silver sky turned dark and went straight up to my room. No rain meant no leak, which meant I might snag a peaceful nap after a sleepless week. My room was inky black when I woke up hours later, illuminated only by the hazy red light of the digital clock. Ten p.m.? I'd been more exhausted than I'd thought.

In jeans and an old flannel shirt, I descended to the dining room in search of food, expecting to find it empty this late on a Monday night, but when I stepped down from the lobby, Domino sat at the bar, head in her hands, her hair shiny in the pendant lights that hung above. Fern, seated next to her, shrugged when she saw me, her ponytail drooping to mid-height. A half-empty bottle of tequila in front of them told me all I needed to know—that I should walk straight past them to the kitchen.

Domino barely lifted her head as I went by. Fern wrapped an arm around her and gave her a squeeze, then hopped off her stool and followed me through the swinging door. "Leftover soup in the walk-in," she said, indicating the walk-in refrigerator on the left-hand side of the kitchen. "I'll cut some bread. I think all of us could use something to eat."

I said nothing, just lifted an eyebrow as I brought the big soup pot from the fridge and placed it on the stove, turning the gas on high. I shoved my hands in my pockets and leaned against the wall, watching as Fern cut into a crusty French baguette from Pies & Otherwise, our bread supplier.

"Don't you want to know what's going on?" she asked, looking up at me.

I shook my head.

"But it's—"

"None of my business," I interrupted. "None of our business. Not the best idea to get drunk with the customers, Fern. Especially not this one." At the glare she leveled at me, I added, "You said yourself she has influence."

"I'm not drunk."

I lifted an eyebrow again.

"I'm not! Really. I had one glass. She needed someone to talk to, and there I was."

I grabbed a soup ladle from where the cooking utensils hung on a magnet above the stove and stuck it in the soup, stirring in a giant circle to distribute the heat. "Whatever it is can't be that bad. She's rich and famous, right?"

My sister nodded as she slid past me and into the walk-in, returning with three ramekins of whipped butter.

"Then she's just fine." With bubbles forming in the pot, I was satisfied it was hot enough to serve. Fern pulled soup bowls and plates from the tall stack to my left and placed them on the long stainless table that divided the kitchen in half. I ladled three portions of steaming squash and lentil soup; Fern added the bread and butter. I grabbed one plate in each hand, and she followed me with the other.

Things had gone from bad to worse in the dining room. When I pushed through the swinging door, I could see Domino had rested her head on the bar and appeared to be sleeping. At the sound of my throat clearing, she lifted it halfway up and looked at me, unfocused, eyes half-open. "You," she said, then promptly put her head back down.

I felt a pang of empathy, despite my contention nothing could ever be *that* bad for someone who'd achieved whatever golden status meant your picture was in magazines and you were paid millions of dollars. I walked behind her stool and set the two soups on the bar in front of me. Fern put hers down on the other side, gently placing a hand on Domino's back.

"Domino? We're having a late dinner. Why don't

you join us?"

"Hmm?" came a muffled voice from under the mess of shiny hair splayed over her face. Fern brushed it back and behind her ear, then wrapped an arm around Domino's left shoulder and guided her upright. Domino held her eyes closed for a moment longer, and I watched as she sniffed the air. Her eyes popped open in search of whatever smelled so good.

I slid the plate of bread and soup across to her. "Go on, eat."

She did—we all did. With coconut milk and warming spices, the soup was a perfect antidote to cold, damp January in the Pacific Northwest.

"God, this is good." Domino broke the silence, laying down her spoon and ripping a piece of baguette in half to dip in the soup. As the minutes ticked by and she got closer to the bottom of the bowl, it fueled her to sit up taller and take in her surroundings. She caught me eyeing her but glanced away quickly.

"Feeling better?" Fern's spoon clanged against the empty bowl.

"Think so. You people here are all so nice." She waved a half-eaten piece of bread in my direction. "Except you."

"Don't let him fool you. He's a big softie," Fern said, reaching to separate a strand of Domino's hair from the bread she held.

I wasn't sure how to respond, so I just kept scraping the last of my soup with my spoon. From Domino's perspective, I probably *wasn't* nice. I didn't know much about movie stars, but I imagined she rarely encountered someone who didn't bend to her every need.

"I'm not 'Depressed Domino,' you know. I'm not," Domino said before finally connecting that piece of bread she'd been waving with her mouth. She stared straight at me as she chewed.

I ran a hand through my hair, suddenly conscious I'd come straight from bed to the dining room. My hair was probably sticking up at all angles. "If you say so."

Fern moved around the bar, filled a tall glass with water for Domino, and began to collect our dishes. I murmured thanks and spun on my barstool to face the windows, where the docks were dry under the lights of the marina. The stillness of the boats indicated the wind had held off as well. Damn. If only I'd gone to Anacortes for supplies—tomorrow could've been the perfect day for repairs.

"You know you're lucky, right?"

I turned back to look at Domino. Our stools were pointed in opposite directions—hers the bar and mine the windows—but with our heads facing inward, we met in the middle like yin and yang. Her makeup was smudged, giving her already intense blue eyes a sultriness she probably hadn't intended, shadowed by her dark fringe. The effect was incredibly sexy. She'd pursed her lips in a little bow, which only made her cheeks mold into perfect curves. "How do you mean?"

"You've probably never been humiliated in your whole life." She broke our gaze and tipped the water glass back, drinking half of it.

I heard the kitchen door swing open. Fern crossed in front of me, headed for the lobby. "I'm beat. You okay here, Domino?" she said as she passed. *What about me?* I didn't say it out loud. She did look tired. We all did.

I thought Domino would follow her, but she didn't stir from the barstool next to me, just eyed me expectantly.

Maybe she's waiting for me to stand first, I thought, so I got to my feet. Nope. She remained seated. I leaned my elbow on the bar. "Sure, I'm lucky. I live here, on the prettiest island in the Pacific. I have everything I need. But I've been humiliated, trust me."

"I bet no one's ever called you Foolish Forest."

What the hell? "I bet they've thought it." A beat passed, me leaning against the bar, Domino starting straight ahead. "What's this about?"

"You really don't know?" She angled her face toward me, eyes questioning. When I shook my head, she picked up her phone off the bar, brought up a photo, and held it out. There she was, on the porch at Grange Hall, hands on her hips, eyes narrowed at the camera, mouth downturned. Big white letters across the top and bottom read DEPRESSED DOMINO.

It wasn't the most flattering photo. "Who took that?"

"You tell me," she said, turning the phone back and looking at it herself. "God, what an asshole."

"Hey, easy. I know I'm cranky, but—"

Domino laid a hand on my wrist and let it linger there. The warmth of it surprised me. "Not you. Harry fucking Roman. This is all his fault." She lifted her hand and set her right elbow down, leaning her chin in her hand.

Again, I found myself feeling compassion for this person who'd materialized from the pages of Fern's magazine to be sitting beside me in my family's hotel in the middle of nowhere. "Listen, I don't know what you're going through. But I do know you're obviously talented. And dedicated. And incredibly beau—" I stopped myself from saying it. "This humiliation? You'll get past it. No one'll even remember it. You'll make your next movie, shine your light on the screen, and bury Harry fucking Roman in the sand."

Domino's eyes went shiny, then impossibly bluer.

Shit. "I didn't mean to upset you." I had to turn away from her intense gaze. It was raw with emotion, something I wasn't good at dealing with.

"I know." When I looked back, she was wiping her eyes with her fingers, smudging her makeup a little more. Damn, she was sexy. Then she laughed, lifting her eyes to the ceiling. "I'm sorry. I'm never like this. I swear. It's hard to explain. It's just all so...mortifying. And isolating." After a moment of assessing me head to toe, sending a rush of blood through me, she added, "Tall, handsome, and confident as fuck. Nope. Definitely you've never been this humiliated. You don't strike me as someone who cares what other people think."

I didn't know why I felt the need to comfort this woman, to explain we all went through the same emotions, no matter our lot in life. I grabbed her hand from her lap and tugged her to stand, then let it go. "Follow me."

"Wait, I shouldn't have said... I guess I'm still a little drunk. I'm sorry," I heard her mumble as I headed for the lobby. At the arched doorway I turned to find her standing in place, regret written all over her face.

"Come on."

She smoothed her bangs, stood taller, and walked toward me, elegant and graceful despite all the tequila and sorrow.

110

CHAPTER 8

Domino

"Where are we going?" I asked Forest, following him through the lobby, where he opened a closet by the front door and rummaged around. He reached back with a black knit hat and held it in the air, head still stuck in the closet. When I took it, he passed an enormous insulated plaid flannel jacket that dwarfed my frame as I slid into it. It smelled amazing—like sea salt and pine needles.

He grabbed a jacket for himself, too—a thick Patagonia fleece the color of moss—closed the closet, and tugged open the front door, ushering in a blast of cold ocean air. Without a word he held it for me as I filed past onto the dark front porch. I wasn't worried about my safety with this man, I realized. He might be grumpy as a grizzly bear, but I just felt...secure with him. I trailed him down the few stairs and along the short path from the hotel to Water Street.

We trudged up the hill I'd come down almost two days ago when I arrived. I gave up waiting for Forest to tell me where we were going and instead reveled in the silence. The shadows of the streetlights grew tall and then receded as we passed each one. LA felt very, very far away, with its never-ending hum of traffic, people, and persistence. We were alone out here, kept company by the gentle lapping of waves against the shore and the hooting of an owl as we walked farther from the marina.

Forest stopped at the top of the hill, digging his hands in the pockets of his fleece, his breath visible in the night air. I glanced around me, unsure where I should be looking. "Why are we here?"

"Right after high school, I drove up here with friends. We were catching the ferry to see a basketball game. I parked right there." He pointed across the street from where we stood, shaking his head.

"O...kay?" I still wasn't sure what we were doing. I wrapped my arms around myself, my hands swimming in the too-long sleeves of the enormous flannel jacket.

"Everyone got out. I grabbed my stuff and locked the door. Followed my buddies to right about here. That's when I heard someone yelling. I—everyone— turned around to see the truck rolling backward down the hill, where it disappeared into that row of bushes. My friends and everyone around howled with laughter, watching me tear down the hill after it."

He looked miserable telling the story, but I couldn't help but laugh. The release of emotion was cathartic. I laughed so hard I bent over double, hands on my knees, the enormous sleeves of the jacket flapping halfway down my calves.

"Ohmygod, I'm so sorry," I said, trying to rein it in. "Was anyone hurt?"

"Just my pride. And a 1987 Ford Bronco I'd saved up for four years." Forest finally cracked a smile. "See? Embarrassing."

"Oh, you think so, but it doesn't compare. That was your friends laughing at you. Perfect strangers are laughing at me."

He grabbed for my hand, pushing up the coat sleeve until he found it, and tugged me down the hill. His grip was big and strong in mine. I took two steps to his every one, pushing back the knit hat with my free hand where it had slid down my forehead.

"Now where are we going?"

Again, Forest lumbered on without a word, leading

me past the Driftwood and beyond, until we came to a stop outside a coffee shop. The sign above the door read Grind House. It was dark inside, except for a single light above a tablet propped on a stand on the counter.

"A little late for coffee, isn't it?" I wasn't sure what time it was, I realized. Where was my phone? I let go of Forest's hand and patted around the back pocket of my jeans, where I was relieved to feel the familiar shape of the device—padded by the huge coat I wore.

"I, uh…" I waited while he reached up and scratched the back of his head, as if trying to decide something, then started talking. "I was here last summer. A family came in at the same time I did. They weren't local. They were visitors from out of town. Detroit."

I pushed the knit beanie back again. "And?"

"The dad—he was a big guy. Construction worker maybe. Lots of muscles, rough around the edges." Forest shoved his hands in his pockets again, rocking back on his heels. I let the silence pass until he was ready to continue. "Anyway. They're standing in front of me in line, and I notice this guy's tattoos. He catches me staring, and he doesn't look all that pleased. So I point at one of the tattoos on his arm and say, 'Nice tattoo. Who is that, Alice Cooper?'"

Sounded simple enough. "Is that bad?" I asked.

Forest locked me in his sight, humor in his eyes, then chuckled. "That's when the guy told me it was his mom. Thought I was a goner. The whole family turned to me with daggers for eyes, the son in particular. How was I to know? Bad tattoo of a long-haired, eyeliner-wearing, aging rock star. That could've easily been his mom."

I broke into another fit of giggles. This time, though, Forest joined me. We kept pulling it together, but as soon as we looked at each other, we were off again.

"I was just trying to be friendly," he said, catching his breath. "Never was one for small talk."

That rang true with what I'd seen the past two days. But I was also learning he wasn't all scowls and growls. He just wasn't nice for the sake of it. It was the polar opposite of what I was used to in Hollywood, where people were quick to say yes and afraid to contradict. The more famous I got, the more agreeable everyone around me became.

"Okay, fine, that *is* embarrassing. You get a point. Still, the only people who know about it are you, Alice Cooper's number-one fan, and his family. It's not like it was broadcast on the news or anything."

He thought for a moment, then something dawned in his eyes. "You got one more stop in you?"

I had as many stops in me as this guy wanted to make. I was having *fun*. More fun than I'd had in weeks. Maybe months. He held out his left hand, and I pushed up the long sleeve to reveal my right one and grabbed hold. There he was again. Warm. Strong. Safe.

He walked slower this time, continuing down Water Street, and I kept pace with him. To our right, across the road, the boardwalk followed the curve of the bay. The sound of rolling waves trailed us; the streetlights above were our beacons. Alone here in the dark of night, on this tiny island at the edge of the ocean, it felt like we were cocooned in our own little world. The quiet between us wasn't uncomfortable. Not at all. Being next to Forest, his hand in mine, grounded me in a way I hadn't felt since... I couldn't remember when.

We passed art galleries and lovely little storefronts I wanted to return to in the light of day, including a bookshop housed in an old bank building and a furniture store with a window filled with vintage pieces and beautiful linens. I was busy craning my neck at a lamp that caught my eye and didn't realize Forest had stopped until I bumped into the back of him.

He reached out to steady me. Our gazes caught, and there was nothing between us but the puffs of our breath, particles mingling like clouds in the night sky. I found myself leaning forward as Forest angled his head down, his eyes trained on my lips. The energy sweeping between us was electrifying. *Kiss me kiss me kiss me*, my brain willed, mesmerized by the hunger of his stare. A long, low horn sounded in the distance, breaking the spell. He stopped within an inch of my lips and pulled back, as if startled awake from a dream.

"What was that?"

"Foghorn." He dropped my hand and turned away, looking out at the rolling black sea.

"No, I mean, what was *this*?" I placed a hand on his shoulder and turned him back to me, indicating the space between us.

He cleared his throat. "Sorry about that."

"Don't be sorry—"

"I was out of line." He let out a deep, rumbling laugh. "I brought you here for one more embarrassing story, then made a fool of myself. Go figure."

His eyes were twinkling, his smile wide. It *was* funny. And charming. And so fucking sexy. "Forest—"

He held up a hand and shook his head, so I let the thought linger unsaid. Hands in his pockets, he indicated a restaurant up ahead with a shrug of one shoulder. "That place is owned by my friend River."

"Another earthy name." I kept my voice steady

despite the desire rocketing through my veins like a double espresso.

He nodded. "I was helping out one night when he first opened. I'd been home from tree planting maybe a year. I was happy to see an old friend having dinner, holding a baby in her lap. She introduced me to her husband and the baby. Plum, the baby was called. I leaned down to kiss the top of Plum's head, only I didn't realize she was breastfeeding."

"Oh no."

Even under the dim street lamps, his cheeks flushed pink. "Oh yes. Let's just say it wasn't the baby's head I kissed."

I shrieked, then clapped a long coat sleeve to my mouth when the sound echoed off the water and back against the windows on Water Street. My eyes were round with surprise. I dropped my hand and whispered, "Wow. Just...wow."

Forest squared himself to me, crossed his arms, and tilted his head. "I think I take the prize for humiliation. Would you agree?"

I closed my eyes and pictured those paparazzi photos—of a woman whose expression said one thing but whose insides felt another way altogether. Despite how I appeared in them, I didn't give a shit about Harry Roman. Whether it was Forest's stories or the tequila or the dark and fog around me, I didn't give a shit about those Sad Affleck memes or *Inside Holly-wood* magazine's take on my breakup. I wasn't depressed at all. In that moment, the cold sea air stealing the heat from my breath and the feeling from my toes, I felt free, untethered from the octopus grip of life as a celebrity.

When I opened my eyes again, Forest was staring down at me, concern wrinkling his forehead. I smiled, and the creases smoothed. I grabbed his hand and spun us in the direction of the Driftwood. "Pretty good effort, Forest... What's your last name?"

"Russo."

"Pretty good effort, Forest Russo. I think maybe you squeaked into the lead. I might be the butt of a nationwide joke, but at least I didn't insult some guy's mom or kiss my friend's boob over dinner." I kept a straight face and eyed him sideways. When our gazes caught, I burst out laughing.

The return trip to the hotel seemed so much shorter than the journey out. Wasn't that always the way? The air somehow felt warmer, and I tingled from the inside out, my hand in Forest's, fingers entwined like ivy around a tree.

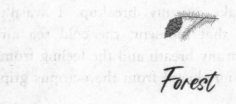

Forest

At the Driftwood, I snaked an arm around Domino and pushed open the front door, holding it wide with my palm while she walked through ahead of me. Inside, she turned to face me, slowly unbuttoning that enormous flannel jacket. She slipped it off her shoulders and held it to me, hanging it from the end of her pointer finger. Grabbing it from her, I watched in admiration as she pushed the knit beanie back and off, shaking her dark shiny hair around her shoulders and smoothing out her bangs.

There was no denying the feelings she aroused in me, feelings I usually tamped down. Relationships—entrusting my heart to another human—I didn't do them. I'd never been comfortable hanging my love out like a leaf on the end of a branch, vulnerable to whatever wind came along and swept it in the ocean.

I was happy with my own company, anchored by the giant evergreens and jagged shores of Orcas Island. Once in a while I hooked up with a woman—never a hotel guest—but exposing myself to things I couldn't control? Not on the table. Domino West had me right up against those self-imposed boundaries.

She was here for a short time, I reminded myself, and on the heels of a breakup. The last thing she needed was some guy in the middle of nowhere crushing on her while she worked.

I hung up our coats while she waited, twisting a strand of hair between her fingers. Squinting over her head, I strained to read the time on the wall clock behind the desk using only the streetlight filtering through the windows. Domino turned to see what I was peering at—and gasped.

"Shit! Shit, shit, shit shit," she said when she saw the clock: 4:15. The lightless sky was deceiving. In summer months it took on the orange cast of day-break right about now, beckoning sunrise, but in midwinter, there was no sign of light until well past seven, which meant hours on end of gloomy darkness.

I came to stand beside her. "Everything okay?"

She pulled the phone from her pocket and checked the time there, too, as if disbelieving what she'd seen. "No. Yes. I mean, it will be. It's just... I have a production meeting in five hours." She flicked a glance at me. "I'm not exactly prepared."

"That's my fault." My shoulders dropped. "I didn't realize—"

"Don't apologize, please." She laid a hand on my arm, sending a skip of desire to my heart like a bolt of lightning. When I startled, she pulled it away again quickly but held my gaze. She'd felt it, too.

Neither of us spoke for a minute, just let the electricity flow between us, but when her eyes left mine and darted again to the clock on the wall, I broke the quiet. "Let's call it a night."

She nodded. Was that disappointment in her eyes? She turned away before I could be sure. We took a step forward in unison. Then another, and another, until we were side by side at the elevator doors, the glassy eyes of the taxidermy deer peering down at us. When a ping announced the elevator's arrival, I moved aside as Domino entered.

"Coming?" Her intense blue eyes, still smudged with mascara, told me she felt the same way I did: like she didn't want this night to end. Her finger poised on the button, she waited, willing me with her stare to step into the elevator—and beyond. Being the focus of her attention felt like sunshine on a winter day.

It took everything I had not to. Instead I shoved my fists in my pockets and held my ground. "You go on ahead. I have a few things to do here." She dropped her head in disappointment, and it almost broke me. "Good night, Domino." I knew my limits. I recognized if I fell into this woman's bed, I might fall in love forever.

She let go of the button, and the door slid shut,

leaving me, my ramped-up desire, and the taxidermy deer alone in the dark lobby.

I climbed the stairs to my room on the fifth floor and tried to sleep. Without rain, there was no dripping water, and the silence was deafening. Eyes closed, I replayed the evening in my mind like a movie: her laughter, the way her hand felt in mine, that almost kiss. My erection pressed against my boxer briefs. Ignoring it seemed impossible. But pleasuring myself to fantasies of Domino seemed...like an invasion somehow. She'd already had her privacy encroached. I resisted the urge to reach down, even though my cock throbbed with need.

An hour passed, maybe more, before I gave up on sleep and switched on the light on the bedside table. I sat up and shoved my feet into woolen socks, then moved to the window and lifted the shade. Outside the sky was still dark, the docks quiet, but the moon shimmered off the Pacific in a silvery beam. A single star twinkled brightly. I let the shade drop back into place.

To expel the energy coursing through me like bees in a bottle, I dropped to the floor to count off some push-ups. Balancing my weight over my wrists, keeping my muscles engaged, forced my thoughts to stay in the moment. If I closed my eyes, though, there she was, looking back at me from the elevator, the air charged with lust. I worked until I lost count and my muscles burned. When I could do no more, I grabbed my phone and sat on the floor, back against the bed, sweat beading down my face.

Roof repair, I typed into a search engine. Nothing like roofing to get your mind off sex. I waited in vain as the browser hung in inactivity, the blue loading line across the top stuck at halfway.

Fern was right. We had to put fixing the Wi-Fi at the top of our list. What if there was an emergency? People, especially travelers, depended on their phones for everything. And I'd be able to find things on YouTube when I needed to.

I called up my images folder and scrolled through photos from my last year of tree planting. The memories of hiking uneven terrain with only a shovel and forty pounds of saplings strapped around my shoulders reminded me of what was most important in life: working hard, my friends and family on Orcas Island, and building a sustainable business with the Driftwood.

I rested my head against the bed, memories of wide open spaces, breathtaking views, and camping in the wilderness in my mind. I must have drifted off, because the next thing I knew, I was awoken by steady drips of water hitting the bucket. The rain was back, and the clear, dry night I'd spent on the streets of Bayview with Domino West felt like a dream.

CHAPTER 9

Domino

"What do you mean, you're not sure yet?" Arthur Dragon's voice snarled through the speakers on my phone. I wondered if the vein pulsing in his forehead would burst now or sometime later. "You're wasting my time." His accusation fanned a flame in the pit of my belly that sent heat rushing to the tips of my ears.

This meeting wasn't going well. I'd been late to join, not because I overslept—I didn't—but because I couldn't get a solid internet connection on my laptop and had to resort to using wireless on my phone.

A row of open mouths stared back at me from tiny squares on the screen. I shouldn't have phrased it that way. Arthur didn't do well with uncertainty, and I didn't do well with confrontation.

"It looks promising." I changed my tack. "I've been here for two days, Arthur. I need more time to find out."

Arthur grunted but didn't press me further. That answer must have satisfied him, because the pulsing vein retreated into his forehead and I no longer feared he would jump through the phone and scream at me in person.

"I'll come and join you?" Marc's optimism cheered me up a little.

I moved from the bed to sit in the window seat, bringing with me the latte Fern had delivered after I'd called down this morning. Rain trickled from the dull sky, puckering the ocean's surface with disappearing circles. I needed Marc to know I wanted more time without disappointing him or irritating Arthur. "That sounds great," I agreed. "Let's connect offline." Marc smiled hopefully. I was on a roll. "Trudi?"

With her brown hair tied back this morning, Trudi's glasses appeared to dwarf her face when she leaned in close to the camera. "Good progress, Domino." We'd texted before the call so I could tell her how the location scout was really going. In other words, she knew why I wasn't sure. I hadn't found a boat or a suitable place for a production headquarters, and the hotel was still a question mark.

Forest and his sister presented a strong front, but what was the deal with the tarp? The lack of a centralized booking system or website was concerning—not to mention the unreliable Wi-Fi. Could they handle the likes of Arthur Dagon? Alex needed to account for every penny, and without a computerized record system, that was going to be hard for the Driftwood to accommodate.

I hadn't even thought about whether they could handle catering. We'd be bringing union crew with us to operate craft services on set, but we still needed a local provider for larger meals and off-set food. Everything I'd eaten at the Driftwood was great, but I worried about its capacity. So far I'd seen only one server and two cooks. That was hardly enough to feed the locals, never mind thirty plus people for six weeks. And who was cleaning the rooms?

I needed to at least consider these issues before Marc flew out to Orcas.

Alex took over the call with a financing update. Before my ability to focus on numbers left me entirely, I heard her say she'd secured another significant financer. Which was good news and bad. If Orcas Island wasn't the right location, we'd have to delay the whole project by another month while we searched for another. Financers didn't like delays.

A knock at the door made me jump and sent coffee dripping down my arm. Emery and Trudi looked up with interest. If I ignored it, maybe whoever it was would go away.

Rap, rap, rap. The knock sounded again. Putting my cup down, I held up a finger and went to answer it. I hit the mute button but didn't put the call on hold; I didn't want to miss Emery's casting update.

"Good morning." Forest towered above me, a wall of muscle and strength. His gray-blue eyes traveled from my face to my feet and back again, watching with interest as I licked coffee from my arm. He looked tired, as I'm sure I did, but on him exhaustion was sexy, his voice slightly hoarse but still deep and rumbling. His gaze ended on the phone clasped tightly in my hand. "I'm interrupting."

It was only then I realized they'd all stopped talking in the meeting. I tapped the screen to turn the sound on. "Excuse me a moment. I'll be right back." They watched as I searched, awkwardly, for how to put the video call on hold. When I finally did, the screen faded to gray, and I made sure the little microphone icon had a strike through it to indicate it was off.

"Morning." Butterflies fluttered around in my stomach. I felt my lips tug into a smile.

We stared at each other, me holding my phone

with one hand and the door handle with the other, him crossing his arms in front him, his dark hair wet.

"I won't keep your—" he indicated the phone with a nod "—friends waiting. I just wanted to tell you..." He cleared his throat. "I had a great time last night."

I was ready to haul him into the room and throw him on the bed, but that would be inappropriate for a number of reasons, least of which was the business call I was in the middle of. "So did I. Thank you."

He waited a moment, then tucked two fingers to his forehead and tipped them in salute before he started backing away.

"Wait." I stepped into the hallway after him. "I have some questions for you. And Fern. You around later?"

"Should be." Then he turned, sucking away his heat and intensity, and stalked toward the stairwell at the end of the hall. I retreated to my room and shut the door behind me, leaning my back against it and inhaling deeply. How could this handsome, grumpy stranger have such a strong effect on me? I shook my head, chalking it up to all the oxygen in the air here in the wilderness.

I tapped the video call app to rejoin the meeting. Emery was speaking. *Shit.* I'd missed the part I was most looking forward to. He stopped midsentence when I reappeared. "Who was *that*?"

Four pairs of eyes peered back at me. Not Arthur's of course. He seemed to have entirely disengaged from the conversation. "Yes, tell us, Domino," Alex teased. "Who was that?"

"Calm down, all of you. It was just one of the hotel managers."

"He can knock on my door anytime." Alex made a fanning motion with her hand.

"Can he act? He'd look amazing on a big screen." Emery appreciated handsome more than most women did.

"Oh, please." I did my best to downplay everything to do with Forest, his looks, and the way he made my stomach do flips. Trudi raised an eyebrow. "Emery, go on," I said.

Even in his tiny square on the screen, I could see Emery's big brown eyes glinting, but he continued. "The underwater scenes—I was just saying I have a lead on a dive team."

Many of the scenes in *Shore Thing* needed to be shot underwater—following the two lead characters as they dove for treasure. I'd been worried from the start about finding underwater camera talent who would fit within our budget. It was a highly skilled job, and people with those specialist skills usually came at a steep price.

"Team?" The implication in Alex's question was

obvious: Did we need—and could we afford—a whole team?

Emery chuckled. "I get your concern, Alex. Let me clarify. This is a group of three people. They come as a group—all of them or none—but *Shore Thing* will be only their third shoot, so we can afford them."

Three previous shoots made me nervous. We were looking for skills here, even more than affordability. Seeing Trudi's concern and Arthur's scowl, Emery explained further. "They're very experienced—the best there is, I would say. Former USERT divers who are making a career move."

"You what?" Trudi asked.

"USERT. Stands for Underwater Search and Evidence Response Team. FBI."

That sounded encouraging. "But can they *shoot*?" Trudi asked.

Emery nodded confidently. "And then some. Their reels are excellent—"

"Have I heard of their other projects?" Arthur interrupted.

Again, Emery exuded confidence. This guy knew how to handle an old grizzly bear like Arthur Dagon. I was beginning to understand he responded to certainty above all else. "Most definitely. *Blue Abyss*?" Emery named one of the most successful indie movies of the past year. Arthur grunted. "And *Chasing Coral*."

Another impressive title. I felt better about this team than I had a minute ago.

Even Arthur appeared satisfied—as evidenced by his disengaging from the meeting once again.

Alex mimed clapping. "Sounds promising," I said. Trudi was typing notes.

"You'll be interested in this, Marc," Emery said. "One of them's very familiar with the location you suggested."

"They are?" Marc and I said in unison. What were the chances?

Emery smiled. He'd nailed it again. I was flooded with gratitude for the mighty little team Trudi and I had assembled. He picked up his phone and searched for something. "Born and raised on Orcas Island, it says here in the packet they submitted."

What a coup. A local connection was always a good thing. Early in my career it'd helped that I knew Toronto well. When I'd worked with American producers or directors unfamiliar with the city, I always made myself available to answer questions, make suggestions, or call on friends to help with props, locations, logistics... It all made a difference to the authenticity of a film—and the bottom line.

"Fantastic. Thank you, Emery. Coming through with good news for the second week in a row. Domino, can you be ready this time next week to approve Orcas?"

"Absolutely," I said with confidence I didn't quite feel.

Marc held up a finger. "Vashon Island also has potential. It's closer to Seattle—which would be good for proximity to the mainland. It also has a big sheltered bay. I can stop there on the way to Orcas, if you like?"

I felt a twinge of panic in my chest. Despite having been here only two days, I'd already grown attached to this little island—and its people. One person in particular. But I couldn't let personal feelings cloud my professional judgment. What was best for the film was most important here—not how unbelievably sexy the local curmudgeon looked in his jeans. The butterflies buzzed around my stomach again. Before I could respond, Trudi jumped in. "You know what? Why don't you do that, Marc. Between the two, one of them will work for *Shore Thing*."

Marc seemed genuinely thrilled. I tried my best to match his enthusiasm—at least outwardly. We wrapped up the call with almost everyone feeling a rush of excitement about how things were going. We had financing. We had a superstar male lead. We had a respected director. We had a dive team. And we had two good options for a location. So why wasn't I feeling pumped like they all were?

I had my work cut out for me now—and not much time to do it. Find a boat, find a space for a production headquarters, and figure out what the heck was going on with this hotel. Fast.

Forest

I felt surprisingly energetic despite the lack of sleep and the dark, dreary weather. Fueled by coffee and unadulterated lust for the woman in 204, I called the cable company right after I left Domino's room, pleased to learn they could send someone out within the hour.

Why had I put off Fern when she'd offered to call a half dozen times over the past month? It was another of those things I'd convinced myself I could fix on my own. But when the rep from Orcas Online showed up with a laptop and other electronic equipment in place of the tool belt I'd expected, I realized what my sister tried repeatedly to tell me was true: I didn't know half of what I thought I did.

I could connect cables and run wire, but I knew nothing about router channels or wireless networking.

It was a lesson in humility.

The rep stuck out her hand in greeting. She wore fatigue-green cargo pants, a tight-fitting thermal shirt, and a bright-orange wool hat—and looked like a teenager. She seemed familiar, but I couldn't have crossed paths socially with someone so much younger. "Aubrey," she said.

Recognition smacked me like a hand to the face. "No." It couldn't be.

"I assure you, I'm Aubrey." When her eyes searched the ground in front of her, I realized my stare was making her uncomfortable.

"You're Aubrey? PJ's daughter?" That would make her... I did the fast math. Nineteen.

She began setting up her computer and other equipment on the long lobby desk. "How do you know my dad?"

I scratched the stubble on my chin, still comprehending how the daughter of a friend from my mountain-biking days was old enough to know how to solve the hotel's Wi-Fi problems. "We used to ride back in the day."

Aubrey laughed. "Ah, I thought you looked familiar. Anyway, I can already see you have some security concerns I need to address."

Fern came up from the dining room and stood nearby, arms crossed, as Aubrey launched into what we needed to fix and how she was going to do it. At least Fern didn't actually *say*, "I told you so." She didn't need to. What we needed was for me to listen to my sister more often.

"You know what you're doing," I said when Aubrey finished her explanation. Figuring she didn't need me breathing over her shoulder, I backed away and left her to it.

Next on my own list was testing the hot water in all the rooms fed by the heat exchanger I'd fixed. I started on the third floor, going room to room, throwing open the windows to let in fresh air while I ran the shower for ten minutes before closing up and moving onto the next. Once the third floor was done—and feeling pretty satisfied with my DIY repair—I climbed the stairs to my room on the fifth floor to empty the rain bucket, then descended to the dining room for lunch with my sister.

She was on the phone as I passed through the lobby, camped out on the stiff-backed chair at the end of the desk while Aubrey worked. She held up three fingers to indicate she needed another few minutes. I sat in a booth by the window, watching the rain pelt against the glass, driven sideways by the wind. A lone figure stepped cautiously along the docks in the marina, trying to keep balance on the wet wooden platforms that heaved with the waves below. Whoever it was didn't look familiar from this distance. As they neared the harbor entrance, I recognized the Dodgers ball cap, dark hoodie, and red-and-white sneakers. It was the strange guy from the coffee shop yesterday.

He made his way up Water Street toward the Driftwood, stopping under a tree near the end of the hotel walkway to bend down and look for something in his backpack. When he straightened again, I was surprised to see him hold up a camera with an enormous lens and point it directly at the hotel. Who the fuck did this guy think he was?

It all came rushing at me: the furtive staring around at the coffee shop yesterday. The gray truck I didn't recognize. The photos of Domino on the docks and at Grange Hall. Paparazzi had landed on Orcas Island for the first time...ever?

Just as I leaped up and grabbed for the jacket I'd slung over my chair, I felt a hand on my shoulder. Fern. "There's nothing we can do."

"Fuck that! He has no right—"

"Turns out he does. I googled. We can't stop someone from taking pictures of the hotel. He's not on our property, so he's not trespassing. It's just like any tourist can take photos of whatever they want." She dragged out a chair and laid the magazine she had rolled up in her hand on the table. She gestured to my chair, encouraging me to sit.

I was rooted to the ground for a moment, anger hot in every cell of my body.

"Come on, sit. It's fine. I'm sure she's used to it."

Reluctantly, I hung the jacket back over the chair and sat, crossing my arms in front of me. "Doesn't seem right."

"I thought that, too, this morning when I noticed him creeping around. But then I remembered she lives in LA. She probably has more cameras in her face before breakfast than you can do push-ups. Comes with the territory."

I glared at the tabloid on the table. "You're as much to blame as anyone. That crap you buy—it's why he's here."

My sister studied me with interest, twirling the end of her ponytail with her finger. "Why do you care so much all of a sudden? I thought this was the last thing you worried about."

Why can't I play it cool? I shrugged, feigning apathy. "I don't." I looked out the window again to see the guy walking away, camera in hand, down Water Street. "Our guests have an expectation of privacy is all. No matter who they are."

"Hmm." Fern narrowed her eyes before her attention was drawn to the door, where Bluebell had arrived to work the lunch crowd.

The dining room was filling up fast. In fact, it was

busier today than I'd seen it since the holidays. More than half the tables were occupied, and another group was making its way up the walk toward the front door. Behind the bar, Bluebell tied on her apron, a satisfied smile on her lips. It *was* nice to see the place buzzing.

"Told you having an actress here presented a unique—" Fern discreetly waved a finger around the room "—opportunity."

"You think *she's* why all these people are here?" I swiveled my neck to look around. Our usual customers were here—Angela and her group of friends included—but I also spotted locals we didn't usually see in the hotel dining room. Poppy Willoughby. Marigold Kipling. Juniper Eliot. Even Rocky Black was here, with some of the town's councillors. Zoe Blum, a tarot card reader I never saw except at the Winslow Farmers Market, sat alone near the fireplace, a deck of cards and several crystals laid out in front of her.

"Um, ye*ah*. I know you almost literally do live under a rock, but even you know celebrities are celebrities because people like to look at them. Right?"

She had a point, but I just didn't think Orcas Island folks cared about that kind of thing. It was silly to think everyone stuck their head in the sand the way

I did. Fern stood to hug Bluebell when she approached to take our order.

"Trouble sleeping last night?" she said to me once Fern sat again.

"What?"

Her eyes glinted with amusement. "You look tired." She raised one eyebrow but didn't press further. "Soup is spiced parsnip." When I grimaced, she added, "Don't knock it till you try it. Parsnips from Big Oak Farm."

"I'll have that. Everything Rose grows tastes perfect," Fern said. Bluebell tipped her chin in agreement, regarding me expectantly.

"Vegetable omelet."

"You got it." Bluebell turned to face the dining room entrance, where a few of our parents' friends were shaking the rain from their jackets and waiting to be seated.

With the fire crackling at the far end and the room humming with cheerful voices, it was impossible to pretend Fern wasn't right. I saw many—most, really—of the diners periodically look up from their tables and around the room like meerkats, searching for someone. Searching for Domino.

"The phone's been ringing all morning. Starting this weekend, the third floor is fully booked, and the fourth floor's halfway there. Call it the Domino effect or whatever you want, but we're gonna have to pull our shit together sooner than we thought."

That was good news and bad. Mostly bad if we didn't get the roof fixed and had to turn people away. I decided focusing on the good was the right thing to do. "Spent the morning testing the hot water system. Heat exchanger's fixed."

Fern clapped her hands together, whether because she was pleased to hear my update or in admiration of the bowl Bluebell had placed in front of her I wasn't sure. Fresh cilantro accented the middle of a hearty-looking soup, swirled on top with yogurt and chili oil. Ribbons of parsnip decorated the edges of the bowl like the corkscrew arms of a cartoon sun. "Wow." She stared at the soup, then up at Bluebell, who set down my omelet. "George is full of surprises."

Bluebell winked. "Actually, Tommy did that. Nice, huh? You all good here?"

Both of us nodded, Fern holding a spoonful of soup in front of her.

The omelet was impressive today, too, served on a round plank of wood and heaped with arugula and grated parmesan. I wasted no time digging in. It was light and fluffy and stuffed with red and yellow peppers, onion, salty tomatoes, and a handful of peas.

Between bites I asked, "So how many guests?"

Before she could answer, a hush quieted the room,

and all the oxygen felt like it was sucked toward the entrance.

Domino stood at the top of the three stairs from the lobby, bewildered at all the faces staring back at her. Even in an emerald-green sweater and black leggings, she looked like she belonged in the pages of Fern's magazine rather than on our rain-soaked little island in the Pacific. Her hair fell around her shoulders in dark, shiny waves. She quickly gathered her composure, smiling broadly and waving at the lookie-loos in the dining room. Spotting us by the window, she threaded the tables toward us, saying hello to each group she passed with a warmth and sincerity that caught me off guard. She must genuinely *like* being recognized. I'd sooner face off with a mountain lion than be gawked at the way she was.

I stood as she approached and pulled out the chair to my left. She sat, smoothing her bangs into place, a simple gesture that made her appear smaller somehow. I couldn't wrap my head around how beautiful she looked after our late night. I rubbed my hand absently over my stubbled chin. She was glowing, even in the diffused gray light coming through the window.

"I'm so sorry about..." Fern put one hand to her chest and subtly indicated the roomful of guests with the other. Her glance darted to the table, where she placed a hand on the copy of *Inside Hollywood* magazine she'd brought and discreetly flipped it facedown.

Domino shrugged and shook her head. "It's okay." Watching my eyebrows rise in question, she added, "Really. It's lovely to be welcomed. People here are so nice."

"Have you eaten?"

"I'll grab something later. I need a favor." Domino answered Fern's question but kept her gaze directly on me.

CHAPTER 10

Domino

I had to get serious about finding a boat and a place that could function as a production office for *Shore Thing*. By this weekend, preferably, before Marc went to Vashon Island and decided it was a better spot to shoot. That meant I had three days. Three and a half if this afternoon counted. I figured Forest was my best chance at help. He knew the place inside out, could introduce me to the locals, and seemed like he'd be honest with me—probably to a fault.

Forest and his sister exchanged a barely perceptible glance. I could've sworn Fern slightly nodded.

"What's the favor?"

"It's not so much a favor, I guess. More a blatant plea for help." My desperation must've been plain for him to see; he almost melted in his chair a little, his gray-blue eyes kind.

"I'll do my best."

"I need to find a building, or office, or some kind of space that could be the production headquarters for my movie. Then I need to find someone with a boat who's willing to rent it out for five or six weeks beginning in late spring." I set my hands on the table. "They'd be well compensated."

"As in *this* spring?"

I nodded, biting my lower lip. Fern obviously hadn't told her brother much about why I was here.

"And you want me because...?"

"You love this place. You know everyone here—and every building. I think you can help me persuade whoever needs persuading that it's a good idea to shoot a movie here."

He considered what I'd said, scratching the back of his neck. Again, I thought I saw Fern tilt her chin slightly in approval.

"I'll do what I can. But I don't promise to sugar-coat things."

I reached over the table and touched his forearm. "That's exactly what I hope." The sleeves of his sweater were pulled up, exposing strong, muscled forearms. Why was it so sexy when a man rolled up his sleeves? "One more thing. I need at least a verbal agreement for both these things by this weekend. Oh, and the boat? It'll actually be *in* the movie."

"Shit." A wrinkle appeared between Forest's eyebrows. I assumed he was worried about the short notice, but I followed his gaze through the window to see a man in all black standing on the lawn in front of the hotel, camera in hand, squinting to see into the dining room. He wasn't dressed for the weather. The hood of his sweatshirt hung heavy over his forehead, soaked with rain. It didn't take a brain surgeon to figure out this guy was looking to get a photo of me.

That's who got those photos yesterday, I realized—and who must've followed me to Grange Hall in the gray truck.

"Shit," I echoed, then drew in a breath and sat up straight. "You know what? Fuck that guy. I have stuff to do and not much time to do it. If he wants to chase me around the island, good luck to him. He's not going to find anything more boring—or less likely to sell to the press."

Forest's irritation eased. He searched the room and waved someone over to our table. A slight woman with angular features and cool-girl style stood from her table and weaved her way to ours.

"Excuse me," Forest told me. He stood and whispered in this woman's ear. She glanced outside as he spoke, eyes narrowing when they landed on the photographer. Then she smiled and nodded, sending her gold threader earrings swinging. Forest moved to sit back down, but she grabbed his arm and pulled him up again to whisper in his ear. He pinched his lips in a tight line.

"Domino, this is Poppy. Poppy, Domino." Poppy pushed past Forest, leaving him to take a step back, and sat in the seat he'd vacated next to me.

"Hi!" she said. Intelligence and curiosity radiated in her green eyes. I took the hand she offered and shook it.

I couldn't explain it, but something in me recognized a kindred spirit in this stranger. "Hi, I'm Domino."

Poppy grinned. "I know. That's why I shoved this guy out of the way." She gestured behind her to Forest, who stood with his arms folded, looking territorial about his seat next to me. A kaleidoscope of jitters danced around my heart. "Stand down, Forest," she teased him. "Anyway, I'm Poppy Willoughby. I'm a writer, and I'd love to—"

"All right, that's enough," Forest interrupted. He took Poppy's arm and encouraged her to stand. "Remember we agreed..."

Poppy peered out at the front lawn again, where

the photographer was now bent over his camera, rain dripping from his forehead to the ground. He had to lean quite far over to avoid water hitting the lens. "On it," she told Forest. "Nice to meet you! Big fan. *Big fan*," she said to me as she turned to leave. "I hope we get to talk more."

"Me too!" I said, and I meant it. From all my encounters with the people of Orcas Island, I'd learned they were just what they seemed. Poppy was no exception. Genuine, interesting, and kind. What was it with this place? I knew for sure what it wasn't: the weather. Unless these folks liked days on end of dreary skies and near-constant precipitation. It must be all the greens and blues that were everywhere here. I'd read somewhere about the powerful effect of colors on mood. Since I'd arrived, my nerves had stilled more with each passing day. No car horns honked. I had no stress about wearing the right thing to the right place. No Deidre to tell the agency where I was, which meant no photographers trailing me everywhere I went. Well, just one.

A flash of olive green outside caught my attention. A figure in a raincoat, hood up, walked confidently to the photographer, who was still crouching over his backpack, trying to tuck the camera inside it. He was startled at their approach. When the person in the green coat turned slightly sideways, I saw it was

Poppy. I looked at Forest sitting next to me, smug satisfaction on his face. Poppy held an umbrella toward the guy, then opened it over him.

Poppy kept a conversation going. He squinted again through the window, at her, and finally at the sky before he shrugged dejectedly, as if giving in. He picked up his backpack and took the umbrella from Poppy, and they walked up the path to the hotel entrance.

"That's our cue." Forest grabbed my hand and pulled me to my feet. Fern waved us off, a sparkle in her eyes as he led me to the swinging door near the bar. Once through it, we entered a kitchen far different from the one I'd seen yesterday. Today it was bustling with activity: big pots steamed on the stove, and the curly-haired waitress—Bluebell—called orders to a pair of men, one older and one younger, who wore chef's whites and barely glanced in our direction.

When we reached the back door, Forest stopped in his tracks. "You don't have a coat."

I looked down at my sweater and shook my head.

"Here. She can wear mine." Bluebell held out a yellow rain jacket.

"But I can't—"

"You sure can. I'll be here for hours. If you're not back when I go, Fern'll loan me something."

I reached out to take it, then hesitated. "You sure?"

Bluebell laughed. "Are you serious? Wait till I tell my friend Rose that Domino West wore my jacket. *My* jacket."

I pulled her in for a hug. "You're amazing. Thank you."

Forest shoved open the back door and held it. "Ready?" Rain pounded the concrete behind the building, and a steady stream of water gushed from the gutters.

"You need a jacket, too."

"In the car."

I slipped into the yellow coat and lifted the hood over my head. Forest reached into his pocket for his keys, hitting a button on the fob that triggered the lights on the jeep to flash.

I hurried around to the passenger side while Forest headed for the driver's-side door. We slid into our seats in a rush, the yellow jacket rustling around me. It was drenched with rain even from that short sprint.

"Not the best day for sightseeing." Forest pushed the button to start the car, adjusting the controls to get the wipers going and the defrost on. "Seat warmer?"

"Absolutely." He hit two switches in the console to turn on the seat warmers before he put the jeep in reverse. Although it had a backup camera, it was evident from the way Forest slung his arm around my seat and swiveled to peer out the back window that he preferred to do things manually. I caught his eye as he twisted. "Thanks for that," I said, referring to the little scheme he'd concocted with Poppy.

"No one deserves to be treated like a zoo animal." He stepped on the gas pedal, and we backed up, then headed out of the parking lot and down Water Street. Raindrops hit the windshield like little pebbles, quickly wiped aside by the rhythmic swishing of wiper blades. We stopped at the light at the first intersection. "A boat, huh? What's this movie about, anyway?"

I studied him as we waited for the light to change. The fingers of right hand hung over the top of the steering wheel, his wrist resting against it. His left elbow was propped on the door where the siding met the window. His hair was damp. A shadow of beard darkened his chin. The crewneck sweater he wore was a shade of red that reminded me of paprika. When the light turned green, he swung left onto Ellison. Sensing my attention on him, he cleared his throat. Right. He'd asked me a question. "It's... I guess the best way to describe it is an underwater rom-com."

"A funny *Titanic*?"

I laughed. "Sort of. Damon Mann—he plays a marine archaeologist who lives on this island."

"The guy from the Star Force movies?"

"Yes." Oops. That wasn't public yet. "I shouldn't

have told you that. Please don't mention it."

Forest took his eyes off the road and turned them on me as if to say, "Duh." He wasn't a frivolous guy prone to gossip, that much was obvious.

"So anyway. His character—he can't find a girl-friend. His friend comes up with the idea of a wanted ad. That's where I come in. But the catch is I'm secretly a marine archaeologist, too—one who's searching for the same buried treasure he is."

"You need a power boat." Forest said it confident-ly; it wasn't a question.

It didn't escape my notice he hadn't reacted at all to the storyline of the movie, just went right to practical things.

"Yes. Can you help?"

"I have an idea."

We drove in silence for the next ten minutes, lulled by the cadenced swishing of the wipers, the hum of the hybrid engine, and the raindrops pinging against the windshield. I peered out the passenger window, watching as we passed a cluster of impossibly tall trees in a blur of dark green, punctuated with the strong brown lines of tree trunks. Their thick, sturdy branch-es held boughs heavy with water.

"What kind of trees are these?"

Forest looked through the window where I point-ed, his eyes lighting up at the question. "Douglas firs, mostly. Sitka spruce and western red cedar. Incredible, aren't they?"

"Mm-hmm." I didn't say anything else, just nodded, struck by their majestic beauty. "Are these old growth? I remember seeing a show—we have a nature program in Canada called *The Nature of Things*—where they showed a satellite image of all the trees in this area that've been lost to logging."

He glanced at me sideways. "You know about this stuff?"

"Of course. What do you take me for, an idiot?"

"It's just—I guess I wouldn't have thought people in LA cared about old-growth forests in the Pacific Northwest." He shrugged. "Not that I'm not glad to hear it. Just surprised." He flicked on the turn signal and slowed to stop at a pullout on the side of the road.

"Around thirteen percent of old-growth forests have disappeared in the past decade due to logging. And that doesn't include wildfire loss. It's unconscionable. Here in the San Juan Islands, the few old-growth forests that are left provide a unique habitat, different from the wetter mainland forests. Some trees in these pockets have been here over 300 years." Forest's eyes were icy blue with determination. This was a subject he was passionate about.

"The area lost most of its virgin growth during the

early twentieth century, especially on San Juan Island itself. The trees there were dry—ideal for burning in lime kilns. Trees that weren't used for kilns were taken to make barrels to ship the lime in. Logging was also a problem, but less so than on the mainland.

"Today most of the old-growth trees in the Pacific Northwest are here on Orcas. The forest on Tyee Mountain, for instance."

"Wow." I gazed out the window again. Now the jeep was stopped, I could take in details like the lichens hanging from gnarled branches like lace curtains. Birds darted among the stands, taking shelter from the rain. The shades of green ranged from emerald to nearly black. Up close like this, the variation was astounding.

"We have to protect the remaining forests if their ecosystems have any chance for survival." Forest's hands gripped the wheel tightly.

Then his expression became apologetic. He laughed uncomfortably, which had me aching to reach out and rest my hand on his thigh. He must have noticed my focus travel downward, admiring his legs. "Rant over."

Eyes back to his face, Domino. Something about this man drew me like a flower leaning for the sun. I'd never felt this way about Harry Roman. He was handsome, and talented, and made all the girls scream.

But I liked the quiet strength of Forest Russo. The way his sweater clung to his muscles, and how his jeans fit like they were made just for him. He wore the clothes; the clothes didn't wear him. His eyes were like a vast blue ocean, seducing me with their mystery and depth. I liked that he cared about things. Cared about the hotel. Cared about its guests. Cared about his sister. And cared enough about me to concoct a scheme to throw a photographer off my tail. He cared about where he lived and what made it the very special place I'd come to know since I arrived.

"You're full of surprises, Forest Russo." I couldn't resist this time. I laid my hand on his thigh. The muscle jumped under my touch. Whatever this was between us, it was kinetic. The hunger in Forest's eyes told me he felt it, too.

He dropped his hand from the steering wheel and rested it on mine. It was warm and calloused, but I loved its roughness. This was a man who worked hard with his hands—and a man whose hands I wanted to work hard on me.

We were both focused on the feel of each other's touch, neither saying a word as the rain pounded the roof of the car, big drips from the branches above us peppered among little drips from the sky. A single car passed by, kicking up a spray of mist from its back tires.

The buzz of my phone broke the bond. He lifted his hand away and flicked on the turn signal, steering back onto the road. I poked around in the pockets of Bluebell's coat to find where I'd tucked my phone when we left the Driftwood.

Trudi. Heard from Marc. He'll be on Vashon on Friday. No pressure. Just thought you should know.

All good, I typed back, but a twinge of anxiety had my right leg bouncing.

Forest cast a sideways glance at me. "Everything all right?"

"Yeah. Or it will be." I watched the trees thin out and huge swaths of farmland whip past the window. "Where are we going?" I deflected his concern with a question.

"To get you that boat."

We approached a stop sign. Ellison Road continued on the right, paved and smooth with a double yellow line down the middle like stripes on a bumblebee. Forest veered left onto a gravel road that cut apart big, empty meadows like the halves of an apple. On the right side, an industrial tractor was shrouded in mist among the green and brown stripes of a field left to fallow. Three crows foraged in the dirt, their feathers black and glossy. I ducked my head to see a tree-covered mountain in the distance on the left, veiled in fog. In the foreground, a split-rail fence lined a property that seemed to stretch for miles. We continued on for another ten minutes, the jeep bumping over mounds in the gravel as Forest steered around sizable puddles. I watched quietly as we drew closer to what looked like the end of the world.

At a break in the split-rail fence, he turned left into a driveway. We drove for another few minutes over a gravel path. Knotty branches of shore pine appeared to reach for the jeep until we arrived at a clearing, where a sprawling house loomed in front of us with red-cedar siding and oversize windows. Fog wrapped around the edges of the building. Only a faint blue delineation indicated the break between sea and sky beyond.

Forest came to a stop and turned off the engine. The stillness around us was astounding. Even the rain fell softly here. It was a stark contrast to the near-deafening wash of tires flying along the wet highway.

"LA has a lot of nice houses," I said, pitching forward in my seat to gaze up. "But this is something else. Who lives here?"

"Henry Black."

"He's important?"

Forest laughed. "You could say that. We're sitting on the largest parcel of individually owned land on the island. But whether he's important or not is beside the point. He's rich, and he has a boat—several." He grabbed the keys from the center console and swung open his door. "Come on. I'll introduce you."

Forest

I hurried to the back of the jeep and opened the rear hatch to get my rain jacket while Domino waited, hood up, by the passenger door. I grabbed her hand, and together we sprinted to the cover of the portico that framed the front door of Henry Black's home in thick wooden beams. I wished I'd called ahead, but I'd spent a lot of time here as a kid with River and Rocky, and Mr. and Mrs. Black—Henry and Olive, they insisted I called them now—had always said I was welcome anytime. Today was a test of that theory.

Domino stood close, grasping my one hand in both of hers. I rapped on the door with three firm knocks, then faced her. How was it possible to look sexy in a bright-yellow raincoat? Water rolled from the peak of the hood down the front of her jacket. With my free hand I pushed the hood back now we were out of the rain, revealing that mane of shiny brown hair. She gazed up at me with striking blue eyes, sending an ache of desire through me. It hadn't been some trick of the dark last night that had catalyzed the connection between us.

The door swept open. "Forest! What a surprise." Olive's eyes brightened at the sight of me. I watched as she turned her focus to Domino, raising an eyebrow slightly. It was evident Olive recognized her, but she didn't make a fuss of it, just stepped back and welcomed us in. "Get in here. Let's leave that misery outside," she said of the rain.

"Can I offer you coffee? Or perhaps a glass of wine?" Olive disappeared with our wet jackets into a coat room to the side of the entrance. She touched a hand to her perfectly styled blonde hair on her return. Even midafternoon on a random weekday, she was dressed in crisply pleated, wide-leg black pants and a white cashmere cardigan with a string of pearls around her neck. Her makeup was perfect. "I think I'll have a glass of wine."

She led us through a foyer with vaulted ceilings and leather armchairs positioned on a beautiful Oriental rug to the massive kitchen, with panoramic windows that overlooked the ocean. It felt like we were perched out over it, and in fact we were. The Blacks had had the house built to fit into the landscape but also make the most of its stunning location. Olive collected a bottle of white wine from the fridge and held it in front of Domino and me.

I let Domino decide for herself. I didn't want my choice to make her think she couldn't indulge.

"Oh, thank you. That's a very nice bottle of wine. But I'd love a glass of water, please. I have a lot of work to do today." Domino smiled that megawatt smile, which seemed to thaw even the unflappable Olive Black.

"Same, thanks, Olive. Tap water is great." I anticipated her next question and headed her off.

After filling two tumblers with filtered water from a spout at the kitchen sink, she removed the cork from the wine bottle and poured herself a glass. Olive gestured to the stools that flanked the giant kitchen island, crafted from rich-looking walnut. "What brings you here?" She looked in particular at Domino, who flicked a glance at me before I answered.

"My friend Domino here is scouting the island as a potential place to shoot a movie."

Olive nodded as if that were something she heard everyday.

"In particular she'd like to rent a boat—for five or six weeks. Is that right, Domino?"

Domino nodded, her eyes shining like cobalt against her green sweater in the natural light that bathed the space. "Yes. To be clear, the boat will actually be *in* the movie. We'd pay for the rental, of course."

Olive tapped a manicured fingernail against the marble countertop. "We might just have something for you. Let me see where Henry is. He can show you the boats." She set her wineglass down with a ting and glided to the top of an open staircase beyond the double-wide refrigerator. "Heeen-ry?" she called down, bending forward as if it would carry her voice farther.

"Down here!" a voice returned from below.

"Can you come up here please, darling?" Olive returned to the island and patted her hair once more before she picked up the wineglass.

Footsteps sounded on the stairs, and a head of thick white hair appeared, revealing the fit-looking Henry Black. A grin spread across his face when he saw me sitting at the counter. "Forest, my boy. Come over here. Let's get a look at you."

I went to the top of the stairs. Henry chuckled and wrapped me in a strong hug, then leaned back and clapped my shoulders twice. "You're looking good, son." He looked past me to the island. "Hey now, if someone told me Domino West would be sitting in my kitchen this afternoon, I'd have laughed them out of town." He strode toward her, holding out an arm. I thought for a minute he would pull her into a hug, too, but was relieved when he gently touched her shoulder instead. "Welcome to our home, Ms. West."

Seeing my surprise, he added, "Relax, Forest. I watch movies, too. Now, what are you doing on our beautiful little island?"

CHAPTER 11

Domino

I repeated what I'd told Olive about why I needed the boat and quickly outlined the plot for Henry. He had a smile on his face the whole time. For a man in his mid-eighties, he was sharp as a pin. I liked him instantly. His face was etched with the lines of someone who'd spent years on the water.

"You've come to the right place," he told me. "Come on, let's have a look." He headed for the stairs, indicating we should follow. "Olive, will you grab their coats?" I noticed a hint of annoyance that he'd interrupted her glass of wine, but Olive got up from her seat and bustled out to the coat room. Forest and I trailed Henry down the stairs into a games room, which replicated the wall of windows in the kitchen. A charcoal-gray-felted pool table sat in the center. On one side of the room was a bar made from the same walnut as the kitchen cabinetry, and on the other a half dozen deep, cozy-looking armchairs were arranged in front of the windows.

"This is beautiful," I said, admiring the views inside and out.

Olive stepped down the stairs, holding our coats at a distance so they didn't drip on her clothes. Henry grabbed them from her arm. "Cheers, Livy. Thank you." He pressed a kiss to her cheek that turned her scowl to a smile before she disappeared up the stairs.

Henry threw open the glass doors, stopping in front of an umbrella stand to pull out three identical black umbrellas. He gave one each to Forest and me.

"Rocky for Mayor?" I asked when we popped them open in unison to reveal each had the phrase printed around the edge in large white letters.

"That's right," Henry said proudly. "That's my boy."

"Henry and Olive's oldest son, Rocky, is mayor of Bayview. These are leftovers from his election campaign?"

"You bet. Now, come with me, and I'll show you what we've got." Henry bounded along like a man decades younger.

We walked across a concrete patio that had two gazebos, one covering an outdoor kitchen. A set of stairs bordered in ornamental grasses led down to a dock. On the arm of the dock closest to us was what I could describe only as a superyacht. Not that I knew what a superyacht was. But this boat was spectacular.

"The *Cloud Nine*." Henry came to a stop in front of it. I stretched the sleeve of my sweater to cover my left hand and juggled the umbrella into it, immediately tucking my right hand into my jacket pocket in a tight fist to warm it up. "A hundred and fifteen feet. Five state rooms, plus crew quarters, of course." Henry gazed up at it, tilting his umbrella back to take it all in, enamored with what he saw.

Forest raised an eyebrow at me in askance. I shook my head. "Wow. She's a beauty," he said. "How long have you had her?"

"About a year and a half now. Westport. Made right here in America. We're planning our first real trip next summer down to Baja. When did you say you'll need it?" He finally tore his gaze away from the *Cloud Nine* and focused his attention on me.

"This June and July. If all goes well," I told him. Henry's forehead furrowed. "But to be honest this is more than we need. Much more. I was thinking something—"

Henry lifted a hand. "Of course. Follow me. I think I have what you need." He touched a hand to the side of the *Cloud Nine* before he led us around the giant boat to another arm of the dock. The *Cloud Nine* was so big it had hidden from view a second, smaller powerboat, this one less than half the size, all white with a black hull. *Redemption* was spelled in block letters across the stern. "Forty-five footer." He gestured to it. "Too basic for your needs?"

I shook my head. "It's perfect." It looked to me like the boat an underwater treasure hunter might use, yet it was big enough to accommodate cast and crew members. "Are you sure you can manage without it for six weeks?"

Henry laughed. "Are you kidding? When I've got my new toy to play with? She's all yours."

I exchanged an excited look with Forest. "Fantastic! I can't thank you enough." I hoisted my umbrella in the air in celebration, looking up at the sky and letting a few drops of rain wet my face. "About payment," I added when I'd lowered it again. "I'll put you in touch with our financer."

Henry squinted at the rain, too, waving a hand to encompass us. "Let's get inside before we're washed away." He let Forest go first so he could walk next to me to the stairs. "Tell you what. Before you go I'll connect you with my investment manager. You can introduce her to your financer when you're ready."

"Perfect. Thank you. Again. I can't believe my luck." We climbed the steps together.

He put a hand on my shoulder. "That's what we do on Orcas Island. Haven't you noticed?"

He was right—and then some. Collectively, I was sure I'd never met a group of such kind, helpful, friendly people. Even Forest's sharp edges seemed to be softening.

Henry and Olive walked us to the door, Olive still clutching her wineglass. He wrapped Forest in another bear hug, patting him on the back. "Good to see you, son. Come by anytime." Olive held out a hand, which Forest clasped for a moment.

To my surprise, Henry enveloped me in a warm, strong embrace as well. "What a treat to meet you," he said. "Isn't it, Olive? A movie star right in our own home." I blushed and thanked them again as Forest guided me through the door.

It closed behind us, leaving the Blacks to their beautiful home and expensive wine. I couldn't help but let out a whoop of relief. One to-do down, two to go as the weekend loomed and Marc made his way to Vashon Island.

I pulled up my hood and gripped Forest's hand, and together we high-tailed it for the jeep, its ocean-blue exterior cheerful against the muted green trees and gravel drive. I yanked open the door and jumped in while Forest ran to the other side. The rain was inescapable. The front of my leggings were soaked, and Forest's jeans had patches of dark blue where they were wet.

He shifted to slip out of his wet coat and tossed it on the back seat, nodding at me to do the same. I balled up the yellow jacket to keep it from dripping all over the console.

Forest flipped the defrost controls on high to clear the fog that had immediately bloomed across the windows from our hot breath and damp clothes. Turning the jeep around, he headed out the way we'd come, plops of rain pelting the roof as enormous tree boughs, heavy with moisture, brushed along the top.

When we reached the end of the drive, where the trees gave way to open fields, the rain suddenly stopped. Forest leaned forward to peer through the windshield as the clouds parted and a sunbeam burst through. The wet grass in the fields around us glistened brightly. He looked at me and laughed. "I have an idea. Got time for a detour?"

With the boat taken care of, I was happy to play tourist for a while. "Show me what you've got."

Instead of making a right turn out of the driveway, Forest went left and drove to where the gravel road ended at another split-rail fence. He shut off the engine and hopped down from the jeep, leaving his wet jacket in the back. "I think we'll be okay for five minutes," he said into the cabin after assessing the sky, where the clouds were the color of charcoal in the dazzling break of sunshine. I followed his lead, slipping out the passenger side and closing the door. I folded my arms around myself. It might have stopped raining, but it was still cold.

I tailed him along the length of a dirt path edged in lime-green grass, the blades glossy with moisture. Forest veered left around a big boulder that marked, I could see now, a short trail to a beach. We came up to a concrete ledge. Forest stepped down a set of log stairs and reached back to help me down.

I filled my lungs with fresh, salty air, scented with wet logs and seaweed. Stones shifted below my feet as we walked, the sound masked by the constant roar of waves breaking on the beach. The push and pull of the rocks along the shore had the sound of muted applause, and the seagulls that followed you everywhere you went on Orcas Island glided along the wind above us like kites in the sky.

The sun glinted off the ocean. Shading my eyes with my hand, I watched the surf churn. The water nearest the beach was Caribbean blue, contrasted against the sapphire shade of the depths beyond. The effect was breathtaking. Growing up in Toronto, I never understood the allure of living near the ocean until I moved to LA. I realized only now, away from the sandy, manicured beaches of Southern California, what it really meant to live with the Pacific. It was a powerful, heaving force. Whether it was the hypnotic effect of the endless blue or the meditative rhythm of the waves, I felt relaxed. Creative. Connected. Less like my life was something to conquer and more like my purpose was to live in harmony with nature rather than in opposition to it.

A flicker of brown broke the surface of a wave, then disappeared. At first I thought it was a log, but it resurfaced, and this time I saw eyeballs. "What's that?" I shouted at Forest. I shielded my eyes again and pointed.

He followed my finger. "What?"

The creature popped up once more, swiveling and looking around. "That!" I jumped up and down as I said it, still pointing.

Forest smiled, his teeth white in the sunlight. "Oh, that. A sea otter." He laughed at the wonder on my face. "Look, there's another." Now it was his turn to point.

"I don't see anything." I searched, squinting against the bright sun. Forest came up behind and wrapped an arm around me, reaching forward to point. There it was, floating on its back, bobbing in the waves while its partner dived and surfaced around it.

I melted against him. "I see it now," I murmured, reveling in the warmth of his chest. He circled me in his arms, wrapping me in strength and safety. I closed my eyes, feeling the sun on my cheeks, and rested my head against him. He tucked me in even closer until I felt his erection stir at my back. Logically, this man I'd known for three days shouldn't make my insides dance like the sugar plum fairy, but instincts—emotions—weren't always rational.

I twirled in his arms to face him, gazing into his round blue eyes. He clasped his hands together low behind me, and I ran a finger along his jawline, enjoying the tickle of his beard. He leaned his head down, touching his nose to mine, and held it there as we breathed in the wholeness of each other. I pressed forward, wrapping my arms around his neck, angling my lips toward his. There was a pause—a breath—the attraction zapping between us suspending time and space, and then we connected, our lips tangling with need.

With the surf crashing on the shore, the insistent wailing of seagulls, and the wind tossing my hair around us like streamers, we kissed. I held the sides of his face. He cupped my ass in his big, strong palms. Our desire flowed like the waves, building and cresting, dipping down to my toes and out through my lips and flowing across his body and back.

We pulled apart, breathless and startled, when a thunderclap crackled through the sky. In seconds, rain poured over us in sheets, pummeling the rocks on the beach and the surface of the ocean in a loud white hiss. I threw my head back and laughed, smoothing my wet bangs back off my face.

Forest tightened his grip and lifted me. I wrapped my legs around his hips, gazing down at him, planting shivering kisses on his eyelids, his cheeks, his lips. Two thoughts raced through my mind: how much I wanted to tear off his clothes and lie next to him, skin to skin, exploring the muscled shapes I could feel under his sweater, and how standing here, in the pouring rain, wrapped in the arms of a man, reminded me of my favorite scene in my favorite film, where Ryan Gosling and Rachel McAdams crash into a kiss that defines the movie.

What the movie didn't show, I was learning, was how cold and wet and sticky it was to be out in a deluge of rain with no cover and no jacket and no fire to warm ourselves by. The cold air rushed into the space between us as Forest set me down and we giggled and shivered. I was giddy with the rush of it all. He grabbed my hand, and together we raced over the rocky beach and back up the log stairs, around the boulder and to the shelter of the jeep.

Forest

It went against every instinct I had to open myself up to this woman. In the jeep, Domino pinned me with a stare, her chest heaving, yearning in her eyes as strong as my own, her dark hair black with moisture and stuck against her sweater like a stream of wet ink. Water trickled down her nose, and her eyes were ringed with smudges of makeup. But her cheeks were rosy as little plums, and her eyes sparkled like labradorite. She literally stole my breath. A shiver shook me out of the trance I was in. I started the engine and blasted the heat.

"Quite a detour," Domino said as I edged the jeep back onto the gravel and headed for the main road. She giggled, her own shivering now abated. She gathered her wet hair over one shoulder and flipped down the passenger-side visor. "Oh!" she cried at the sight of herself, wiping her smudged makeup as we bumped along the gravel.

"Glad you liked it." I smiled, but making out with a guest wasn't my proudest accomplishment. I'd allowed instinct to take over, let my body dictate its desires before my brain laid out all the logical reasons it was a bad idea.

"Were you *trying* to recreate *The Notebook*?" Domino let out another sweet giggle when she saw my confusion. "Oh, come on. You've seen it, haven't you?"

A memory rang somewhere in the recesses of my brain of the movie Fern mentioned the other day. Something about… Allie Hamilton. When I stopped at the intersection of Ellison Road, I turned to Domino. "Allie Hamilton."

Her eyes twinkled. "Isn't that why you—"

"Counter to what you're thinking, I haven't seen it." I made a right toward Bayview, the wipers working double-time now I could drive faster on smooth pavement. Rain streaked horizontally across the side windows. The defrost was on high to keep our wet clothes from fogging the windows completely. With the sky the color of lead as the last of the light drained from the day, I had to keep my eyes squarely on the road.

"You haven't seen *The Notebook*?" The register of Domino's voice indicated her disbelief.

"Nope."

"We'd better fix that. You can't kiss a woman in the pouring rain without knowing what she's thinking—and how unbelievably sexy she finds it." Domino reached for the controls. "It's hot in here. Isn't it?"

I took one hand from the steering wheel and rested it on her thigh. "Understatement of the year."

She dialed the heat to low. "What are you doing tonight?"

CHAPTER 12

Forest

Back at the hotel, the reality of what I'd done crept along my bones like a ghost in the night. Fern glowered at me as we traipsed through the dining room, eyeing the clothes glued to our bodies and the pink glow that'd settled on Domino's cheeks.

Shit.

I didn't stop to be reprimanded, just pointed to the wet jeans chafing with every step and beelined for the lobby, Domino leading the way. She pressed the button to call the elevator, and I willed it to hurry under the lifeless eyes of the taxidermy deer. Domino stayed quiet, sensing the change in my demeanor, but she delivered a sexy smile when the elevator dinged its arrival.

Once the door slid shut, cocooning us inside, she grasped my index and middle fingers, sparking the embers still smoldering in my belly to a flame. I couldn't deny I had feelings for her. Could I stop them? Or was I careening forward like a roller-coaster hurtling around a bend, sending my heart in swoops and jumps?

At the second floor, Domino took a step out and lingered, eyeing me over her shoulder and swinging our hands where they joined. "See you later?"

It took everything I had not to step out next to her. "I'll come find you." I cleared my throat and dropped her grip. "I have a few things to do."

She nodded, pursing her lips in a pretty bow. Then she was gone from view as the elevator door shut again, leaving me in a space that suddenly felt cold and empty.

The bucket of rainwater in my room was nearly full to the top. Emptying it down the shower drain was a necessary dose of reality. Domino wasn't just any guest, as Fern had pointed out on day one. Her stay here could change the game for us—but not if we didn't get our shit together so we were ready for it. A movie filmed on Orcas Island—with Domino West and Damon Mann—would bring attention to our little paradise whether we wanted it or not. The situation wasn't one I could cross my arms and ignore. I'd just helped her find a boat, for Christ's sake. What was that, if not an indication I was helping move it all along?

I peeled out of my wet clothes and flung them in the bathroom sink while I showered, steam billowing around me. My body vibrated with desire—mixed with anxiety about bringing the attention of the world to the family business when we weren't prepared for it.

My stomach rumbled with hunger as I toweled off. Intending to stay in my room for dinner, I tugged on sweatpants and my favorite PNW hoodie, a gift from Fern over the holidays. It had a graphic of a vintage blue jeep against a backdrop of trees with the words Upper Left USA emblazoned across the chest. I picked up the phone to call to the kitchen and discovered Fern had texted while I was in the shower. Six times.

WHY were you both wet?

We need to talk.

I know you have something to tell me.

Hey don't ignore me.

Coming down for dinner?

And finally: **What the fuck are you doing, Forest?**

I debated about heading downstairs to face my sister in person but decided against it. The dining room was open to the public, and it had been busy these past few days. There was no point in making a scene. I dialed the kitchen as planned and requested one of my favorite things on the menu: a burger and fries. While I waited, I flipped on the TV news and sent a text to Fern. **I'm beat. Eating up here. Talk tomorrow.** Then I turned off my phone.

The weather woman appeared onscreen with a forecast that only ratcheted up my anxiety: rain for the next four days. I eyed the bucket catching steady drips from the ceiling. When I answered Tommy's knock on the door, my teeth were clenched. Setting the covered plate on the table by the window, I vowed to convince Fern in the morning we couldn't afford to wait until Domino left. We needed to get the roof patched—pronto.

The burger was hot, the bun perfectly toasted. Fern sourced meat from a nearby farm, and it made all the difference, elevating the classic cheeseburger with range-fed beef, ground fresh daily. Combined with American cheddar from Tillamook Creamery in Oregon, roma tomatoes, pickles preserved in-house, and our own burger sauce, it was perfection on a bun. The fries were just as I liked them, crunchy on the outside with a light, fluffy interior. The potatoes, too, were grown right here on the island.

I popped the last fry in my mouth and wiped my fingers on a napkin as the news ended and an entertainment program began. I loathed that kind of programming—its sole purpose, it seemed, was to parrot what celebrities posted to their social media and dissect their challenges in excruciating detail. What I found most egregious was it was all a distraction from the issues that really mattered to people around the world. Clean water. Fresh air. Wildfires. Deforestation. Food security. In a nutshell: the climate crisis. Who Brad Pitt was dating—or who Taylor's latest song was about—did nothing but deter attention from the real issues.

Another knock on the door interrupted my irritation. Dropping my napkin to an empty plate, I went to open it, sure I'd find a fuming Fern. But it was Domino on the other side, her bright eyes dimming a little when she saw the annoyance on my face.

"Is—is now a bad time? I'm sorry. I could—" She left the word hanging but turned to the side, indicating the elevator. Her hair was smooth and shiny again, reflecting the lights in the hallway. She had on a silky black dress—or was it a slip?—with a long cardigan.

My irritation softened in an instant. "Not at all. I was just—" I ran a hand through my hair, remembering I'd stepped from the shower without brushing it "—watching the news."

Domino cradled her hands together in front of her, twirling a gold ring on her finger.

Invite her in, you idiot. I held the door open.

"Come in."

The hollow sound of rain dropping in the bucket startled me into reality. Just as Domino took a step forward, I took a bigger one out of the room and toward her, quickly drawing the door shut behind me. She jumped back, surprise etched in her features.

"You know what? It's a mess in there. Let's go to your room?" I touched a hand to her face, tracing her soft cheek, hoping she didn't sense my panic.

"Yeah." Domino hesitated a minute, searching my eyes, then shrugged. "Yeah, sure. I have something I want to show you, anyway." The edges of her lips curved up in a smile. She grasped my fingers and whirled around, tugging me down the hall.

Thank fuck, I thought as I followed her. The skirt of her dress draped temptingly around her legs as she walked. Fern would've killed me if Domino had seen the leak. Killed me dead.

Domino

That was weird, I thought of the awkward exchange at Forest's door. But as the elevator slid closed and he wrapped his arms around me, my concern evaporated. I inhaled deeply where my face pressed against his chest. There it was: that intoxicating mix of pine trees and sea salt.

He trailed slightly behind me down the hall, hand at my low back. At my door he spun me around and pressed me against it, running the back of his hand down my cheek and farther, along my neck and collarbone, slightly grazing my breast and ending at my hip. My nipples peaked like pearls under black silk. Forest angled his head, leaned his left forearm against the door behind me, and brought his other hand to tilt up my chin. He caught me in a mind-melting kiss that stirred every nerve ending in my body. I watched his lips, hypnotized. His mouth hung open with a need that matched my own.

When he drew back, I fumbled in the pocket of my cardigan to find my key card as I whirled around to open the door. It clicked closed behind us, and we stood there in the entranceway, gaping at each other, lust prickling my limbs in pins and needles. He cupped a hand around each side of my face and bent to kiss me again. I closed my eyes, letting our connection wash over me. It felt different. Primordial. Like we were made for this.

Our breathing intensified as we kissed. I barely wanted to come up for air. I grabbed the hem of his sweatshirt and tugged it over his head. Our mouths reconnected quickly, my hands exploring the smooth curves of his chest while the rain drummed steadily against the window.

He slid my cardigan down first one arm, then the other, his hands slipping over my dress like butter on ice. He walked me backward, dropping kisses on my lips, my cheeks, my neck, my shoulders—anywhere with exposed skin. When we reached the bed, he gave me a gentle push, and I landed on the soft duvet. I leaned back on my elbows, letting my legs fall open.

Hunger flared Forest's eyes, an animal stalking its prey. He knelt on the bed before me and flicked the delicate silk skirt of my dress so it rested around my hips.

"Okay?" he asked, his eyes hooded, his hands resting on my knees. I leaned on one elbow and tugged the thin straps of dress off my shoulders. My nipples were dark and swollen.

I guided his hand to cover my breast until one nipple was in the center of his palm. With a groan he squeezed. "Yes," I murmured.

He leaned forward to kiss me again, the outline of his cock warm and hard where it met my core. Instinct had me rocking my hips to grind against it, sending swells of need through me each time the thick tip grazed my clitoris.

I moaned when he leaned back on his knees again and trailed a finger up and down the wet lace that covered my pussy. My skin tingled. I wanted to be fucked so badly it hurt. I'd never felt so switched on. Forest hooked a finger around the waistband of my thong and tugged it off. My heart beat so hard I could hear it.

"Condom?"

I indicated the bedside table, shimmying out of my dress. He stood and stepped out of his sweats and boxer briefs, revealing a perfectly hard, perfectly thick cock, pointed at the ceiling, throbbing in anticipation. In an instant he was back with me, filling the void he'd left, kneeling in front of me and stroking my breasts.

"Fuck, I want you." He tipped his cock inside me, pushing in slowly until it felt like he'd split me in two. He groaned, echoing my own sounds of pleasure.

We clutched each other, my legs around his hips, driving his cock into that spot that pitched me closer to the edge with every thrust. I writhed along with him. He didn't pound me like a sledgehammer. He fucked me like his cock was a bow and I was a violin, vibrating at a frequency that was warm and sweet and lyrical. We heaved and groaned, me arching into him, his hands framing my head.

I ran my fingers over his back, loving the feel of his

muscles moving, shifting, working. He dropped his forehead to my shoulder as we neared the point of ecstasy. His cock grew impossibly harder, and my pussy impossibly wetter, as he began to pulse with release. I clenched around him, climaxing in rhythm. Everything fell away in that moment, leaving us spilling over the edge of rhapsody.

He caught his breath, and I did, too, his forehead still on my shoulder. He looked at me with such raw vulnerability I thought my heart might burst. Still inside me, he bent again to kiss me, not rushing, lingering tenderly on lips that felt bruised with passion.

I sighed as he pushed himself up, then out of me. He flopped on the bed next to me, his hands on his forehead. "Wow."

I laughed, shifting my knees left and right. Was I nervous? Maybe. Things you do and think in the heat of the moment always seem a little silly after the peak, when you're descending back into the valley.

I slid to the edge of the bed and headed for the bathroom, stopping to drop the dress that'd been clutched in my hand while we fucked. It fell to the floor in a puddle. I lingered there, enjoying Forest's eyes on me, feeling more beautiful than I'd felt with any man.

Forest passed me on my way back. I climbed under

the sheets, leaned against the headboard, and held up a corner to invite him to join me when he returned. I cradled my body around his, all limbs and skin and afterglow.

"This is what you wanted to show me?" His heart thumped beneath my ear, and the sound of his laugh vibrated through his chest.

I shifted to straddle his hips with mine, crossing my arms over my chest. It had the opposite effect of what I'd intended. Instead of attitude, I'd shoved my tits up and out. Forest's cock jumped under me.

"Of course not," I said, cheeks burning as I fumbled around on the bed for my cardigan. Feeling the cashmere under my fingers, I untangled it from the sheets and wrapped it around myself. To Forest's protest, I lifted off him and stood, searching the room.

"Aha," I said when my gaze landed on the remote.

He slid back so he could lean against the headboard. He pulled the sheets to his waist, covering his beautiful cock, and watched with interest as I aimed the remote at the TV and hit the Last button. "You want to watch a movie?"

"Not just any movie." I went to the closet to find the thick woolen socks I'd had on earlier, then bounced next to him on the bed. "Turn out that light, would you? There's a glare."

Forest plunged us into darkness before the room

glowed orange. On the screen a setting sun lit a wide sky and the ocean below the color of fire. When Rachel McAdams's name appeared, Forest groaned.

"*The Notebook?*" I could almost hear him rolling his eyes. "I'd rather stick needles in my thumb." But he reached out and pulled me to his chest. He kissed my forehead, and I took a deep, contented breath. With rain pelting the window, the distant sound of lanyards clanking on masts in the marina, and this man's arms around me, I was about the happiest I remembered being in a very long time.

I was asleep before Ryan Gosling's Noah had lunch with the Hamiltons, but Forest woke me by gently running a hand over my arm. I sat up and straightened my bangs, certain I looked a mess. But Forest simply pointed to the screen, where Noah and Allie were locked in a kiss, drenched in the pouring rain, her legs circling his waist, blue dress glued to her skin.

"We did it better."

"We did." I wrapped a hand around his forearm. "But I'm afraid we might be biased."

He tossed his head back, his laugh resonant in the dark room. "And their kiss isn't realistic. No shivering? Come on."

Now it was my turn to laugh, and as I did, I leaned into his side, finding my nook again.

At the end of the movie, when Noah and Allie died hand in hand, Forest let out a groan. I glanced at him sideways, but he just shrugged. "Hey, I sat through it, didn't I?"

The credits rolled, and Forest padded to the bathroom naked, his muscles lit blue by the glow from the screen. Everything about this guy screamed "I'm a man"—his strong, calloused hands, his muscled forearms, that deep voice, his gruff attitude—and his beautiful cock.

I was still staring when he returned, scratching his head, searching around the room.

"They're over here." I pointed to a pile of his clothes on the floor.

"What time is it?" He picked apart the items to find his underwear.

I'd spun the digital clock around to face the wall the first night I was here. I hated the red light it cast in the darkness. I grabbed my phone from the bedside table. "One fifteen."

Forest went stiff. He tugged on his sweatpants and pulled his shirt over his head, followed by his hoodie. Was this guy for real?

I sat up and pulled my knees to my chest, wrapping my cardigan around them. "Where are you going?" My voice sounded screechy even to my own ears.

"I, uh... Well, I have to..." His expression was hangdog, his eyes guilty. "I'm sorry. I have to go." He looked ready to pounce for the door, but first he leaned over the side of the bed and planted a lingering kiss on my lips. Then he was gone.

CHAPTER 13

Forest

I knew I'd left Domino feeling...weird. But I'd last emptied the bucket around six, and rain had been pounding down for the seven plus hours since then. Once the door snicked closed behind me, I sprinted down the hall to the stairs and climbed them two at a time to the fifth floor, chest heaving with effort. Outside room 502, my hand trembled as I slid in the key card, nervous about what I'd find. I let out the breath I hadn't realized I was holding at the sight of the full bucket, a small puddle about six inches wide around it.

It could have been worse. *Much* worse. I raced to

the shower stall with it, doing my best not to spill over the edge. After a week of this routine, I'd honed my water-carrying skills more than I ever thought I'd need. Empty bucket in hand, I grabbed a towel from the railing and rushed back to mop up the puddle.

I tossed the wet towel in the bathroom sink with my clothes from earlier and stood for a minute to let my heart rate slow. Gathering the heavy, sodden pile, I slipped on a pair of boots and traipsed the elevator. In the basement, I threw the lot in the washing machine.

A shelf beside of the dryer held laundry soap, dryer balls, and a basket of odds and ends like dish towels that needed to go back upstairs and a couple of Fern's shirts, ready for ironing. Domino's face stared back at me from the top of the pile. I picked up the *Inside Hollywood* magazine and read the headline: "Depressed Domino: Where Is She Now?"

Against my better judgment I flipped through the pages until I found the cover story. Two photos spanned the header: one of her smiling, radiant in an impossibly tiny bikini, carousing on the beach with Harry Roman, and another on the docks outside the Driftwood, eyes closed, gray sky swirling around her.

"Once half of Hollywood's hottest couple—and we do mean *hot*—Domino West has disappeared from public life, retreating to a small island in the Pacific Northwest," the article began. I skimmed the rest, the spark of anger behind my rib cage bursting into a flame.

Farther down the page was a series of four photos of Domino with a different man in each. "Domino's Dating History," read the caption, along with their names, which didn't mean anything to me. I figured they must be famous, too.

I'd seen enough. I closed the magazine and tossed it back where I'd found it, determined now to see the situation with Domino for what it really was. She was here—temporarily—for work. And I was a diversion— a distraction from the circus of her real life. It was obvious she was attracted to men who ran in her circles, who looked good on a red carpet, who could help elevate her career. Her own Hollywood happy ending.

I stalked through the basement back to the elevator. On the ride to the top floor, I was filled with intention about how to move forward from this clumsy position I'd put myself in. Now I had perspective, maybe it wasn't a bad thing I'd left Domino's bed in the middle of the night.

Rain continued to fall as Wednesday morning dawned, although the deluge had lightened, and the sky was more silver than slate. I found a clean pair of jeans and slipped back into the Upper Left USA hoodie, stuck my phone in the front pocket, and took the stairs to the basement to throw my clothes in the dryer. But the dryer was already on, the washer churning away on another load. The magazine was gone, too. Fern must have been here before me.

I steeled myself for The Talk I expected her to deliver. But the dining room was bustling this morning, and Fern was all smiles behind the bar, steaming milk at the La Marzocco. "Morning, brother," she said when I approached, her blonde ponytail neat as a pin.

I gestured to the room behind me. "What gives?" I said quietly so only she could hear.

She shrugged. "The Domino effect," she whispered back. "I know I shouldn't enjoy saying I told you so. But I love it."

Bluebell came through the kitchen door carrying plates loaded with food. She tipped her chin in my direction. "Bluebell's here, too, huh." I stepped behind the bar, hoping to take a turn at the espresso machine.

"Called her in a half hour ago when it started to get busy. Here." She hip-checked me out of her way and plucked a mug from where they hung on a rack on the wall. I held up two hands and backed away. As I slid out a barstool to sit, I returned a wave from Poppy, who was curled up in one of the big leather chairs by the fireplace. "So we gonna talk about it?" Fern pushed a button to pull a shot of espresso.

I shook my head. "No need. I know where my

priorities are." My sister eyed me sideways but didn't interject. "I'll call around to find a roofer this morning. Get an appointment set up for next week."

Fern set a steaming mug in front of me. She leaned back against the bar and folded her arms in front of her. "Did you hit your head? What have you done with my stubborn, do-it-all-himself brother?"

I chuckled, lifting the cup to my mouth. The coffee was perfect—nutty sweetness and acidity mixed together. "Still here. Just noticed the bucket in my room is filling faster now than it did three days ago, and it'll only get worse. Our guests deserve a certain level of experience. Particularly if those guests bring with them all kinds of attention."

"Now you're speaking my language. Remember I said more guests are due this weekend? The phone rang practically off the hook while you were gone yesterday. The lull we were expecting—the lull we were counting on to get our shit together—it's gone. We're booked clear through till May."

"Oh fuck." The reality of hosting the movie star in room 204 was finally sinking in. Whether the attention would last didn't matter at this point. We had this week, and next week, and the following five months to worry about. Beyond that, no one could predict.

"I'll tell you what else. We are *going* to get with the twenty-first century. This pen-and-paper stuff is ridiculous. We have no way to collect data, no way to save guest preferences—no real way, anyway, other than in here." She tapped a finger against her temple. "And don't get me started on reviews. In this day and age? We *need* to collect our own reviews. They're useful for so many things—social media, customer experiences, website testimonials—"

Fern's voice drowned out as Domino appeared in the coved entrance to the dining room, a smile spreading her cheeks when she saw me. She looked even more beautiful this morning. Was it the sensory memory of feeling her next to me, her naked body curled around mine, her breath coming in hot little puffs as the movie played? Or did she actually just get prettier by the day?

It didn't register that nearly every head in the room turned to look at her. But she had eyes only for me as she descended the stairs and came forward, her eyes sparkling, her bangs shiny. "Good morning." She ran a hand across my shoulders, then rubbed the space between them under the hood of my sweatshirt. I stiffened and pulled away, and she dropped her hand, the light in her eyes dimming.

"Morning," I said politely. I picked up my mug. "I have some calls to make. If you'll excuse me?" Domino nodded, crestfallen. As I left, Fern instructed her to take a seat and settle in for an almond-milk latte.

Domino

"Oh my god, I love your top," Fern gushed. "Free & Easy, right?"

The hopeful gleam in her eyes gave me a reason to smile and pay attention to her rather than following Forest's back as he walked away. Her enthusiasm for my clothes was endearing.

I slid onto the barstool Forest had vacated. "That's right." I straightened one arm, where the words California Poppy trailed down the sleeve in orange cursive letters. The other sleeve was the same. "I love their stuff. Even though I'm from Toronto, I can't get enough of surf culture."

Fern filled the espresso basket with grounds. The scraping of barstool legs against the floor to my right drew my attention.

"Morning!" Poppy's intelligent green eyes bored into mine. She put a hand to her chest. "Poppy."

"I remember." I spun on my stool to face her. "I owe you an enormous thank-you for yesterday."

She shrugged, tucking her brown hair behind her ear. "Eh, no big deal. He was kinda cute without that enormous camera crammed in his face," she said of the photographer she'd played decoy on.

Fern set a latte on the bar, shaking her head at Poppy. "To each her own," Fern said.

"Really, though—I owe you one. Anything you want."

Poppy eyed me, then Fern, then me again as if she couldn't believe her luck. Then she pitched me: "Actually, there is something. Let me profile you."

"Profile me?"

"A feature story."

I hesitated. Deidre would pull out her hair if I said yes without her approval.

"She's a great writer," Fern said over her shoulder as she cleared away a handful of mugs Tommy had dropped on the bar.

Poppy gripped her hands together in front of her in a silent plea. What did one local article matter? Deidre would probably never even hear about it. I smoothed my bangs. "What the hell. Okay."

"Whoop!" Poppy fist-bumped the air. "But first you need to tell me about that sweatshirt." She reclined so she could see the back, where a giant California poppy graphic spanned the length, the words Free & Easy in turquoise capital letters across the bottom.

"You like it?" I glanced down at the smaller version of the poppy repeated over my heart.

"That's me." She pointed a thumb at herself. "I'm named for the California poppy."

"You are? I thought you were all named for indigenous plants or something. This is the state flower of California."

Poppy held up a finger. "Little known fact: it's naturalized all over the Pacific Northwest—even north of here on Vancouver Island. People always think I'm named for the red poppy—you know, the remembrance one?"

I'd always thought they were the same, just different colors, but I nodded anyway. Botanical knowledge wasn't exactly my strength, although I was learning more about plants that grew here on the island just by meeting the people named for them.

"Oh shit." Fern's forehead wrinkled in the middle, her gaze directed outside, her hands clasped around the edge of the bar.

Poppy and I rotated on our stools. "They're multiplying," Poppy said, seeing the photographer from yesterday flanked by two others. They were taking full advantage of a break in the rain, standing around, staring in, then pointing and gesturing now I'd turned to face them.

"Wave." Poppy lifted her arm high and flung it around wildly. Seeing her, Fern did the same.

"Everyone, wave!" Poppy called to the others in the dining room, who did as she directed. In a second the photographers had more than they'd bargained for. If there was one thing paparazzi *weren't* looking for, it was a big group of people smiling and looking happy. They were after the money shot: a celebrity doing something scandalous or even completely banal, provided they looked miserable. But a roomful of people madly waving their arms in the air, grinning like idiots? The three men lowered their cameras in unison. After that, every time one of them lifted a lens, a shout would echo in the dining room to get everyone's arms back in the air. By the time I finished my coffee twenty minutes later, the three men had collected their stuff and retreated down the street, shoulders slumped.

"Where are they staying? Not here, I gather?" Poppy asked Fern.

She shook her head, ponytail swinging. "Surf Motel?"

"I thought you were the only hotel on the island." I didn't remember seeing a Surf Motel when I googled accommodations.

"The only hotel worth staying in, you mean." Fern was back in front of the espresso machine, the aromatic smell of coffee filling the air again.

"It's a run-down old place at the other end of Water Street. I can show you sometime."

"What are you doing today?" I asked. Poppy didn't seem to be in a hurry to get anywhere. With Forest avoiding me, I needed her help scouting for a production headquarters.

"Interviewing you?" she asked hopefully. She reached into the tote bag that hung from the back of her stool and dug out her phone.

"How about you show me around Bayview, help me find what I'm looking for, and we can talk on the way." I stood, stretching my legs.

Poppy didn't need to be asked twice. She jumped up, too, and grabbed her bag and the leather jacket she'd flung on the bar. "Where to first?"

I laughed at her enthusiasm. "Hold on. I need to run something by Fern before we go, plus grab a coat. Meet you in the lobby?"

She walked away, jacket over her arm, texting. Fern's expression held a mix of worry and interest. "Is this about my brother? Because I—"

"No." I shook my head to ease her concern. "Nothing like that. It's about the movie."

Fern visibly relaxed.

"I like everything about the hotel. My room is comfortable, and the location is central—we're right by the marina, which means it'll be easy to get crew and equipment on the boat. And the food so far has been amazing."

Fern beamed with pride, her cheeks like two ripe peaches. "So that's all good, right?"

"It's great. But I need to ask if you—and your kitchen—could handle catering." She was already nodding, but I continued before she could agree to the idea without thinking about it. "It's more than you think," I continued. "On set we'll have craft services for fruit, coffee, snacks, that kind of thing. They'll need your help sourcing food. But I'm talking about catering larger meals—both here and on location if we need it." Again, Fern looked ready to jump in with a yes, but I held up a hand. "It's a lot. Before you agree you should talk with Alex and Trudi. Alex handles our finances. Trudi's my coproducer."

"Okay. I'm sure that's the smart move." Fern balled her fists in the pockets of her apron. "I need to check with our suppliers, make sure they can handle it. And George."

"We can talk more about it later. You'll think about it?"

"Are you kidding? Our little hotel as part of a big movie production? It's the opportunity of a lifetime. I'll do everything I can to make it work." Her attention shifted to the lobby. I followed her gaze to see Forest behind the desk, brows furrowed as he read something on his phone. "Including getting Mr. Grump over there on board."

I picked up my own phone off the bar. "You're wonderful," I said before I headed for the lobby.

"Wave!" Fern shouted as I went. The paparazzi had returned. I smiled as the roomful of people lifted their hands again, and the photographers lowered their lenses, their faces falling, too.

As I walked through the lobby, Forest held his phone to his ear, speaking quietly. I rested my hands on the long desk, happy to wait, but he lifted a finger, his expression harried. As I turned to walk away, though, I caught a hint in his eyes of the lust I'd seen there last night. His grouchy demeanor couldn't hide the way his body reacted to mine on a baser level.

I didn't have time to think about whether I'd done something to anger him. Poppy was waiting. The most important thing today was to find a production headquarters. I had no doubt Marc would nail down everything he needed on Vashon Island the minute he had the chance, but I was determined to bring *Shore Thing* to Orcas Island, with or without Forest's support. The coastal ambiance, the small-town charm, the rural setting—it all reflected the script exactly.

I wrapped my wool coat and scarf around me, glimpsing a streak of blue sky through the window. The rain had eased, but I realized I hadn't asked Poppy if she had a car. Big oversight. If we were on foot and it started raining again, I'd be screwed.

I needn't have worried. Poppy wasn't in the lobby when I returned, so I swung open the front door to see a little red Miata at the curb, exhaust billowing from the tailpipe in the cold air. She leaned across and rolled down the passenger-side window, her arm heaving circles to move the hand crank. "Jump in!"

The paparazzi scurried over and lifted their cameras the minute they saw me. I beamed a happy smile—one I genuinely felt. I needed to change the narrative of Depressed Domino. Now was as good a time as any.

I lifted the latch to open the door, which creaked with age. Gathering my coat around me, I lowered into the tiny cabin and slammed the door closed. The interior was all black, the gear shift rattling in the console as the engine rumbled. "This is so cool!" In Toronto there were no old cars on the road. The weather was too hard on them; winter salt rusted them out in a matter of years. And in LA the cars were all shiny and flashy. The first word I thought of when I saw a red convertible in Hollywood was *douchebag*. But I meant it when I said Poppy's Miata was cool.

She already knew it, though. She was a cool girl. Smart, curious, self-assured, and ambitious, if asking me for an interview point-blank was anything to go by.

I watched in the side mirror as the photographers

chased after us, snapping photos until the Miata zipped away, leaving them in our trail. Poppy expertly worked the clutch and gear shift, and even though the car was built more than thirty years ago, she told me, it hummed like a bee.

CHAPTER 14

Domino

Poppy drove along Water Street, past the restaurant where Forest kissed his friend's breast instead of her baby's head. That night the streets had been empty beyond seagulls and streetlamps. In the middle of the day, though, locals smiled and waved from the sidewalks at the sight of the red Miata.

"Been there yet?" Poppy pointed to Grind House, the coffee shop Forest had walked me past on his tour of embarrassing moments.

"No. Fern makes such good coffee, I haven't branched out." I finger-combed my bangs. The vinyl roof on the convertible rattled, but the heat worked well, and it wasn't raining, so we were warm and dry inside the car.

"True. But you haven't lived until you've had a Grind House doughnut." Poppy changed gears and slowed as we passed, glancing sideways to assess me. Was I the type of woman who ate doughnuts? Or did I count every calorie? Deciding I must be the former, she said, "That'll be our last stop of the day." She sped up when the shopfronts thinned out a few blocks beyond. At the very end, where the road stopped and the wilderness began, a three-story blue-and-white building was set back from a parking lot. As we neared I could see the paint peeling off in places and a couple of windows boarded up. An old vertical sign projected off the front near the doors: Surf Motel.

Poppy stopped the car, letting it idle at the side of the road. "This is the place Fern was talking about. The photographers must be staying here. Cheap, not so cheerful, but no one asks questions."

"It's open?" Nothing about the place suggested open for business. But when I leaned forward in my seat to see more of it, I noticed lights on in a couple of rooms. At the back of the lobby, a single lamp illuminated a small desk.

She laughed. "I know. Not my first recommendation." She pulled into the motel parking lot. Two cars were parked at the far end. The pavement was cracked with age and salty air, the parallel lines faded to near invisibility. She reversed quickly and retraced the route we'd come for a couple of blocks before making a right.

"Where to now?"

"Winslow. On the other side of the island."

"I went on Monday. Checked out Grange Hall and the fish restaurant. What's it called?"

"Cottle's. Isn't it the best?" Poppy drummed her fingers on the steering wheel. "I was thinking Grange Hall might be a good place for your production headquarters. Did you go in?"

"Just looked through the windows."

"I can do better. I know the owner." She wound the little sports car through residential streets lined with trees, their bare branches arching over us like arthritic fingers, until we reached Ellison Road. She floored it on the main drag, and the Miata shot off like a tiny red rocket toward the other side of the island, zooming past stretches of farmland, stands of enormous trees, and intermittent glimpses of the Pacific.

At Grange Hall Poppy introduced me to the manager—her mom, Georgia, an older version of Poppy with silver hair and the same intelligent green eyes. Caretaker was a better description, Georgia told us. My gut feeling had been right. The old agricultural building would be perfect for production. It was big and clean, equipped with tables and chairs, and it had a kitchen. But it wasn't a slam dunk. The grounds were used for weekly farmers markets every Saturday from April to October. In the winter months the market moved inside. If everything went on schedule, we'd need the space in June and July, but the way Georgia explained it, the volume of people who shopped at the market every week could be prohibitive to moving cast and crew in and out of the grounds. And then there was the distance from Bayview. Ideally we needed somewhere near where the boat would be docked. Still, I got Georgia's contact information and vowed to put her in touch with Alex and Trudi.

We stopped for lunch at Cottle's, where I was happy to see Angela again. She was on her own, her helmet on the table, her notepad in front of her, pen in hand, but the minute she saw us, she flagged us over, making room for us to eat Cobb salads with smoked salmon lox, shrimp, and a hard-boiled egg dressed with spicy harissa vinaigrette. Like my last meal here, it was divine. I decided that if the Driftwood couldn't handle catering for *Shore Thing*, I could ask Mary and Louis.

"What are you working on these days?" Angela turned her curious gaze on Poppy, who held up a finger while she chewed a mouthful of salad.

"Oh, I have a little project I'm chipping away at. Plus, you know, my usual column for the *Chronicle*," she said after she swallowed. "Damn, that's good. Got anything you'd like me to share?" She eyed Angela inquisitively. "If you want any info about the island, Angela knows all."

Angela let out a lilting laugh. "I told Domino the other day, so I suppose it's not a secret. I'm writing about a murder. Right here on the island."

Poppy's fork clanged against her bowl as it dropped. "Say what?"

I touched Poppy's arm, laughing. "I had the same reaction. But it's old—a cold case, right, Angela?"

"That's right. I'm still in the research stage. Taking notes, reviewing police reports. Nothing for your column—yet."

"And observing all around you. That's what you do best." Poppy turned to me. "The thing I admire most about Angela is how she takes an interest in her surroundings—people and places—without being intrusive. Everyone loves her. Everyone trusts her. Wherever she goes, doors just...open."

Angela's cheeks turned a shade of pink that matched my scarf. "Thank you, dear. You're earning quite a reputation yourself." Now it was Angela's turn to share what she admired about Poppy. I was struck once again by the way the people of Orcas Island truly cared about and liked one another. After LA, it was almost hard to trust it was real. "She's smart as a whip, this one. And funny."

"That's what I'm learning." I smiled at my new writer friend as she fidgeted with the ends of her thick brown hair. "In fact, she's writing a piece about me. Aren't you, Poppy?"

Poppy's eyes lit up like fireflies. "Does this mean I can start asking you questions?"

I laughed. "The whole ride home."

Poppy held up an open hand in front of Angela, who despite her age knew right away what was expected: a high-five.

Since leaving the Driftwood this morning, we'd been miraculously free of a tail of paparazzi. I felt refreshingly normal—just a woman having lunch with two new friends. An hour and several cups of tea later, we stuffed ourselves back into the Miata and headed for Bayview, reversing our route like a video played backward. Poppy hit a button to press record on her phone and asked questions as thoughtful as any interviewer I'd met, and I found myself sharing more about my private life than I had with any other reporter since "making it" in Hollywood.

As the road weaved among the giant trees, she asked me about growing up in Toronto, about my parents and what they were like, about working toward a goal that seemed almost impossible to achieve, about moving to Los Angeles and the differences between Canadians and Americans—and about my very public romance and breakup with Harry Roman. I was relieved to tell my side of the story, trusting Poppy would treat it with respect rather than salaciousness and be fair and honest to both him and me.

Not for the first time I wondered about the serenity I felt on this wonderful island at the edge of the world. Something about the place felt right, felt innate, felt like *me*. "It's like I've never belonged anywhere—not the grind of Toronto or the sunny veneer of LA," I told Poppy.

"This place'll do that to you," she said without a hint of surprise. "Make you wonder why people live anywhere else."

The twenty-five-minute drive passed in what felt like five, and suddenly we were back at Water Street. Poppy took a left. "Isn't the hotel that way?"

"I promised you doughnuts!" She expertly parallel parked across the street from the café. Daylight was just beginning to fade, but it hadn't rained all afternoon. I stood for a moment on the sidewalk, staring out at the steely gray ocean.

"Domino!" a man shouted behind me. I turned as a camera flashed, then another, and another. The trio of photographers weren't wasting any time now they'd spotted me. Their little group spread out wide so they didn't all get pictures from the same angle.

"Over here!" came a second man's voice. "Domino! Talked to Harry?"

"What's it like to be dumped?" the third guy yelled. They were trying to get to me, to catch a shot that would net them big money, but I flashed them a brilliant smile, posing next to the Miata. If they were going to get a picture of me, they might as well get a good one.

Poppy stood patiently to the side, taking in everything happening in front of her. "Okay, thank you," I told the photographers after a few minutes. "My friend is waiting." I walked around to join her, grabbing her arm to jog across the street. A bell above the café door jangled as we entered.

A few faces watched us approach the counter after the commotion outside, but again the people of Orcas Island were respectful. No one came rushing up for a selfie; no one stared for more than a few seconds. At the till, Poppy introduced me to Ginger, a happy-looking woman with beautiful red hair cut short and wispy around her face.

"Are you a rare instance of someone your age *not* named after a plant?" I assumed she was named for her copper-colored locks.

Ginger laughed and put her hands to her hips. "No, but you're not the first to make that mistake." She explained her namesake was a plant called western wild ginger, which was, of course, native to the island and not the root ginger used in cooking. "You might miss it unless you're looking for it. It's an evergreen that carpets the ground," she said, "although it does have a burgundy flower when it blooms in spring."

"Either way, it's really pretty. It suits you," I told her. She smiled, bowing her head slightly. "Poppy tells me you make the best doughnuts."

"Best in the state, and I don't mind saying it." She gestured to the display case beside the counter, where a half-dozen kinds of doughnuts were organized neatly in rows, like little planets in a pastry solar system. She eyed me thoughtfully. "I know the one for you. Take a seat. Coffee and doughnuts on me."

Within minutes she arrived at the table we'd chosen near the back, a tray expertly balanced on her right hand. She set coffees in front of each of us, then thunked down a couple of heavy plates. Mine held a pastry about three inches in circumference and nearly as tall, coated in a crinkly sugar glaze. "London Fog," she said before I asked. For Poppy she'd brought a classic French crueller, hand-piped to double height so the extra swirls soaked up the shiny glaze. "Hope they live up to their reputation." Ginger rested her hands on the back of my chair for a moment before she retreated to serve the next customer.

"Your eyes are almost the size of that doughnut." Poppy laughed. "What are you waiting for? Try it."

I lifted the London Fog doughnut, heavy like a paperweight in my hand. Beyond the delicate crunch of the lemony glaze, the dough was fluffy and golden brown. The first bite was heavenly, but it wasn't till I took a second that I hit the Earl Grey pastry cream in the center. It was smooth and rich without being too sweet or heavy. I'd found my nirvana. I must have closed my eyes for a second to savor it, because when I opened them, Poppy sat grinning across from me, chewing her own pastry, amused.

"When I'm right, I'm right," she said before sinking her teeth into her crueller. Then something drew her attention outside. She stood in place, lifting her arm in the air and waving it wildly, yelling, "Everyone, wave!"

A few at a time, the patrons around us joined in, craning their necks to see who they were waving at. Poppy pointed outside to where the three photographers lurked across the street like night crawlers, their cameras aimed at Grind House. Quickly everyone caught on and flagged their hands back and forth, both obscuring the paparazzi's view and spoiling whatever candid scenes they hoped to capture. I giggled at the scene around me, hand on my chest. What a special, uniquely compassionate place I'd found myself in.

Forest

There were two possibilities for roofing repair on Orcas Island: the Fly Guys, a company run by Rupert Byng, an old friend of my dad's, and Jack Woodhouse, who'd moved here last spring and so far was somewhat of a mystery. I'd hoped to book the former, but when Rupert explained his team couldn't do a site visit for at least two weeks, I decided to take a chance on Jack and arranged for him to come by on Monday, crossing my fingers for fair weather for the next five days—or until whenever Domino left.

In the meantime we had guest arrivals to prepare for, beginning tomorrow. I did my best to shake the visions of Domino's naked body from my head, willing the memory of her impossibly soft skin and the subtle smell of lilacs that followed her to the recesses of my brain. I went methodically from room to room on the third and fourth floors, checking they were clean and stocked, the bathrooms had hot water, and the Wi-Fi signal was strong. A few of our summer staff were arriving today, too, to help with housekeeping.

Coming for dinner tonight? Fern had texted when I finally looked at my phone a few hours later. **I need your help with something.**

My gut said to keep out of Domino's way for the remainder of her stay. I figured if I kept out of sight, I might stand a chance of getting her out of my head.

Can you get away for an hour? We could eat up here.

Like old times, she messaged back. When we were kids we often had dinner in my room while our parents were busy with guests. It became a ritual, especially on weekends: my mom laid our food out on big wooden trays, which we set in front of us on the bed while we watched movies like *Jumanji* and *Free Willy*. Some aspects of growing up in a hotel sucked, but Jack and Judy made it fun.

I showered while I waited, letting the hot water loosen where my shoulders were knotted from hard work and push-ups. The tension eased as I ran soap over my tired muscles, but one body part refused to relax. My cock was hard and heavy in my hand as I stroked it, slowly at first, remembering the way Domino's pink nipples peaked into rosebuds just before she came, how warm and wet her pussy felt around me, how flawless her naked body looked in the morning light. I found a faster rhythm, pumping my cock with my hand as pressure welled in my sac. Images of Domino on the bed beneath me, shoulders bare, back arched, lips swollen with need played on my eyelids like a movie. My sac tightened, and my mind and body went numb as every cell in my body seemed to rush for a single point of exit. I rode the contractions, pumping cum out of my cock, watching it shoot into the stream of water from the shower head.

I leaned against the tile wall, letting the endorphins work through me. One thing was obvious: it was going to be a while before I wrested control of my mind back from Domino West.

Towel around my waist, I picked up the clothes from the floor where I'd tossed them and tidied the bed. I drew on jeans and an old T-shirt and grabbed the remote to search for something to watch while we ate.

A thud sounded on the door. "Sorry. Elbow," Fern said. I held it open while she carried in two trays of food and set them on the bed. Each held a grilled salmon steak, crispy around the edges and seasoned with kosher salt and black pepper. "That's quinoa with fennel and mixed herbs." She pointed to the delicate-looking grain salad on the tray closest to her as she kicked off her sneakers and climbed on the bed, crossing her legs yoga-style in front of her. She wore a sweatshirt and stretchy black leggings.

My stomach grumbled in anticipation. I'd been too focused on checking the third and fourth floors to eat anything past breakfast.

"*Catch Me If You Can*? God, I loved this movie. Turn it up, will you?"

We laughed as Leonardo DiCaprio's Frank Abagnale fooled a Secret Service agent and evaded capture for forging checks. Dinner finished, I pushed my tray away and watched as my sister took her last bites, eyes barely leaving the screen. It really did feel like old times.

She did a double take when she caught me looking at her. "Do I have something on my face?" She felt around for a napkin and wiped her mouth.

I leaned back against the headboard, kicking one foot over the other. "Nah. Just remembered the time you spilled tomato soup all over the bed because you were scared in *Twilight*."

Fern pouted. "I was only fourteen."

"Oh, no. That's not an excuse. It was *made* for fourteen-year-olds. You're just a wimp."

She tossed the napkin on the tray and shimmied back so she could lean beside me. "Whatever, tough guy." She shoved my shoulder. "You cried in *The Blind Side*."

"Did not."

"Did, too."

Knowing we could go back and forth forever, I changed the subject. "What did you need my help with?"

She reached for the remote and hit the mute button, bending her knees to her chest. "Domino asked if we could handle catering."

"What, like a dinner?"

"Like the whole movie production."

"Absolutely not."

"Come on, Forest. Why not? I've already spoken to George, and he says we can—"

I folded my arms over my chest. "I don't care," I interrupted. "What the hell does *George* know? How quickly he forgets how crazy it is around here come tourist season."

"But listen, I have a plan—"

I held up a palm. "No way. Look at this place. Look around you." I motioned the floor, indicating the bucket, then the water stain on the ceiling. "In case you haven't noticed, things are falling apart at the fucking seams. Literally. The list of shit to do is a mile long. We're barely ready for the people who're coming tomorrow, never mind a crew of Hollywood clowns with their heads up their asses."

Fern cast her eyes to the ceiling and sighed. "Once you see it, you can't look away, can you?" she said of the dingy gray stain the shape of an inkblot, edged in brown. "Guess we gotta paint, too, huh." She tightened her lips in a line, resigned. On the TV screen, Frank Abagnale climbed through a bedroom window to flee his engagement party. "Fine," she added a minute later. "But I'm going to put her in touch with River. This isn't going to ruin our chances of hosting the movie."

"Suit yourself." I shrugged, but I knew River Black would be thrilled at the chance. Isola was always busy in the summer, but they catered weddings and events around the island as well. They'd be perfect. Despite my protestations, there was no denying this movie would be a coup for the Driftwood, catering or no. If Domino's presence this week filled the dining room and brought bookings through till May, the boon a whole production would create seemed unfathomable.

And my stomach dropped at the idea of never seeing Domino again.

I was in trouble. Big, pathetic, soul-squeezing trouble.

220

CHAPTER 15

Domino

We stayed at Grind House until it closed. Poppy kept asking questions about acting and producing. I found I was eager to share both the good parts of my journey and the bad. Her enthusiasm for the creative process reminded me of the grit with which I'd started my career and made me even more determined to be taken seriously in my industry. It felt now like my detour with Harry Roman had been just that—a temporary deviation from what I really wanted in life. I wanted to make movies—good ones—and have a career that lasted beyond youth and the nebulous label of "it" girl.

The more time I spent with Poppy, the more I liked her. Her confidence was inspiring. She told me about her writing and promised to send me links to her favorite recent pieces. She was funny, too, with a dry sense of humor and a deadpan delivery that had me in fits of laughter. In everything we'd done today, she'd shown me she was my opposite: 100 percent *not* a people pleaser. She didn't seem—or need—to care whether anyone liked her.

"Ever ghost-written for anyone?" I asked as we collected our belongings. Ginger had flipped over the Open sign and begun cashing out the till.

"A book, you mean?" She slipped into her leather jacket and waited while I tied my scarf.

"No." I'd wound the pink wool too tight and struggled to loosen it. "I mean for appearances, interviews, stuff like—" I stopped when she wrinkled her nose.

She paused at the door, leaning back against it. "You mean the monthly quiz nights at my grandma Honey's house? You wouldn't believe how wild those octogenarians get."

"Ah, shit." Her lips twitched, and I felt my cheeks burn. "My bad. But I'm serious, Poppy. Would you be interested in doing some ghostwriting for me?"

"You need a writer for appearances?" She opened the door and stepped into the frigid night. "What a weird concept."

The photographers were huddled together under the awning of the shop next to Grind House. Only one lifted his lens when they spotted us; the others kept their arms wrapped tightly around themselves. They looked positively frozen. "Hang on," I told Poppy, then retreated into the café. "Ginger?" I called, not seeing her or Julian. She poked her head above the display case from where she was working behind it. "If you've got three hot drinks and three doughnuts left, would you let these guys have 'em? On me." I motioned to the three figures silhouetted under the streetlights.

"Of course." She grabbed three paper cups from the stack to her left.

Outside, I posed for a couple of photographs on my own before I linked arms with Poppy and pulled her in. I laughed at what I was learning was her typical reaction to things: cool and indifferent. She must have really wanted to interview me, I realized now, given how enthusiastic she'd been the first time we met. We crossed to the Miata as Ginger brought out the coffees and doughnuts.

"If I'd known a week ago I'd be feeling sorry for paparazzi..." I shook my head as I gathered the bottom of my coat and lowered into the convertible. "What *is* it about this place? Being in a small town has gone to my head or something."

Poppy snorted. "Yeah, gets a little much, doesn't it? Sometimes it feels like we're all trying to out-Pollyanna one another." She pulled a U-turn and pointed us in the direction of the Driftwood. "So about this ghostwriting thing."

"Come have dinner with me, and I'll explain."

"Sure." She hit the gas pedal, zipping us toward the hotel.

Over a meal of Salt Spring Island mussels and scallops seared with potatoes and beet greens, I told her how actors have writers on call to help them prepare for appearances like late-night talk shows, award ceremonies—even social media. Once she got past the initial shock that Ryan Reynolds, and Kristen Bell, and Damon Mann aren't *actually* effortlessly funny or interesting, and their casual anecdotes on Kimmel and Fallon are carefully planned down to the minute, she jumped at the opportunity. I sensed not for the first time she was yearning for an escape from Orcas. She told me she hadn't had time to travel but instead had focused on her writing career, establishing a regular column in the local paper and writing pieces for mainland publications like *Portland* magazine and *Seattle Weekly*.

"I've been busy since the minute I started writing ten years ago," she said. "I'm one of those people who's romantic about the work. You know, whiskey, cigarettes...the Bukowski of it all." She stared across the dining room to the big fireplace at the far end, twin flames reflected in her eyes. "I believe with all my heart if I write something that's undeniably great, people want to read it."

She shook her head and let out a snort. "I don't mean some random story about how the Seattle music scene's changed since the nineties."

"You're talking about the project you mentioned to Angela."

"It's a..." She fiddled with the napkin in her lap. "Feels a little silly to say it to you now. But it's a script."

"A movie script?" When she nodded, I said, "I'd love to read it."

"You would?"

I settled back in my chair and savored what was left in my wineglass. "Of course."

"I would love that. But it's not ready," she hastened to add.

"Yet."

She straightened the utensils on her empty plate. "Yet." She lifted her eyes to mine, grinning.

I'd hoped to see Forest at some point tonight, but the barstools where he usually camped out remained empty. Fern had disappeared shortly after we'd sat down, too, leaving dinner service up to Bluebell. She seemed to relish in the task, running back and forth between the bar, kitchen, and dining room with purpose. Poppy told me about Bluebell's side hustle, an organic skin-care line infused with local seaweed.

After Poppy left, and we'd made plans to meet up again the next day to finish her interview, I lingered awhile longer, chatting with Bluebell as the last dinner guests wrapped up their bills and trickled out. But a half hour later, with still no sign of Forest, I thanked her and headed for my room.

It'd been a long day, after a long night, without a lot of sleep. I flopped against the crisp white pillows on the bed in room 204, thinking carefully about why I was here. I'd desperately needed to escape the relentless motion of LA and the aftermath of Harry Roman. But most importantly I was here to scout a location for *Shore Thing*, not to moon after a man I barely knew—and a whole crew of folks were counting on me to do it.

From now on that needed to be my focus. I was here for such a short time. There was no point getting caught up with someone that, once the shoot was over, I'd likely never see again. Especially not one who seemed to despise the idea of celebrity and everything it represented.

Friday morning began with a text from Trudi, asking how things were going. **Found a boat and the**

perfect spot for headquarters, I messaged back, sipping the delicious coffee Fern had delivered at eight a.m. Poppy's comment about Pollyanna echoed around my head. **Working on catering,** I told Trudi.

Two out of three ain't bad.

Marc? I suspected the real motivation behind her check-in had something to do with him.

On route to Vashon Island.

Orcas is it. I know it, I texted.

Anything to do with the hunky hotel guy? The three emojis she followed up with made me laugh: the smiley face with heart eyes, the winking face, and the eggplant.

In spite of, I replied. I knew she was hoping for details but I kept them to myself.

Marc's worried.

I've read the script, remember? Marc hadn't laid eyes on anything beyond the synopsis and the first set of storyboards back in November—a fact I planned to use to my advantage if push came to shove.

I stretched my arms wide and yawned. Outside rain was falling again, and seagulls floated low in the mist. It was a two-cup morning. I planned to spend an hour answering emails before I met Poppy in the dining room for another jolt of caffeine.

My stomach flipped seeing the name of the script writers we'd hired at the top of my inbox. They'd finished their revisions. *This is really happening.* "Yes!" I cheered aloud in the quiet room. *I'm making a movie.* I'd allowed the circus around Harry and the distraction of Forest dim a little of the fire I had inside to bring this project to life.

Deidre had sent a long message detailing how she and TBA had "handled" the Harry situation, how she hoped I didn't "undo all her hard work" with a public fling with "some lumberjack in the woods." For a PR professional, she wasn't very professional. Still, I kept my response upbeat and friendly, holding up my end of the bargain to always be likable and easy to work with. It'd been apparent from the day I'd moved to California that one thing I should avoid at all costs was the label *difficult.* No matter what Deidre, or the press, or the likes of Arthur Dagon said to me, I kept my head up and my smile easy—which often meant I was like the proverbial duck with a serene exterior, my insides frantically flapping below the surface.

Answering emails was like having a bucket of ice water poured over me. *Buck up, buttercup,* I told myself as I stood from the window seat and slid into sneakers. *This is your shot.* It was hard to come back from a role in a bad movie, or a bad role in a good movie, and it was even harder if your name was in the credits as a producer. Trudi and I wanted to make our mark in Hollywood by developing films with a strong female point of view. If *Shore Thing* flopped, it was going to be even tougher, if possible at all, to find financing for whatever we wanted to do next. All my career eggs—and Trudi's—were in a basket so delicately woven the bottom might fall out at any minute.

As I left the room and closed the door behind me, I steeled my nerves with determination. I wanted to see Forest in the dining room, but more than that, I *needed* to see Forest. I needed to tell him this fling, or whatever he wanted to call the thing simmering between us, was over.

Forest

"I'm glad to see you," Domino told me as she took the barstool next to mine. I'd lingered over coffee with Fern, discussing how we could reupholster the old red-vinyl seats and booths in stages and buff the floor in the dining room late one night.

"That'll never work." As usual, Fern had rebuked out of hand any idea that involved me and YouTube. "What about the social media person you agreed to hire?"

"You mean the social media person *you* agreed to hire." A lot of other improvements needed to happen before I wanted to spend a dime on social media.

"Hmph." Seeing the resolve in my eyes, Fern had stomped off to the kitchen, wisely sensing a sibling argument on the horizon.

I stood abruptly and moved around the back of the bar. I was happy to see her, too—too happy. I'd made a decision last night, and I was determined not to be swayed by Domino's intense blue eyes. Or her pretty pink lips, pursed in a bow. Or the way her faded Levi's hugged her perfect ass. I stuck my hands in my pockets, suddenly conscious Domino was looking at me differently this morning. As if some window between us had closed.

"Coffee?"

"You know how that thing works?" Her smile threatened to crumble the wall of determination I'd built. I made sure to look her in the eyes rather than the outline of her nipples in the white T-shirt she wore. There definitely wasn't a bra under there.

"Read the directions and everything."

Domino narrowed her gaze. "You read the directions?"

I laughed, running a hand through my hair. "Normally I'd take offense, but in this case you're right. Fern made me. I usually figure things out on my own."

"That checks out." She pursed her lips again, which twitched at the edges until she broke into a smile. "In that case, yes. I'll have a—"

"Latte with almond milk. I know. Half the caffeine, right?"

When she nodded, I filled the basket with fresh grounds and hit the button to pull a shot. Grabbing almond milk from the bar fridge below the counter, I set the steamer jug in front of me and glanced around the dining room. It was unusually quiet after the past week. The breakfast rush was over, and Bluebell was perched in her usual spot by the fireplace, deep in a phone conversation.

Domino peered around, too. "I know. The Domino effect has worn off."

"You know about that?" I looked up from steaming the milk to catch her expression.

She shrugged. "Poppy told me." Which meant Fern must've told Poppy—and who knew who else. Seeing my dismay, she rushed to add, "Hey, I'm all for it. If I can bring attention to local businesses—to *your* business—I'm happy to be of service."

My cock stiffened at the thought of Domino servicing my business. I poured hot milk over the espresso shot, closed my eyes, and forced my thoughts on something less X-rated before I turned around and set it in front of her.

"I can't do that fancy stuff on the top like Fern. But see what you think." I watched as she took a sip, raising her eyebrows. "Okay?"

"Better than okay. It's great."

Fern came through the swinging door from the kitchen. Seeing us at the bar, she hesitated a split second, as if deciding whether she was intruding. She proceeded toward us.

"Will you come join me in a booth?" Domino asked me then. "If I'm not interrupting."

"He's all yours." Fern came around the back of the bar and playfully shoved my arm. I followed Domino to a seat by the window.

"God, it really does rain a lot here, huh," she said, staring out at the leaden sky.

I shrugged. "This time of year, yah." I watched her drink her coffee, doing my best not to notice the pink stain her lipstick left around the rim. "So listen, Domino—" I said just as she, too, started talking. I let her finish.

"I think you're wonderful." I felt my cheeks flame. "This whole place is wonderful—the hotel, the island, the people..." She turned to take in the room around her, Fern behind the bar, Bluebell curled up on an armchair by the fire, the big picture windows that overlooked the marina.

"I think you're—"

Domino interrupted me. "Uh-uh. Let me finish. Please." She cleared her throat, reached across the table, and rested a hand on my forearm. "It's because it's so wonderful I have to end whatever this—" she motioned the space between us "—is. Orcas Island *is* where I'm going to shoot *Shore Thing*. And because of that, because this movie is so important to not just my career but those of quite a few others, I need to be serious. Professional." She locked eyes with mine as she said the last word.

I let out the breath I'd been holding, relieved her feelings aligned with mine, then laughed. Domino's expression turned to surprise. "It's not what you think," I said. "I've been thinking about things, too. About how important your movie is to us. How Fern would kill me if I ruined it, scared you away from shooting here." Domino looked at my sister behind the bar, who smiled and waved, her neat blonde ponytail shiny under the pendant lights. "She might not look it, but she's a killer."

Domino smirked. "If only you knew what a killer *really* was. She's a pussycat." Her eyes became unfocused, as if she was thinking of someone in particular.

"Anyway. We're worlds apart, aren't we? I live in the middle of nowhere and don't do relationships. You live in Hollywood and date rock stars. How's that for hard to relate to?"

Her lips quirked. "Pretty up there."

"Exactly."

We grinned at each other like schoolkids. I was glad we were on the same page. Though we were opposite in lifestyle, our priority was the same: focus on our businesses first and foremost. Yet sitting across from her, seeing her sapphire-blue eyes flash under that dark fringe, I still felt longing ache through my chest. I locked away the feeling and reached a hand across the table.

She studied me questionably before she grasped hold and shook. Her hand was slender and delicate in my clumsy calloused one. "That was easier than I thought," she said as we let go. Her attention was drawn to the arched doorway into the lobby. "That's my cue." She nodded at Poppy standing there. Domino picked her phone off the table and stood. "See ya around, Forest Russo."

"Yah. See ya...around." She'd walked away before I finished the sentence. I wasn't sure what I'd expected, but just like that she went back to being the movie star in Fern's magazine, not the woman I'd shared a bed with.

Behind the bar Fern caught my eye and raised an eyebrow after Domino and Poppy exited the dining room arm in arm. I shrugged, not in the mood for explanations. I glared out the window at the rain, coming down in sheets now, washing away the glimmer of hope I'd held I might've found someone I connected with. How on Planet Earth could I have fallen for this woman in under a week?

I dug the phone from my pocket and called up the website of a local equipment rental company. Buffing floors and using my body was the best way to plug the rapidly growing hole I'd let Domino shoot in my defenses.

The rest of the day passed quickly, a blur of guests checking into the third and fourth floors, moving luggage upstairs, and delivering extra pillows and kettles where requested. At quarter to five, I grabbed the fob for the jeep and told my sister I'd be back in an hour. I took my time driving to the outskirts of Winslow to pick up the buffer, Charlie Parker on the speakers and darkness settling in.

CHAPTER 16

Domino

Poppy asked me to meet her in the lobby at 10:00 a.m. Saturday morning, saying she had something interesting planned but refusing to provide details. My only other instruction was not to eat breakfast.

I hadn't seen Forest since yesterday morning—which was both helpful and discomforting, a feeling I pushed to the recesses of my mind. I could examine the emotions it stirred later. I also hadn't had a firm response from Fern about catering. If it was a no, I needed to find an alternative, fast. The fact that Marc was on Vashon Island now, charming everyone there with his perfect teeth and beautiful clothes, working out deals with hotel and boat and restaurant owners, ratcheted up my anxiety tenfold. Setting aside how I felt about Forest was one thing. Setting aside the certainty in my gut about Orcas Island being the *only* place to shoot *Shore Thing* was another. This film was all about falling in love—with the characters, with the story, with the dialogue, with the cinematography, with the setting. All those elements needed to be perfect to deliver the magic and alchemy that separated a good movie from a great one.

Standing on the steps of the Driftwood, sheltered from the rain, I watched a red blur crystallize into the shape of a Miata as Poppy sped toward me. I made a pathetic attempt to keep dry with a hand held over my head as I raced down the front path and tugged open the car door. Inside, Poppy waited until I was settled before she handed me one of the paper cups she'd propped between her thighs.

"You can get after-market cupholders, you know." I laughed watching her reposition her own cup so it was balanced between her legs.

She rolled her eyes, reaching back into the tiny cavity behind the seats to retrieve two wax-paper bags. "Here." I grabbed one of them, which sank into my hand.

"Feels like a frigging doorstop." I peeled apart the paper to see the familiar ringed shape of a thick, golden-brown doughnut coated in crackled glaze. "Good thing I'm hungry."

Poppy smiled, then focused on the road as she pulled out and did a U-turn.

"Want to tell me where we're going now?" I took a drink from the cup she'd handed me, surprised to find instead of coffee it was some kind of tea. "Mmm. What's this?"

"Mulberry tea, Ginger said. Once in a while she tries out new things. Grown locally maybe?" She sipped her own cup and shrugged. "She rattled off a long list of health benefits. Tastes like green tea to me."

I tasted it again, letting the flavors sit on my palate. "Nutty and kinda sweet. I like it." I ripped a sticky piece of doughnut from the bag and bit into it. "Oh, try them together. It's divine."

She took her hands off the steering wheel and balanced it with her knee, fumbling to get the doughnut out of the wax bag in her lap. Left hand back on the wheel, she lifted it to her mouth with her right, sinking her teeth in. "You know—" she said around a mouthful "—you're on to something there." She swallowed. "Ginger always nails it."

"So you gonna tell me where you're taking me?"

"You'll see."

The Miata raced along in a stream of mist kicked

up behind the traffic, the short, squat window wipers working double time. Poppy followed a half dozen other cars turning left into the grounds of Grange Hall. Unlike the last two times I was here, the parking area was full of vehicles, and a parade of umbrellas filed toward the big old building at the center of the property.

"What's with all the…" I said as I looked around.

"Saturday. Farmers market." Poppy angled the little red car between two enormous pickup trucks, a mouse between two elephants.

I clapped my hands together. "Yay! This *is* a good surprise."

"Careful," Poppy warned as I released the handle to open the door. "Not much room here." I eked it open enough to shimmy out without smacking the shiny-looking truck beside me as she did the same on the left. "This isn't the surprise, though." She flipped open the little trunk and grabbed a black umbrella, opening it to cover us. The words Rocky for Mayor were printed along the edge, just like the umbrellas we'd used at Henry's. "You'll like it. Come on."

We joined the queue of people in front of the doors. A few folks near us seemed to recognize me, but under the canopy of the umbrella I blended right in. Not that I minded now. As I'd witnessed all week, island folks had a special way of making me feel welcome and respected here, sharing smiles and hellos without demanding selfies or otherwise making me feel intruded on. They'd all heard I was here by now; I was old news.

Poppy shook off the umbrella once we were under the cover of the veranda and added it to the enormous stand brimming with others. I smoothed my bangs as we stepped inside and looked around the big room at the long, evenly spaced rows of tables. The hum of voices echoed off the high ceiling as folks wandered among the stands, filling carry bags with root vegetables, crafts, and baked goods. I spotted Angela Fletcher on the opposite side of the room, in an animated conversation with a wrinkled but sprightly-looking older guy.

Grange Hall looked entirely different filled with people. It was no longer a cavernous, empty space but one plainly meant for the purpose of bringing people together. Seeing the market vendors' tables filled with one-of-a-kind and handcrafted items reminded me of St. Lawrence Market back home, a landmark at the south end of Toronto we used to visit on Saturdays a few times a year. The memory brought a smile to my face as Poppy tugged me to the far side of the room.

We pushed through the throng until the crowd thinned out enough I could see a woman with long dark hair seated at a table, a stack of three-by-five-inch cards in front of her. She narrowed her gaze as we approached, assessing carefully this stranger Poppy had in tow.

"Hey, Zoe," Poppy said. The woman wore a voluminous black dress and a purple scarf with shimmery pinstripes draped around her shoulders. As she smiled, her face creased with lines, but her eyes were warm, and her interest was piqued. A scruffy little dog was curled in her lap.

She nodded once at Poppy, her dangly earrings swishing forward and back, then turned to me. "Who's this you've brought with you?"

Poppy pointed at the two empty chairs in front of Zoe's table. "May we?"

"You look familiar," Zoe said as we sat.

"Zoe, this is Domino. Domino, this is Zoe Blum, the island's best tarot card reader."

Zoe didn't look like the hand-shaking type, so I smiled and bobbed my head as she seemed to examine every freckle on my face. "Only tarot card reader, you mean. Have I done a reading for you before?"

Poppy lifted a discreet eyebrow in my direction. We were in agreement. If I was going to let Zoe read my cards, the less she knew about me, the better. I shook my head. "No. This is my first time."

Zoe sat still as a statue for half a minute, then closed her eyes and kept them closed for so long I wondered if she'd fallen asleep. Poppy and I exchanged a glance and waited while Zoe inhaled a long breath, held it, and blew it out through her nose before she opened her eyes again. "Ask me a question."

My mind raced. I don't know what I'd expected, but it certainly wasn't to be put on the spot. Two images sprang to the front of my mind: Forest's strong, handsome face—and a purple-cheeked Arthur Dagon, spittle at the edges of his mouth, his forehead beading with sweat. *Eesh, are those images really that close to the surface?* I shuddered.

"Will my project be a success?" Though I desperately wanted to ask if Forest would somehow be part of my future, more was riding on *Shore Thing*.

Gathering a deep breath, Zoe picked up the deck of faded cards and shuffled, split the pile in two, and moved them from one hand to the other. Once she was satisfied, she fanned the cards out with both hands and surveyed them quickly before choosing one, which she placed facedown in front of her. She set the deck to the side and eyed me pointedly, then flipped it over.

On the card was a man seated on a throne in a blue tunic and gold cape, a fish-shaped amulet around his neck. In one hand he held a cup and in the other a scepter. Beyond the throne a fish leaped out of water to his left. A ship was pictured behind him on the right.

"The King of Cups."

I waited patiently while she stared at the card, audibly breathing in and out through her nose. Finally she tapped her finger on it, her bracelets jangling against the table. What on earth did this cups guy have to do with me or my movie?

"The King of Cups is a very influential card," Zoe said. "He represents creativity, emotion, the unconscious. Your project—it's a creative one." I nodded, although she hadn't phrased it as a question. I stole a glance at Poppy, who had leaned back in her chair and folded her arms over her leather jacket. "The King of Cups symbolizes a balance between intellect and emotions. When you see this card, you know you have control over your emotions and can accept them—without them getting the better of you." *Except when it comes to Forest.*

"If you're being challenged in this project," Zoe continued, "be firm in your boundaries. Stay true to your feelings. Don't allow others to steer you off course."

"Oh!" I murmured, surprised. It was uncanny, when I thought about Marc and Arthur and how strongly I felt about the location and the script and all the other details.

Zoe caught my gaze and held it. "This rings true for you." Again, it wasn't a question. She had no doubts about her reading. "You care about achieving your goals, but you're also prone to making sure others are happy." She tapped the card again. "If you sense logic and emotion are out of balance, draw on the energy of this card to realign yourself."

I stared at the card, taking a mental picture, trying to memorize every aspect of it so I could come back to it when I needed. I nodded again, watching as she tapped her finger a third time. "Weird. This is just what I needed," I told her. "My project is—"

Zoe held up a palm to quiet me. "There's more." She closed her eyes again, drawing in another deep breath and exhaling through her nose. "Romance." She opened her eyes wide, searching my face, apparently satisfied with whatever she saw there. I sensed Poppy looking at me but kept my focus on Zoe. "You made a connection—recently, if I'm reading this right?" I hadn't told Poppy—or anyone else—about my feelings for Forest. "Approach it practically but also with compassion and understanding. Combined, the love you find will be deep and rewarding."

I found myself wanting her to say more—to guide me somehow in deciding whether my connection with Forest was real. Telling me to be practical... It was a bit late for that. "But is he—" I paused, glancing sideways. Poppy quickly looked away and stared intently at a spot on the wall. "Is he The One?" I leaned forward and asked Zoe quietly.

Zoe's bracelets jangled as she petted the little black dog in her lap. "Only you know the answer to that." Satisfied with the message she'd given me, Zoe turned her attention on Poppy. "What about you? What can I help you with today?"

Poppy looked between us before she shook her head and got to her feet abruptly, sending her chair skidding backward and startling the little dog. "Oh, no. Not today." She tucked her hair behind her ear. "I'm still reeling from the last one."

Zoe looked perplexed, but Poppy widened her eyes at me, encouraging me to stand as well. "Thank you. It was...enlightening. How much do I owe you?"

Poppy took a few steps back and waited while Zoe dug her credit-card reader out of the depths of a large patchwork bag so I could pay. I left the table in a daze, struck by the King of Cups and what he meant for me, my movie, and maybe my love life.

Though we were stuffed from the doughnuts, I stopped at several stalls, sampling local cheeses, jams, cookies, even gin. For the first time since I'd arrived on the island, two people approached for selfies, both teenage girls. The first one's parents lingered behind, mortified at their daughter's bald courage. The other was with her mom, who smiled from ear to ear and joined us for a picture. Otherwise folks greeted me with smiles and treated me like any other islander, here for the same reason they were on a rainy Saturday in January.

When we left, my bag was brimming with goodies, including a hand-knitted hat for my mom and a pair of earrings made from beach glass for Saylor. Poppy juggled to free her hand at the entrance so she could fumble around the umbrella stand to find hers. In a sea of other Rocky for Mayor brollies, she shrugged and grabbed the closest one.

"You're quiet," she said as we trudged to the car, gravel crunching underfoot. Fortunately she remembered which aisle we'd parked in. We'd never have spotted the tiny red car amid all the trucks and SUVs in the lot. I tucked a bottle of gin under my arm and held the umbrella while she opened the trunk, then snapped it shut and popped it in, along with my heavy bag. We raced to slide into the cabin to get out of the rain.

"Am I? It was kind of overwhelming in there, I guess. You know how it is with crowds."

"Mmm." She let the engine warm for a minute before she reversed out and joined the line of cars waiting to exit the grounds. Once we were flying along toward Bayview, she spoke again. "Anything you want to talk about? Off the record."

I watched the giant evergreens outside the window pass in a blur of greens and browns, listening as the wiper blades whooshed back and forth. "I—I don't know. I guess I'm just...thinking about the reading. It's weird, right? Seems impossible for stuff like that to be accurate. But somehow it just...is."

She gripped the wheel, anticipating the curves and bends in the wet road ahead of us. "Like horoscopes, I guess. They're ridiculous. But somehow they give you a glimmer of hope."

I appreciated she didn't push, just waited to see if I wanted to talk. "With my career, I'm always the agreeable one. Always making sure everyone's happy. Never causing trouble. Which sometimes means I don't put myself first. But this movie—I *know* Orcas Island is perfect for it."

"Someone thinks it isn't?"

"I dunno. Maybe. Our location scout—the *real* location scout—is on Vashon Island right now. We're working with this director, Arthur Dagon? He's kind of a jerk. I worry whatever he wants is what I'm going to get."

Poppy looked at me wide-eyed. "You're working with Arthur Dagon?"

"Uh-huh. You know about him?" I knew he had a big reputation, but I hadn't realized it traveled that far.

"Yes. No. Well, sort of. This writer friend of mine—we met at a conference in Portland last year. He had a…let's just say not-optimal experience with the guy. From what I heard, 'kind of a jerk' is an understatement. More like class A asshole. With a side of giant prick."

I giggled, and when I caught Poppy's eye, the two of us laughed from the gut. Once I caught my breath, I sighed. "Nailed it. Anyway, that's what I'm dealing with. But that card—the King of Cups—gave me the kick in the pants I need to stand my ground, not let his bullshit get to me."

Poppy took her hand from the wheel and held it up for a high five, which I met with enthusiasm.

On Water Street, the rain turned to sprinkles. "And the romance part?" she probed gently. "You weren't thinking of Harry Roman, were you?"

I didn't answer, but my silence spoke volumes.

"Forest is a good guy, Domino. Just don't mess with him if you're gonna run home to Hollywood and never look back. He's a lion on the outside, but he's got the heart of a baby kitten." She stopped in front of the Driftwood and let the engine idle. Seeing my pursed lips, she laughed. "Okay, maybe not a kitten. A great Dane? A big, tough, great Dane. But one with floppy ears, not those mean-looking cropped ones."

She giggled, but there was truth behind her eyes.

"How did you...?" My question trailed off when Poppy rolled her eyes. "That obvious, huh."

"Pretty hard to miss. I bet Angela's got a whole page of notes on it."

I smiled at the thought of Angela writing about my schoolgirl crush in her tidy cursive script. What a mismatch we were: an island outsider, one with big-city dreams and an ex-boyfriend more famous than Elvis, and a quiet, hardworking Pacific Northwesterner with a gruff exterior and a contempt for all things celebrity.

As I stepped out of the car and collected my overloaded bag from the trunk, a question formed in my mind: *Was* this just a crush, someone I could turn my back on and walk away from forever? Or was this little island—and its inhabitants—imprinted on my soul?

CHAPTER 17

Forest

I hung around the dining room after dinner service Saturday night, annoying Fern by drumming my fingers on the bar, counting the minutes until the last diners left. With the third and fourth floors now occupied, and more people to feed, dinner went later than it had in weeks. By the time I lugged the final tub of dishes to the kitchen for Tommy to wash, it was quarter to eleven. My sister and I yawned in unison as she untied her apron and tossed it with the pile of dirty dish towels and napkins. I wrapped my tool belt around my waist and buckled the clasp.

I'd paid Tommy double time to stay an extra hour

and help me move the tables and chairs to the kitchen, the lobby—wherever we could squeeze them. Then I ushered him out the door. It would be a full eight hours before I needed his help again to move it all back in.

I hung a plastic sheet in the arched doorway to the lobby. After filling a bucket with vinegar and water, I wiped the floors in methodical sections using a terrycloth mop, following the steps I'd gleaned off the *This Old House* website. Then I began the task of hand-sanding the perimeter, rubbing the grain four inches out from the baseboards, working over each plank in the floor until the finish was dull.

My mind traveled back to my first encounter with Domino in the lobby, dressed as I was like a drowned rat, clutching my soggy sneakers and pretending not to eavesdrop. How different she looked to me then. I no longer saw her as the spoiled movie star in Fern's magazine. She was a smart, beautiful woman who'd worked hard to get where she was. I leaned the mop against the wall and swiped an arm across my forehead to wipe away the sweat, chuckling. Funny how people become three-dimensional when you let them. Life was all about perspective, I thought as I lugged the buffer out of the kitchen, where I'd stored it since last night.

I reflected on my previous two relationships and

how I'd been so sure I wasn't to blame when things went sour. *You're so rigid.* Kate's words rang in my mind as I looped the straps of a dust mask over my ears and wedged a buffing pad in place on the machine. I remembered recoiling when she'd said it, an invisible hatch sliding into place between me and the outside world.

When Misha came along, I'd barely let her see past that wall, just enough we *seemed* like the perfect couple on the outside, but when she wanted to start building a future together, I froze like a lake in winter.

I moved the buffer from side to side across the floor, following the direction of the grain, overlapping each course by six inches. Just like when I was a kid, using my hands—putting my muscles to work—helped me sort through what I was feeling. The steady sweeping motion was like a tide washing over me, and as the old finish on the floor dissolved into powder, the fear I'd felt all those years seemed to fade away, too. I realized now that'd been the issue all along: fear people would think I wasn't good enough, or smart enough, or worthy of receiving love.

I reached the far end of the room by the fireplace, stopping to survey a floor now blanketed in fine white powder, etched in circles like sand in a Zen garden. With each step I took, my boots left perfect footprints. *I'm foraging a new path.* Maybe it was the vinegar fumes and dust, but suddenly I knew it was time to let go of my fears and start living in freedom.

Vacuuming felt like cleaning a slate. No matter what, I'd always have Domino to thank for getting me to this place—for helping me crumble the walls I'd built long ago. In another lifetime we might've had a real shot. She lived an opposite life to mine, but her openheartedness had shown me I didn't need to approach life with my guard up. I could let go of the idea everyone had some notion of me I needed to counter. She liked me for who I was.

The dust gone, I threw open every window in the room, letting in the sound of rain and the roar of the Pacific pushing up against Water Street. With every gust of wind, a splash of water hit the pavement as waves erupted over the seawall. I shivered as I wrapped plastic booties over my shoes, ripped off the dust mask, and replaced it with a respirator.

Starting at the fireplace, I brushed three-inch-wide strips of finish across the floor, then poured stripes of it along the grain, spreading it with a long-handled roller, careful to overlap each pass and work quickly to keep the edge wet. With wind blasting through the open windows, I had to pay careful attention to how quickly it dried. A solid hour later of focused work, I reached the last section of the floor, by the entrance to the lobby. I surveyed the room, pleased with how it gleamed under the lights.

It would be three hours before I could roll on a second coat. I ducked under the plastic sheeting to the lobby, loosening the straps on the respirator and lifting it to my forehead. The clock on the wall behind the desk read 1:40 a.m. I slumped into one of the two big armchairs Tommy and I had hefted here, the eyes of the taxidermy deer keeping constant watch as I laid my head back and closed my eyes.

The sound of the elevator rattling down the shaft coaxed me into consciousness. Sitting up straight, I wiped the sleep from my eyes as the door slid open. Fern stepped out, her blonde hair loose around her shoulders, her hands tucked into the arms of an oversize sweatshirt.

"What are you doing down here?" I lifted the respirator off my head, rubbing at where the elastic had dug into my skin while I slept. "Shit, is that the time?" It was after five. I leaped to my feet.

"When you didn't text me back, I thought I'd better come check."

I patted a hand over my back pocket. "Must have left my phone on the bar."

"How close are you?" She scanned the tables and chairs piled around the lobby.

"I need three hours. Four including this," I said, waving at the unorganized furniture.

She rubbed her eyes with her fists. "Not ideal."

"Not much I can do about it." I moved to the doorway and lifted the plastic sheeting. "I gotta…" I let the sentence drop and indicated the dining room with my thumb before I ducked inside and fastened the respirator back in place. It was icy cold in the room with the wind coming off the water, but the first coat of finish was bone dry. I set to work applying the second layer, repeating the careful, methodical process of rolling it on with the grain in the wood. The second coat went much faster, and by 6:00 a.m. I was back in the lobby and behind the desk, making a handwritten sign to tape to the plastic sheeting.

Fern returned around six thirty, and together we pushed the tables and chairs to the edges of the lobby, making a clear path from the elevator to the desk and from the desk to the front door.

"I have an idea," she said when I grumbled about coffee. Behind the desk, she picked up her phone and started tapping. I was deliriously tired, operating on fumes and satisfaction with the way a night of hard work helped me clear my mind. Fern murmured something intelligible as she typed.

"You gonna tell me what you're doing?" I stuck my elbows on the desk and rested my chin against my fists. *"Fern,"* I said with meaning when she didn't glance up.

SALLY GLOVER

She ran her pointer finger up my forehead from eyebrows to hairline. "That frown's gonna be permanent if you aren't careful."

"Whatever." I didn't give a shit about wrinkles or much of anything at that point. When I was exhausted like this, irritability usually got the better of me. I exhaled audibly.

Fern put down her phone and leaned forward, pressing her fingers into the desk on either side of her. "Ginger's going to bring stuff over. Coffee, doughnuts, milk and sugar, napkins—all of it." My shoulders dropped a notch from where stress had them squeezed to my ears. "I told George not to come in until eleven."

"But Tommy—"

"Tommy'll be here in an hour." I wanted to wipe the smug smile from Fern's face, but she deserved a pat on the back. As usual, she'd handled a problem with ease. She shone when it came to making decisions on the spot that in my hands would leave me sleepless. She eyed the elevator when we heard it called to another floor, then looked at me. "I got this. Go upstairs and sleep."

I didn't need to be told twice.

When I opened my eyes around noon, the room around me was silent. I dragged myself from the bed, every muscle aching, and drew open the shade. I was pleased to see dry sidewalks; no rain meant I could spend the whole day outside. I wanted nothing more in that moment than fresh forest air in my lungs, the wind in my face, and my feet in the dirt. I texted River. He jumped at the offer of an afternoon hike.

Pick you up in 30, I wrote, then got in the shower.

Downstairs, Tommy and Fern had moved most of the furniture back into the dining room. One long table remained, strewn with empty plates, a few crumbs, and a coffee station. I grabbed a paper cup from the stack and filled it with coffee from one of the urns, reassured to see steam rising from it. One half doughnut remained on a large platter, its open edges even where it'd been cut with a knife. Clutching it in a napkin, I pressed a lid on the coffee.

Standing in the open doorway to the dining room, I surveyed the space, gratified. Most of the tables were full, the diners likely unaware of any difference. But the refinished floor glowed shiny and golden, and the room felt a little less shabby. I stopped at the bar.

"Don't say it." Fern balled her fists into her apron pocket. Gone were the loose waves of blonde from this morning. Her hair was now neatly fixed in a low bun. She smiled wide at someone behind me, her gray-blue eyes glinting.

"What, 'I told you so'? Don't need to. It's obvi-ous." I set the paper cup on the bar and pulled the key to the jeep from my pocket.

"Said it anyway, huh."

Bluebell set her tray down and punched an order into the screen at the end of the bar. "Hey, Forest. Looks awesome in here," she said without looking up from the monitor. "Great job." She twirled on her heel and was gone before I could reply.

"Now will you let me order new vinyl for the booth seats and chairs?" Again my sister sent a flirty smile over my shoulder. I turned to see Rocky Black grinning back. He looked away quickly, as though the most interesting thing in the world had appeared out the window. "Seriously, Fern?"

"What? He's an important customer now he's mayor," she protested. "Plus a big tipper," she added under her breath. "Anyway. I'll think about the chairs. One thing at a time, huh? Roof first. Then social media. Then furniture."

I rolled my eyes. Those were her priorities, not mine, but I had a day off—a day I vowed to spend thinking about anything other than the Driftwood Inn. "Whatever. I'm gone for the day. If you need me, save it." I picked up my cup, half doughnut in hand, and strode for the kitchen door.

In the jeep, I queued up a Miles Davis playlist and cranked the volume as I pulled out of the back lot and headed for River's, a gabled cottage on a bluff that overlooked West Sound, surrounded by madrone trees and towering cedars. It was modest for a guy from the richest family on the island, but it was a beautiful spot. He was on the front steps, pushing a raincoat into a backpack, when I arrived.

"Tyee?" I asked as he slid into the passenger seat. His reddish-brown hair was slicked away from his face. He had on a Patagonia fleece nearly identical to mine.

He leaned forward and peered up at the clearing sky. "Perfect day for it."

The trees grew thicker as we hiked away from the parking lot at the base of Orcas Island's highest peak. Following the gravel path that led north to the start of the loop trail, River filled me in on business at Isola. Running a fine-dining restaurant sounded a lot more complicated than keeping the Driftwood afloat.

The clouds cleared, and sun danced across the treetops, but below the canopy the ground was wet, the air chilly. The trail climbed steeply, and we quickly gained elevation over a series of switchbacks up the mountain. Heart pumping, breath heavy, my lungs were filled with the sweet scent of the forest. The path was soft underfoot, bouncy with moisture and pine needles.

Our conversation fell away as the trail became rocky and we focused on the climb, working our way above the tree cover into the bright sunshine. I stopped to peel off a layer, tucking my fleece into my pack while River drank from his water bottle. We continued on where the sun had dried the exposed rock near the summit.

At the peak we slipped off our packs and sat, taking in the breathtaking views of the trees and hills of Orcas Island, the glimmering blue Pacific, and the Olympic Peninsula in the distance while we ate energy bars and gulped down water.

"So tell me about her," River said, crumpling a wrapper in his palm as he chewed. The fact he didn't mention Domino by name didn't surprise me. Orcas residents might be respectful, but they still gossiped.

I stared at the snow-capped peak of Mount Baker, stark white against the azure sky. How much should I share with my old friend? Since the relationship—or whatever was between Domino and me—couldn't go any further, it seemed silly to discuss something that didn't really exist. "I dunno, man. She's different."

He chuckled. "Uh, yah. She's a movie star." He tilted back his water bottle and swallowed a sip. "But you've been hanging out, right? She as self-absorbed and superficial as they all seem?"

"Not at all. She's just..." A pair of crows swooped and tangled among the treetops below us. "Lovely." I'd settled on the perfect word to describe Domino

West. "And I don't just mean to look at. There's that, too. But she's kindhearted and real. Not what you'd expect."

River dug in his pack for sunglasses. He raised his eyebrows before he slid them on his nose. "I don't think I've ever heard you talk about a woman like that. Not Misha or Kate—usually I don't get more than a word out of you. This one has you expanding your repertoire of grunts."

I shoved the empty energy-bar wrapper into my pocket, pushed to stand, and wiped the dirt from my jeans. "Doesn't matter anyway. It's like Mercury and Neptune. We're light years apart." I hefted my pack over my shoulders. "She lives in LA. I'm out here. In the middle of nowhere."

He straightened his legs and took another drink of water. "Maybe you can make it—"

"Nah, man. Besides, Fern would kill me if I did anything to screw up this movie shoot." I eyed the sun in the sky and checked the time on my phone. "Better go before the light does."

We followed the trail south along a rocky scramble that had us using our hands for balance—and our brains for concentration—until we were below the treeline again. It was cooler in the shade of the enormous cedars and old Douglas firs. We stepped carefully over gnarled tree roots and the loose dirt and gravel.

"Shit," River cursed at one point when he lost his footing and slid on his ass. "The way down is always worse."

I grabbed a low branch to keep myself from slipping, too. "Ain't that the truth." I turned River's phrase over in my mind. I'd reached the summit of my relationship with Domino and was now faced with the slippery, precarious trip down the other side.

CHAPTER 18

Forest

At the base of the mountain, quadriceps screaming from the hard work of trekking downhill, I stopped for water and checked my phone to find a message from Fern.

Dinner?

Shit. Joining my sister in the dining room meant the possibility of seeing Domino—a temptation I wasn't sure I could resist. But the pull to be there for Fern was stronger than the instinct to hide away like a coward, so once I'd dropped off River, I beelined for the hotel as the sun set against an orange-and-purple sky. After a shower, I descended to the main floor.

Bluebell leaned a hip against the bar, foot propped on the copper rail that ran the length of it. She held a tray in one hand, waiting for Fern to finish mixing the drinks she was waiting for. "Hey," she said as I neared. "Ever think about helping your sister back there?" She tipped her chin at Fern, who held a shot glass in one hand and a bottle of gin in the other.

I took a seat on a barstool two down from where Bluebell stood. "Trust me, you don't want that," I said at the same time as my sister said, "Hell no, he doesn't."

Fern glanced up to see my reaction, and we both laughed. "See the muscles under that shirt? That's what his job is around here. The muscle stuff."

Bluebell sidled over to me, wrapped a hand around my bicep, and gave it a squeeze. She jumped back in exaggerated surprise. "Nice guns."

I felt my cheeks heat. "I should make you a drink sometime. You'll wish you never asked." My sister was right; I was good at fixing things, planting things, building things—and not much else. The La Marzocco I could handle. But the last time I attempted to make one of her drink specials, she'd spat it out in front of me, horrified.

"Two Strong Legs and a Pink Unicorn." Fern set three tall glasses of beer on Bluebell's tray.

"What is it, *Game of Thrones* night or something?" I'd been facing Bluebell and hadn't seen Domino come in until I heard her question. Bluebell laughed and left to serve her tables. I turned on my stool as Domino pulled out the one next to mine and perched on it.

She had on a pink sweater that looked as soft as a bunny. It cast her cheekbones in such a pretty shade I felt my resolve melting. But that wasn't what made my mouth drop open: it was the black leather miniskirt that, as she sat, exposed long, smooth legs. She crossed one over the other, and I sucked in a breath. It took a minute to drag my eyes away from them. I shifted on my stool to accommodate the reaction she ignited in my cock.

When I finally shifted my gaze to her face, she smiled knowingly. She knew exactly the effect she had on me. The air between us was charged with energy and raw desire. She raised her eyebrow just enough for me to see it, then turned away to focus on Fern, leaving a hole in my heart like she'd pierced it with an arrow.

"Tell me about this Pink Unicorn."

Fern held a martini shaker in one hand and a shot glass of gin in the other. "Chasing Fluffy Pink Unicorns, it's actually called. Raspberry Gose-style ale from Ghost Runners Brewery on the mainland. Glass or pint?" She resumed mixing the drink, oblivious to the inferno of lust between me and her number-one guest. Talk about pink unicorns. I was sitting right next to one.

"Pint, please." She broke into that hundred-watt smile that felt like sun bursting through clouds on the darkest morning. "How was your day?"

I managed to close my mouth finally. "Grrr—" I cleared my throat around what felt like a ball of longing. "Great." The word came out clearer this time. I looked straight ahead, watching my sister with intent, as if her every move depended on my supervision. *Keepitcool keepitcool keepitcool,* I reminded myself. This woman would be gone from the hotel, from the island, from my life in a few days, and things would go back to normal. The constant erection would fade. The tingling at the base of my stomach would stop. And my sister and I would have successfully hosted a movie star without her finding out about the leaky roof or the feelings I found myself having for her.

"I should thank you." She placed a hand on my arm, sending my hormones into another tailspin. Now I looked at the ceiling, the floor, anywhere but those magnetic eyes. But on the way down, my gaze landed on her legs and traveled up their long inches, remembering how soft they felt. "For introducing me to Poppy. She took me to the farmers market yesterday."

"Huh," I grunted.

"Yeah. I'm hoping Grange Hall will work for a production headquarters."

"Nice."

Fern curled the heels of her hands around the bar and leaned into them. When Domino's phone buzzed and she turned it over to look at it, Fern furrowed her brow, and she mouthed, "What the fuck?" Her eyes went pointedly from me to Domino and back again. I breathed in deeply and looked at the ceiling again. She was right. I needed to pull my head out of my ass.

Domino set her phone down on the bar again. "Did you two get a chance to talk about what I asked the other day?"

Fern shook her head, then nodded. "No—I mean, yes. I spoke with George, our head chef, and a few local suppliers, and I can confidently say yes, we'd love to handle catering. Wouldn't we, Forest?"

I pinned Fern with a look that could burn holes. "Er, Fern? Could I speak with you for a minute?" I got to my feet and indicated the kitchen door with my thumb.

A veneer of panic crossed Fern's eyes, but she kept her voice calm. "Excuse us," she told Domino. She followed me to the kitchen, where George and Tommy were flying around, moving from the grill to the sous station and back, plating meals and sautéing scallops.

They barely looked up.

"I don't know what's going on with you. But. Do. Not. Screw. This Up." She poked a finger in my chest as she said the words through clenched teeth. "We have an opportunity here. An opportunity of a lifetime. I'm going to do whatever it takes to bring Domino back to this hotel to make her movie."

"But there's no way we can—"

She reached up and clapped a hand over my mouth to stop me midsentence. "Yes, we can. And we will. Whatever she needs we can handle. Pick your jaw up off the floor, and get your head screwed on right."

"But—"

Fern held up a finger. "Uh-uh," she said, staccato. "We got this." She spun on her heel and pushed back through the door, leaving it swinging.

I took in a deep breath, willing my anxiety, and the lust that vibrated through me whenever I was around Domino, into submission. My sister was right—again. We could handle it. The shoot was months away. There was no question it would take the hotel to another level. The business it would bring to the entire island was impossible to deny. I could keep my libido in check for as long as it took to make that happen.

Following Fern, I pushed through the door to where Domino sat at the bar, now flanked by Poppy. Fern had resumed mixing drinks for Bluebell. "Hey,

Poppy," I said.

Poppy clasped her hands together. Her leather jacket was on the bar next to her. She looked ready to burst with a secret. "Can I tell him?"

"Of course! I'm just as thrilled as you are." Domino's eyes filled with affection when she looked at Poppy.

"I'm going to be—I am—Domino's assistant. While she's here. And for the movie. Isn't that exciting?" She pulled out her phone and called up a document she began reading from. "'Poppy Willoughby agrees to produce materials and services at the request of Domino West for fees agreed on in advance...'" She let her voice trail off. "Anyway, I'm not telling you about my fees. That's between me and my client. But the point is you can now call me 'assistant to Ms. West.'"

"You're worth every penny. It's not just getting me coffee, if that's what you're thinking." Domino fixed me with a glare. "Poppy is integral to getting this movie made."

"Plus I get to write stuff for you."

"Plus she gets to write for me. It would be a total waste not to squeeze every last drop of talent out of you while I can."

Poppy's eyes took on a shiny glaze. So Domino had the same effect on others, too, which only proved she hadn't become an "it" star without that thing that drew you in, bathed you in light, made you want to do what you could to help her or just gaze at her and wonder how anyone could be so perfect.

"Squeeee!" Poppy shot both her hands in the air, pumping the ceiling with excitement.

"First order of business?" Domino prompted.

"Oh yes. I'm ready to draw up an agreement for the Driftwood to provide production catering. I'll need both your signatures." She pointed at me, then Fern. Fern eyed me sideways.

"No problem. Happy to help," I said simply. Looking around me, at Fern bustling behind the bar, Bluebell and Tommy running orders to the floor, and Poppy and Domino with their heads together, planning the next few days, I decided I'd get dinner to go after all. Another burger in my room sounded perfect right about now. "Excuse me again." I returned to the kitchen to put my order in.

"I'll bring it up," Tommy offered, barely looking up from his prep station. "Might be a bit."

"No problem."

I couldn't help but drink in another eyeful of Domino's long legs twisted around the barstool like some kind of serpentine goddess when I returned. I lingered a moment behind her and Poppy until Domino turned to look at me, warmth in her eyes, pink in her cheeks, her lips pursed in that sexy little bow.

"Let me know when you have the contract," I told Poppy, tearing my focus away from Domino's mouth.

"Cool. You heading off now?" Poppy was no doubt happy to have her superstar friend all to herself.

"Yah. I'll eat upstairs. Have a good night." I strolled to the arched doorway, cooler than a cucumber. But when I reached the top of the stairs, I couldn't help myself. I turned around to see Domino staring back at me. Was she, too, questioning our commitment to stay apart?

My room was deafeningly quiet without the constant sound of water hitting the bucket. A full day without rain in late January in the Pacific Northwest was something to celebrate—especially when you had a leaky roof and couldn't fix it when you needed to. I was pent up with energy, with no good way to spend it. I switched on the TV to the local news, peeled off my shirt, and dropped to the floor to press out push-ups. Ten sets of ten and the meteorologist appeared on screen, signaling nearly an hour had passed. I stood to catch my breath, running the back of my hand across my forehead to wipe away the sweat, when a knock sounded at the door. Tommy. Finally. My stomach rumbled in answer.

But when I opened it, it wasn't Tommy but Domino standing in front of me, one hand on her hip, shades of the other night. Only this time she was holding a plate stacked with fries and a cheeseburger. "Room service," she said cheekily, jutting out her hip. Her eyes traveled from my face down my bare chest. "You're not the only one who's hungry." She said it quietly, almost under her breath, as she fixed my crotch with her stare.

It took me a second to realize my mouth was hanging open again. Damn. This woman made me stupid.

"Aren't you going to invite me in?" She raised her eyebrows suggestively, snapping me back to attention.

"But I thought we said—" I glanced behind me. *Oh shit.* The bucket. "One sec." I held up a finger, letting the door close while I rushed to shove it in the closet. What had the meteorologist said? Dry overnight, showers tomorrow. I thanked the gods of weather and straightened the bed in a hurry, throwing the socks I'd left on the floor under a pillow. I rushed back to the door, pausing to run a hand through my hair.

I swung the door back open and held it, motioning her in. She trailed a finger along my bare stomach as she passed.

"Let me just—"

But Domino pushed the plate of food and a napkin in my hand and sat on the bed. "No, leave it. I like you half-naked." Her smile felt like the cheers of fifty thousand people in a stadium clapping all at once. "Sit. Eat. I'll wait right here." She crossed one of those long, graceful legs over the other, tapping the toes of her shoes together.

I looked around, deciding if she meant I should sit on the bed or at the table by the window. I chose the latter. As much as this incredible woman bringing me dinner was a fantasy I never knew I wanted, Fern's words resounded in my mind. *Do. Not. Screw. This. Up.* All I could think of in this moment, though, was whether fucking our star guest again would screw things up more for me or for her.

I looked at the plate of food. This was a new situation, and the rumbles of hunger in my stomach turned to butterflies.

"You know what? I have a better idea." Domino uncrossed those impossibly long legs, kicked off her shoes, and padded to the table, where she dragged the other chair close, her thighs touching mine. She chose a fry and dipped it in the little pot of ketchup, holding it toward me. I eyed the fry, then her, then the fry again as I leaned in and took a bite.

"I bet you're hungry." I could do nothing but grunt. I was speechless. Domino stood, hitching her miniskirt higher as she straddled me, her legs dangling over my hips. I shifted in the chair, cock hard as marble. With one hand around my neck, she leaned back and picked up the burger. She took a bite first, juice from the tomato running down her hand. "Mmm. God that's good." Holding it out to me, she nodded, eyes fixed on my lips. I bit off a mouthful, hands on her hips, gaze glued to her. The taste barely registered over the lust throbbing in my veins. "Here. More." Her left hand grasped my shoulder as she fed me with the right. Her eyes were like sapphires, flashing under her dark fringe. She pursed her lips cheekily, a smear of ketchup at the corner.

When the burger was gone, she reached back again for the napkin. "I'll take that," I said when she brought it to my mouth. I gently dabbed the ketchup from her lips. She licked them and laughed, enjoying the sweetness of the sauce on her tongue.

Draping her arms around me, she leaned forward, touching her forehead to mine, her hair soft on my face. She pressed a kiss to my lips, then another, and another, and another, until we opened our mouths, tongues tangling, moans mingling. I drew her hips closer, groaning at the feel of her hot pussy grinding against my cock.

Domino leaned back. Her eyelids were heavy, her cheeks flushed, her lips deep red. She hooked the hem of her sweater and lifted it off, hair falling over bare shoulders in dark ribbons. I ran a hand up her arm, nudging her bra strap off her shoulder. "Sexiest thing

I've ever seen," I murmured, seeing her nipples tipped against the black mesh. The bra's black trim cut lines under her breasts and up into delicate straps.

When she reached behind her and unhooked the clasp, I tugged a finger under the wire and gently peeled it away. Her breasts were round and heavy in my hands, and she let out a soft moan as I traced my thumbs over her nipples. I hugged her to me, loving the soft warmth of skin and curves against me as we kissed.

I trailed hands down her back, over the strip of her leather skirt and lower, cupping her ass and squeezing, encouraging the rhythmic groove of our hips.

"I need—" she started but didn't finish, just ran a finger down my chest to the waist of my jeans. With a gentle tug, the first button popped open. She stopped there and cupped a hand over the insistent bulge in the denim where my cock threatened to burst. Her hand felt hot where she teased it around me.

If I didn't get it out soon, it was likely to rip out of my jeans like a fist through a wall. Finally Domino pulled down the zip and released me. I was hot and throbbing and vibrating with need. She tugged my jeans and boxer briefs just low enough she could wrap a hand around my cock and stroke one, two, three times. Precum oozed between her fingers.

With one hand around my balls and the other

gripping my cock, her breasts were pushed together in front of me, round and swollen and beautiful. Moaning, I took her left nipple in my mouth, flicking my tongue across it until it tipped. Then I moved to the other, hands roaming her soft skin until I found her upper thigh. "Yes," she murmured when I let my fingers trail the seam of her thong. "Don't stop."

I pulled the crotch to one side, exposing her pussy as she let out another moan. She was wet and warm when I glided my fingers between the folds, my thumb pressing the sensitive nub of her clitoris. "Ohhh." She was louder this time. She slid forward until I felt the slick heat of her around my shaft. She rocked back and forth, rubbing against me. I rocked with her, guiding her hips, watching her breasts rise and fall with each breath.

"Protection?" I murmured.

She lifted off me and stood, tugging the skirt around her waist back into place. I pointed to the nightstand, and without a word she found what she needed and returned. "Where were we," she murmured, straddling my lap again, black leather riding up her thighs once more. I rushed to roll on the condom before she brought herself down on my cock, taking me deep inside her, letting out a little cry. I groaned, eyes closed as fireworks exploded behind my eyelids. I'd never felt anything like her.

Then she rode me like one of those mechanical bulls you see in movies, but the last thing I wanted was to buck her off. The sight of her black panties pulled to one side was impossibly hot. My finger was still tucked under the elastic, my thumb once again pressed to the bud of nerve endings at her clitoris.

She clutched my shoulders, her breaths growing shorter, her movements intentional, using my cock to find what felt best, eyes closed. Somehow I managed not to explode, instead focusing purely on her. Her moans came closer now, a gentle rhythm, her pussy wet and softer than velvet. Then her eyes fluttered open and gleamed into mine, glinting like jewels, her mouth a little O as I felt her pussy squeeze and release, squeeze and release, squeeze and release. Her breathing slowed and she let herself fall around my shoulders, hair silky on my chest.

"Fuck, Forest," she mumbled into my shoulder. "Fuck."

She pushed up and off me, then settled back on my lap, her underwear sliding back into place. My dick stood at attention between us, aimed straight to the ceiling, the condom glistening with her cum.

"Ugh," I groaned. She rolled the condom off before she clasped her hand around me, fingers pointed at my balls, the tip of my cock in her palm. She stroked up and down, moving her hand to where the shaft met the head, applying just the right pressure. With her other hand she cupped my balls, squeezing gently but firmly, as if willing the cum out of them. The way her hands felt on me, the sight of her perfect nipples, breasts full and round, the leather wrapped around her waist, and the glimpse of black mesh took me to a place I hadn't known possible. The tension inside me grew and grew, my muscles flexing, my heart pounding. With each stroke the sensitivity increased until I reached a place of no return, anticipation building in a rush of lust and hormones. Sensation arose in my balls and thrust through the tip of my cock as cum exploded out.

When it was over, after the endorphins sent waves of relaxation to every part of me, I lifted Domino from my lap and sat her back in the chair. I went to the bathroom to grab a towel. On my return she looked anything but embarrassed about what we'd done. Her expression was one of pure exhilaration, her eyes bright, her cheeks flushed. She took the towel and stood, wiping her hands. Then she smiled and pushed past me, reaching around to unzip her skirt. At the door to the bathroom, she slid it to the floor, along with her thong, so she was gloriously naked. She stepped out of view, and I heard the shower come on.

After cleaning up I pulled on my jeans and under-wear and sat on the end of the bed, at odds about what to do with myself. When a gust of wind rattled the window, I moved to look outside, raising the shade for a clear view. The docks at the marina were dry. Would the rain hold off for the night? A couple hurried from the hotel to the street, coats wrapped tightly, hands in pockets, rushing to get to their car in the cold.

I couldn't take the risk that it might rain in the next eight hours. As steam from the shower seeped across the room, I racked my brain for some excuse I could give for why Domino couldn't spend the night with me.

Maybe I should be honest. The thought crossed my mind, but I quickly dismissed it at the memory of Fern poking a finger in my chest, her words ringing in my head like the hook to a bad song. *Do. Not. Screw. This. Up.*

"Something interesting out there?" Domino startled me back to the present. "Thought you might join me." She stood next to me by the window and hooked my pointer finger in hers. She'd twisted her hair in a knot high on her head. Pink from the shower, she was wrapped in a towel that barely reached her thighs and showed off those long, sexy legs.

"I didn't want to intrude." I shoved my free hand into my pocket, wishing I'd thought to put on a shirt. How could I tell this woman we needed to stay apart after what we'd just done?

She put a hand to my chest. "I think you've seen it all now. Except my toes. Maybe you haven't really seen my toes." She lifted her leg and pointed them. It was a graceful move, just like the rest of her, and in spite of myself I laughed. This woman was full of surprises.

I dropped her finger and shoved the other hand in my pocket. "Listen, I, uh..." But the words stopped coming when Domino leaned against me in front of the window, silencing me with a kiss that sent shivers down my spine. I reached blindly for the cord to drop the shade, then nudged her to the bed, our lips barely separating as her towel dropped to the floor and I unzipped and shimmied out of my jeans.

CHAPTER 19

Domino

I dreamed I was back in LA, getting dressed in my room, when a knock sounded at the door. *Tap, tap, tap* came the insistent rapping. But when I answered it in the dream, a sock clutched in my fist, no one was there—and the knocking continued. I awoke in a foggy haze to realize the tapping was happening real time—in a strange room that felt like mine only it was strewn with someone else's things and a very naked, very handsome man in the bed next to me. I sat up, lifting my hand to see I was, in fact, holding one of his socks.

Morning light filtered around the edges of the

window shade, but it wasn't enough to see where the noise was coming from. I nudged him gently, then with a bit more force when he didn't stir. "Forest," I whispered hoarsely. "Forest!" I said more loudly.

He turned over on his pillow to face me and reached up to tug me down with him. "Morning, beautiful." I didn't resist at first, just nestled against him, but the irritating noise continued.

I sat up again, pulling the comforter around me and smoothing my bangs. "What's that sound?"

Forest's eyes flew open, and he leaped from the bed like a shot from a cannon. In the dim light I couldn't make out what he was doing near the closet, but when he turned back he held a white cylindrical object, which he set on the floor near the bathroom. The tapping sound hollowed. Was that a fucking bucket?

I willed calm into my voice, certain what seemed to be happening wasn't actually possible. "You're kidding me." I slid to the side of the bed and stood, bringing the comforter with me, heading for the window, where I grasped the cord to the shade. I squinched my eyes shut, wishing away the dread building at the pit of my stomach. But when I yanked on the cord, and gray morning light streamed into the room, my heart sank. Forest was standing, naked, next to a large white bucket—that was collecting a steady drip of water from the ceiling. He looked sheepish, and guilty, and apologetic, and impossibly sexy all at once.

"About this—" he started, running a hand through his hair. The muscles in his arms and chest were chiseled like Michaelangelo's David in the silvery light.

But anger fueled me like a volcano ready to blow. I lunged for the table, still wrapped in the comforter, to retrieve my sweater and bra from where they'd been abandoned last night. Clasping them in one hand, the other holding the blanket in place, I careened for the bathroom in search of my other clothes. Enraged and determined, I tripped over the blanket and fell forward in a heap, humiliation burning my ears and anxiety tripping through my veins.

Forest vaulted forward, alarm across his face. He was so apologetic, and his concern so genuine, I couldn't stop tears from springing to my eyes. "Domino?" he said, sitting next to me on the floor.

It was hard to take him seriously, cross-legged on the floor like some naked yogi, and despite the tears a laugh spilled out of me, bringing with it a tiny bubble of snot. *Good lord.* I'd thought Depressed Domino was embarrassing.

"Here. Use this." Forest pried the balled-up sock from my hand and used it to wipe my nose. "It looks bad, I know."

"Are you kidding me? I told my producing partner... I told Arthur Dagon—ARTHUR DAGON—
that this was the perfect spot for *Shore Thing*. That
we'd never find anywhere better."

"It is. I promise." He ran a hand through his hair.
"I wanted to fix it myself last week, but Fern insisted
we had to keep it under wraps while you were here.
She didn't want anything to mess up your plans." I
looked him in the eyes. He was as sincere as the ocean
is deep. "The roofer is coming today. This morning, in
fact. So you see, everything *will* be fine."

"You don't know Arthur." I had to admit I didn't
really, either, but from what I'd learned of him so far,
the slightest trigger set him off. Trudi and I hadn't
spoken it aloud, but I knew we had a silent pledge that
nothing could go wrong with this movie. But how
could I explain that to this bare-assed man with his
hair sticking up at odd angles, whose gray-blue eyes
were wells of care and concern? Water dripped
steadily into the bucket behind him.

Forest reached up and tucked a strand of hair behind my ear, his hand gently caressing my cheek.
"You don't know Fern."

I burst out with another laugh, which quickly became uncontrollable giggles. Forest smiled, looking at
me with wonder at my out-of-proportion reaction.
Once I could breathe again, I explained, "Whatever

you think Fern's got in the way of determination, I would bet money it pales in comparison to Arthur Dagon." In my head I pictured pretty blonde Fern in cartoon form, a giant scary shadow the shape of Arthur looming behind her.

"It'll be fine." Forest leaned forward until his face was next to mine, bringing with him that scent of pine and sea salt and making my heart flutter against my rib cage. He pressed a kiss to my forehead, his lips lingering before he said, "If I don't pull away now, I'll have you back in that bed in minutes." He pushed up to stand and headed for the bathroom. "Jumping in the shower. You okay for two minutes?"

I gathered the blanket around me like a big pillowy dress and found my skirt and underwear. I needed a shower, too, but I could wait until I was in my own room, where I could put on clean clothes. Finger-combing my hair, I glanced around, trying to remember where I'd left my phone.

I found it on the table next to the plate I'd brought up the night before. Turning it on, I moved to the window while I waited for it to boot up, gazing out at the rainy Pacific, where whitecaps crested on the surface and disappeared like soap suds. A string of buzzes indicated texts coming in. A lot of texts.

Who's the new guy? The first one was from my sister, Saylor.

Call me, Trudi had texted, followed by, **Seriously. We need to talk** sent a half hour later.

From my mom: **Are you all right, honey?**

Even Poppy sent a message: **I'm downstairs if you need me.**

Deirdre had included a link to a TMZ post. My heart dropped to my feet as I read the headline—"Depressed Domino finds new man"—before I clicked it. I closed my eyes and drew in a breath as the website loaded. Maybe the photographers had gotten a shot of me with Forest at some point without us realizing. But apart from our walk that second night, I hadn't been alone anywhere with him in public, so whatever it was I could explain away as friendship or even work.

I let out a gasp at what I saw when I opened my eyes. TMZ had several pictures, shot through the very window I was sitting in front of, taken last night. I had a towel wrapped around me. Forest was shirtless. And we were making out like our lives depended on it.

"Fuck."

"Everything okay?" I hadn't even registered the water turning off in the bathroom or Forest coming back in the room. A towel hung low on his hips, and he was using another to dry his hair. A few drops of water trailed down the muscled V in his chest. "Domino?" he asked again when I didn't answer.

"I—I have to go." Desperate not to see his reaction, I avoided eye contact and bounded for the door.

"Domino?" I heard him call after me as it snicked shut behind me. I leaned back against it, closing my eyes, as another series of buzzes vibrated the phone in my hand.

"Fuck," I said again, then stood up straight, smoothed my bangs, and hurried to the elevator. *You can deal with this,* I told myself on the ride to the second floor. I wasn't attached to anyone. It wasn't like I'd been caught cheating on Harry. In fact, I worked hard to convince myself, maybe it was a good thing. Maybe I could use this exposure to my advantage.

When I got to my room, I put down the phone, determined to figure out a strategy before I read any more texts or even considered answering them. I climbed in the shower, letting the heat release the anxiety that had tensed my muscles in the past hour. I thought through what I needed to do, making a mental list and prioritizing what mattered to the movie—and my career—before I worried about the spin the Hollywood gossip mill wanted to put on my personal life.

By the time I got out, I was sure about one thing: my priority was confirming the Driftwood could handle a movie production. Forest Russo aside, I had to be realistic. If he and his sister were hiding anything else from me, or if the leaky roof wasn't fixed right away, we'd have to find another location. Maybe Marc was right. Maybe Vashon Island *was* the better choice. Why try to shove the square peg of Orcas Island into the round hole of all the complex needs of a film production. Whatever feelings I had for Forest were a separate issue.

I pulled on an old pair of Levi's and my emerald-green sweater, slid back into the ballet flats I'd worn last night, grabbed my phone, and headed for the dining room, desperate for coffee before I addressed Trudi, Deidre, or even my sister.

Bluebell, Poppy, and Fern were huddled at the end of the bar when I descended the three steps into the room, Bluebell showing the other two something on her phone. She dropped it abruptly into her apron pocket the minute I approached. Bluebell and Fern had open mouths and red cheeks, as if they'd been caught on the hop. Fern played nervously with the end of her blonde ponytail. Poppy, as usual, didn't seem bothered.

"Guess there's no pretending you aren't looking at my latest humiliation." I dragged out a barstool, its legs scraping along the floor like an old bagpipe, then slumped onto it, dropping my phone to the counter and my head in my hands. I didn't look around me at the other diners in the room—I couldn't.

Fern and Bluebell exchanged a glance, coming to some silent agreement. "At least you look good," Fern said.

"You look *incredible*, actually," Poppy agreed.

"Talk about the best revenge," Bluebell said.

I peered at them sideways, then shrugged. "Doesn't matter."

Bluebell leaned a hip against the bar and dug her hands in the pockets of her apron. "Just saying. If a photo got out of me looking like that—like a divine sex goddess, in the arms of a shirtless hunk—I'd do everything I could to make sure everyone saw it. Fern would do the same. Wouldn't you, Fern?"

"Ignoring the fact you just referred to my brother as a shirtless hunk," Fern said as she scurried behind the bar and pointed at the La Marzocco. I nodded. "I take their side on this one. You really do look incredible. For sure Harry Roman's kicking himself to the moon by now." She tamped the coffee grounds in the basket and secured it in the grouphead, pressing the button for a double shot. Rich brown coffee streamed into the shot glass below it.

I didn't wish Harry any harm, but the thought of the photos on TMZ this morning making him squirm did bring a smile to my face.

"See? Every cloud has a silver lining." Bluebell winked before she pushed through the swinging door into the kitchen.

When Poppy's phone rang, she excused herself and went to the lobby to answer it. "Editor," she explained.

Fern set the latte in front me, the foam on the surface etched with a pattern that looked like the layers of an onion. I sipped and watched as two older men walked in, tipped their hats to Fern, and found a seat at one of the red-vinyl-covered booths that faced the marina. Yesterday's clear blue sky felt like a distant memory now. The rain fell in torrents, drumming against the windows with each gust of wind. It was nice to see the front lawn devoid of photographers for the first time in nearly a week. They got what they needed last night.

I knew I had to confront Fern about the leak, but I wanted to be sure I was calm and rational. I was polite by default; I was a Canadian after all. That, and my leap from Toronto to LA had taught me a thing or two about diplomacy. It used to kill me when my grandmother said, "You catch more flies with honey than vinegar." I'd always thought it was sexist. (This was a woman who'd encouraged my mom *not* to go to university but to dedicate herself to her husband. Fortunately—for me and for her—my mom ignored that advice and became one of the most prominent bioethicists in Ontario.) But now I saw where she was right—when I approached situations big and small with respect and kindness, my chances of getting the outcome I hoped for were ten times better than when I was confrontational or emotional. Zoe's King of Cups card only drilled home how important that was.

Besides, I knew Fern's heart was in the right place. She wanted to help me.

"So, Fern," I said when I was ready. "I know about the leak."

Fern's gaze shot up from her phone, and she clapped a hand to her mouth. "Shit," she mumbled behind her fingers.

"You *were* talking about a tarp." It all made sense now I remembered the conversation I'd interrupted my first morning here.

"It's my fault. Forest was going to fix it right away. But then you came, and I knew you'd walk away from here the minute you found out the hotel has a few...issues. It's just— We had this grand idea about making the hotel more efficient, updating the old wiring. A few things fell by the wayside in the process." Her voice wobbled, and she blinked quickly as if fighting back tears. "It was me who told him not to. I'm really sorry. Does this ruin everything?"

Did it? I hoped not. I wanted more than anything to make *Shore Thing* here. I tapped my fingers on the side of the coffee cup. "That depends."

"We'll do anything to help. Oh, damn it," Fern said when Bluebell asked for coffee for the men sitting by the window. "Hold that thought."

Movement in the lobby drew my attention, where Forest strode toward the front door. Voices sounded as he reappeared, this time with a man in faded utility pants, work boots, and a heavyweight jacket with a sherpa-lined hood. Their voices faded away again as I heard the faint ping of the elevator and the door slide closed.

"Your brother said a roofer is coming this morning," I said once Fern had set two mugs on Bluebell's tray. Her ponytail bounced as she nodded. "That's one problem out of the way. Anything else you need to tell me?"

Her eyes went round like saucers, and she put a hand to her chest. "That's it. I swear."

"You're sure?"

She moved to the side of the bar where a laptop sat atop a stack of papers. "Here. I'll show you." Fern hustled around and settled on the barstool next to me. She flipped open the screen and called up a spreadsheet program, angling the laptop so I could see it, too.

"Roof," I read at the very top of a list of to-dos. "Hot-water heater?" My voice went up an octave on the word *heater*.

"Oh!" Fern rushed to hover the mouse over that box in the spreadsheet and hit delete. "Forest fixed it." Glancing at my knee, which was betraying the calm I wanted to portray by dancing up and down, she added, "Promise."

I scanned the rest of the list: *paint, upholstery, floors, glass washer. Wi-Fi.* Oof, that was a big one. I raised an eyebrow. Fern held up a finger, then repeated the process of hovering over the cell and hitting delete.

"Let me guess. Forest fixed it?"

She laughed. "Not this time. Computers, uh, aren't really his thing."

"What *is* his thing?"

"Pretty much everything else. He's kind of a... What's the word?" She scrunched her eyes shut, popping them open when she remembered. "A luddite." She laughed again. "But if something's broken, he'll try to fix it. The hot-water heater, for example. A flat tire. The grill in the kitchen."

"Something's wrong with the grill in the kitchen?"

She vehemently shook her head. "God, no. Sorry, that was just an example—a bad one. But he's your basic jack of all trades. Good with machines, good with plants, good with cars." She paused, staring unfocused at the kitchen door. "Just not so good with people." She turned to face me, suddenly aware I might be offended. "Sometimes," she corrected.

I shrugged. "Eh, he's not so bad once you get past the gruff exterior."

Fern's eyes sparkled. "Uh-oh. Do I detect a crush on my big brother?"

My cheeks burned. If I hadn't just spent a ridiculously good night with him, I might've been able to play it cooler. *Did* I have a crush on Forest Russo? I felt a pang in my heart when I realized how much I'd grown attached to the guy in the week I'd been here.

Fern stood, clasping both hands on the bar on either side of the laptop. "Wait a minute. *Domino West* has a crush on my brother?" She emphasized my name, remembering I wasn't just another hotel guest. She did a little hop where she stood before she sank back down on the stool.

I leaned an elbow on the bar and rested my chin in my hand. "You know you were telling me about island time?"

"Mm-mm. Why, you think you're on it now?"

"I dunno. Something's definitely happening to me here." At the entrance to the lobby, Poppy stuck her head in and waved. "Call you later," she said, covering the phone with her hand. Fern and I waved back.

"So you do have a crush on him." Fern rested her elbow on the bar, too, mimicking my posture. "God, you're so lucky. You can go to a place, meet someone interesting, fall for a guy. Around here I'm lucky if anyone's single, never mind interesting."

I assessed Fern anew, taking in her slate-blue eyes, pretty round face, and long blonde hair. "You know what? I have a good feeling about you this year. I don't know why. Call it instinct. You're going to meet someone, I know it."

Fern straightened in her seat. "Hey, I have an idea! Have you ever had your tarot cards read?"

I laughed. "Poppy beat you to it."

"She did? Bummer. Tell me you liked it, at least."

I wrinkled my nose. "I think so. It was weirdly accurate."

"That's Zoe. She's been really helpful with her...advice." Fern played with the pendant charm hanging from her necklace. "I find I hear her voice whenever I need it."

I took a drink of coffee and set the mug on the bar. "About that list." I indicated the laptop with my thumb. "You sure that's it?"

She looked it over one more time. "The only other thing I meant to put on here is social media."

I inhaled, thinking. Paint and flooring and chairs were all aesthetic—and wouldn't make or break the hotel's ability to host the cast and crew. Nice to have, sure, but not essential. I felt a lot more grounded than

I had an hour ago when I woke up to water leaking from the ceiling in Forest's room.

My phone buzzed on the bar. My eyes went to where it lay facedown beside me as Fern closed the laptop and stood. "I meant what I said—I'm sorry we didn't tell you about the roof. Thank you for being so cool." I stood, too, and tugged her into a hug. Despite what'd happened, I trusted this woman.

"Partners?" I asked as we pulled away.

"Partners." She squeezed my hands, then let them drop as she picked up the laptop and moved back around the bar.

I turned over my phone. And froze.

Where the fuck are you? Arthur Dagon had texted. **And why the fuck is there a tarp on the roof at this shithole hotel?**

CHAPTER 20

Forest

Jack Woodhouse was as quiet as he was rumored to be, but he was quick and efficient, and within twenty minutes of arriving he'd taken photos and measurements of where the roof needed to be patched and promised he could get the job done in under a day. Together we cleared the area of debris, unfurled a giant blue tarp, and wrapped the end around a piece of lumber to anchor it. Then we nailed several two-by-fours in place so the temporary fix would hold up to the heavy rain and wind we would no doubt get until Jack came back with supplies.

It was rough work in the driving rain. By the time

we were finished, water streamed from my Mariners cap and down the front of the thick fleece I'd worn this morning. Jack had tossed a high-viz rain slicker on before we stepped onto the balcony of room 502. I wished I'd thought to do the same.

He let me scramble down to the patio first. I watched as he followed, nimble as a fox. I lifted the hat from my head and wiped my forehead with the back of my sleeve. Just as I opened the door to get out of the rain, the sound of a man coughing drew my attention.

A taxi was pulled over on Water Street in front of the Driftwood. A silver-haired man had climbed out and waited patiently on the sidewalk, holding a folded newspaper over his head to keep the rain off. The rear door was open and seemed to be the source of the coughing. A big man hefted himself out, leaning heavily on the door as he did—so much the car heaved sideways under his weight. His face was purple, whether from coughing or just ill health wasn't clear.

"What the fuck." His loud gravelly voice carried all the way to the balcony where I stood with Jack. The man seemed to be looking right at us, eyes bulging. The fellow with him, elegant in a toffee-colored coat, shook his head behind his friend's back.

Suddenly I was glad to be out in the rain fixing the roof and not behind the front desk to receive whatever fury this man was about to unleash.

I turned to Jack, who was watching with equal interest, and shrugged. "Fixing a roof in the rain ain't all bad, turns out."

He chuckled and ran his hands down the front of his jacket, wicking off the water, before he ducked inside and I followed behind. "Will you be here Friday when I come to do the job? I could use your help."

I stepped into the bathroom and tossed my wet hat on the counter, calling, "Yah, I can be here. Roofing by yourself, hey—that's hard work."

Jack didn't quite meet my eyes when he answered. "I'm new here—just getting my feet under me."

"You came last spring, right?" I opened the door to the hall and held it while he walked through. "Where're you from?"

"Oh, you know. I spent some time on the mainland and a little overseas. Glad to be here, though."

It didn't escape my notice he was vague about his background. But watching him on the roof told me everything I needed to know: he could fix the leak, and he could do it soon. He knew his way around a hammer and nails—even five stories off the ground.

Once we were in the elevator, I held out my hand to shake his. "See you Friday."

"Friday." His grip was firm.

Before we even reached the main floor, a voice

boomed so loud we heard it in the elevator car. The volume only intensified once the door slid open to the lobby, where the purple-faced man was tearing a strip off my sister. Her mouth was pinched in a nervous smile. Uh-oh. I knew that look. It meant tears were soon to follow.

I looked at Jack, who nodded and high-tailed it out the door as I hurried behind the desk to stand next to Fern. "What's the problem here?"

"This fool claims Domino West isn't staying here." The man's enormous hands were spread wide on the lobby desk. Every time he moved, he left a palm-shaped sweat stain. Up close like this, I could see a vein throbbing down the middle of his forehead.

"I can confirm that—we don't have a Domino West booked into the hotel at this time." I folded my arms over my chest. Technically we weren't lying. We had an *Allie Hamilton* staying with us, but no reservation under Domino West.

"Jesus Christ. Don't you know who I am?" He raised one of his meaty hands and slammed it back down on the desk, making Fern jump. He crooked a finger at me and narrowed his eyes. "I know who you are."

I'd never seen this man in my life. I turned to my sister, thinking maybe she knew who this guy was from her magazines, but she just shrugged, shrinking back. A flash of green caught my eye at the entrance to the dining room. I glared at Domino standing there, shaking my head slightly and waving my hand low, palm down, left and right, hoping she'd pick up on my cue and disappear. But instead she smoothed her bangs and took five determined steps forward until she was standing behind the hulk of a man spitting fire at Fern and me.

"You're mistaking me for someone else—" I began.

"Hello, Arthur." Domino spoke calmly behind him.

He turned around to face her, and she seemed to shrink back a little. When she'd mentioned Arthur this morning, I'd chalked her fear to nerves about the production, but I could see now her warning was warranted. "Finally. Why are you keeping me waiting? Here, take this." He shoved his rolling suitcase toward the elevator and glared in my direction. The man with him, wearing an impeccably tailored suit, simply stood in place, his coat draped over his arm, looking neither at me and Fern nor Domino and this beastly oaf.

Domino moved toward the silver-haired man and kissed his left cheek, then his right. "Welcome." The two seemed genuinely happy to see each other. She slid gracefully between him and Arthur and set her elbows on the lobby desk, clasping her hands together. "Sorry for the confusion. Fern, Forest—this is Marc McCann." She indicated the man in the nice suit. "And this—" she touched the base of Arthur's left elbow, eliciting a grunt "—is Arthur Dagon."

I'd never met someone with a more fitting last name. He was more dragonlike than human.

"Do you have rooms for them for—what? One night?" She directed the question at Marc.

Marc looked around the lobby, his lips pinched together. "One night will suffice."

"Yes, we can certainly manage that." Fern no longer looked like she might burst into tears. She flipped the page of the giant guest book in front of her, running a pen along the left-hand column. "Mr. Dagon, you'll be in room 412. Mr. McCann, you'll be on the second floor with Dom—Miss West."

I opened the wide drawer in the bureau behind me and found the room keys, then slid them across the desk. Arthur turned his back, leading Domino into the dining room. "Deal with it, would you, Marc." It wasn't a question so much as a demand.

Fern took down Marc's information as Arthur and Domino descended into the dining room, where she steered him toward the windows and out of sight of the front desk. "You can charge the same credit card Domino used," Marc was saying.

"You must be here for *Shore Thing*." Fern was downright cheerful now the big red man was out of the picture. "We're so pleased you're staying with us. We've been helping Domino with her location work. She seems to really like it here."

"I'll bet she does." Marc cast his eyes my way. Fern's cheeks burned red. He shook his head and tsked. "I'm sorry. That wasn't fair." He held his hand out to me. "Nice to meet you. It's been a long morning."

"I'm sure it has." We shook cordially. "I'll take your bags up. Enjoy your stay."

Marc smoothed a hand over his hair, which lay perfectly, like he'd just come from the barber. For a brief moment he seemed unsure what to do but ultimately decided to join Domino and Arthur in the dining room.

Fern blew out a breath when the lobby was empty. "I'm not cut out for people like that." She placed a hand over her stomach. "Feels like I drank a gallon of coffee."

I squeezed her shoulder. "We're fine. You did great." I took a few steps toward Marc's and Arthur's luggage, then stopped. "Fern?"

"Mm-hmm?" she said, picking up her phone.

"What am I missing here? Both of them acted like they know me."

Fern's mouth twitched at the corners. "You don't know?"

"What?"

"Come look." She tapped the browser on her phone and brought up the *Inside Hollywood* website.

"What the..." There I was, shirtless in a window, arms wrapped around Domino West, lips locked in what I'd thought was a private moment. "Jesus." I felt the tips of my ears burn red.

"You're famous now, big bro." With that she snatched her phone back and walked into the dining room, leaving me openmouthed, embarrassed, and, I had to admit, a little impressed with myself. From what I'd seen, the pictures, though illicitly gained, only hinted at the hot, lustful night I'd spent with Domino West.

When I'd managed to pick my jaw up off the floor, I grabbed Marc's sleek suitcase—Rimowa, it said across the top in discreet lettering—and Arthur's shabbier but still expensive-looking bag and wheeled them to the elevator.

Something about their arrival left me feeling eerie. The air felt different now—charged with an energy at odds with island life. I shuddered as the elevator door shut and it began its ascent to the second floor.

Domino

What else would this day bring? I stared across the table at Arthur and Marc. First my photo was splashed all over the internet—again—and now the meanest guy in Hollywood had shown up unannounced. I'd thought I still had a day before crossing all the t's and dotting all the i's on my plans for Orcas Island. Doing it without full preparation wasn't my first choice.

I didn't like the expression on Arthur's face as he peered around the dining room. With him here the furniture looked more worn than it had before; the vinyl seemed to have more rips and tears. Marc, too, looked as if he'd bitten into a sour cherry. The constant thrum of rain outside didn't help. Neither had said a word since we sat down, just eyed the people at three other tables like kings staring down from their castle.

Angela was here, too. She seemed oblivious to the conversation her two friends were having at her table, just watched Marc and Arthur with interest. She reached into her pannier bag and pulled out that dogeared notebook and a pen.

I sipped the water Bluebell had set in front of me.

"Get me an espresso." Arthur didn't even look her in the eyes, just demanded what he wanted with a growl.

To her credit, Bluebell didn't bat an eye. "And for you?" She turned her attention to Marc.

"You probably don't have oat milk here." At her nod, his eyes brightened a little. "Wonderful. I'll have a flat white, then. Thank you."

"I'm fine with water," I said. The last thing I needed was caffeine when my stomach was doing dips and swirls like a boat on a stormy sea.

"Your judgment is shot," Arthur said when Bluebell walked away. "We're shooting the movie on Vessel Island."

"Vashon," Marc corrected him.

"Whatever. Marc has it all set up." In the gray light coming through the window, Arthur's skin looked like a mottled bean, patches of flaky red on his cheeks and chin.

I glared at Marc. "Orcas was your idea. You sent me here."

"You volunteered."

I swallowed over the lump of anxiety that had formed in my throat. He was right; of course he was right. I needed to set aside whatever personal feelings

I'd developed during my week here and focus on what was best for the film. However fucking impossible that felt right now.

I looked at Angela. She'd stopped scribbling in her notebook, just held my gaze and tipped her chin. *You got this*, I imagined her big green eyes were telling me. I straightened my shoulders and sat taller. *"Control your emotions and accept them—without them getting the better of you."* Suddenly I heard Zoe's voice like she was next to me.

"How about this. I'll show you around today, explain what I've learned about this place and why it's the right place for *Shore Thing*. Tomorrow we can go to Vashon. If I have it all wrong, you can show me why."

Bluebell returned with an elegant little espresso and Marc's flat white, in which she'd etched a tree on the surface of the microfoam. His eyes grew wider at the sight of it. "This looks..." He searched for the right word. "Delightful," he told Bluebell. He smiled at Fern, who stood behind the bar by the espresso machine.

Arthur picked up the tiny cup in his enormous hand, a child's toy in a giant's grip. He tipped it back in one gulp, slamming the cup on the table. His breathing was audible—shallow and nasal. Not for the first time I wondered what redeeming qualities Arthur

Dagon possessed. He was married to a stunning violinist. He must have done something good to attract her and keep her by his side, but I'd yet to discover what that was.

"Well, what are we waiting for?" He bumped against the table as he stood, sending the water in my glass sloshing over the rim.

"Uh, okay." Panic shot through me. My feet felt numb. "Please wait here. I'll be right back." I managed to maintain a calm facade as I got up and somehow made it to the bar without dropping to the floor. Now my back was turned to Arthur and Marc, I squeezed my eyes shut and forced a few deep breaths in and out, my lips in a circle as I imagined breathing through a straw. It worked in yoga to calm the heart rate. I hoped like hell it would work in real life, too.

When I opened my eyes, Fern stood in front of me, her head slightly tilted, concern wrinkling her forehead. "You all right?"

I nodded quickly. "I will be." I did another round of straw breathing as she watched, grasping the edge of the bar. "What are the chances I can borrow the jeep?"

"I think Forest was going to..." She stopped mid-sentence when my eyes went round with panic.

"It's important. Like, make or break production on Orcas Island important."

Fern dug the phone from her apron pocket and typed a message. "C'mon, brother. Please get this," she muttered under her breath. Three seconds later, she slid the phone back in her pocket. "He's coming down with the key."

I held my hands in front of me in a prayer position. "Thank you, thank you. You have no idea how much—"

"First I can't see the script, and now you're keeping me waiting." I whirled around to find Arthur standing behind me, his hulking figure casting a dark shadow. Marc stood slightly behind, shrugging apologetically.

"If you'll come with me, gentlemen, I'll show you around the hotel while Domino gets her things." Fern came around the bar, all warmth and professionalism. I could have kissed her in that moment. "After all, we hope to host you again for a longer stay. Right this way." She indicated the door to the kitchen. Amazingly, Arthur and Marc followed her orders like good soldiers.

"Where are they going?" Forest said as he approached.

"Fern is..." I hesitated. Fern was what, exactly? "Showing them the kitchen, I think." Gazing into his confident blue eyes, the cut of his jaw shadowed with the hint of a beard, I realized I needed more than just the key to the jeep. "Come with us?"

"Think I'd rather jump in the Pacific," he said.

"He's not that bad."

"He *is* that bad."

I laughed. It felt good to break the tension that'd built in my chest. "Okay. He's pretty bad. But you're a fellow grump, right? You can bond over scowls and crossed arms. While you help me show them the boat and Grange Hall and the marina and everything that makes this island the perfect place to shoot my movie."

True to form, he crossed his arms, shaking his head. But he didn't say no.

I leaned in toward him and grasped his elbows. "Please? I need you."

Whether it was the callback to last night or the pathetic look on my face, he shrugged, his lips quirking to one side. "You owe me."

"I'll make it up to you." With a glance behind me to make sure Arthur hadn't reappeared, I stood on tiptoe and planted a kiss on his lips. When his eyes darted sideways, tracking the tables of guests to see if they'd noticed, I said, "They know already. Everyone does. Thanks to those assholes." I pointed out the window to the front lawn, where the three photographers had set up again, this time with umbrellas. "Guess they upgraded now they made some money off invading my privacy."

"Wave!" Forest hollered into the room. Eleven sets of hands shot in the air, flailing back and forth. Again, it seemed to work. The paparazzi lowered their ridiculously big lenses.

Forest brushed a strand of hair from my eyes. It was impossible to ignore the sparks zinging between us, even now. That wall he'd had up when I first arrived—the pretense of being someone who didn't want to know or care—had slowly crumbled over the past week. I hoped it was something he was happy about. I hoped he knew I saw him for who he really was—a smart, caring, capable man, who just happened to be incredibly handsome and able to bring me to orgasm like no other.

The whoosh of the kitchen door had me leaping a foot back from him, though. I needed, desperately, for Arthur to see me as the professional, determined, hardworking woman I was. I set my shoulders back, trained my face into a calm, confident smile, and brushed my bangs into place. "I'll be back," I told Forest before I strode for the lobby and upstairs to change my shoes and grab a coat. *"Be firm in your personal boundaries,"* I heard Zoe say in my head. *"Stay true to your feelings. Don't allow others to steer you off course."*

CHAPTER 21

Domino

I was impressed with Forest's quiet fortitude as he guided the jeep around the curves of Ellison Road on route to Henry Black's. Arthur sat in the passenger seat next to him, the seat belt stretched taut over his protruding belly. Even from the back I could hear his heavy breathing, punctuated by grunts of disapproval when he saw something through the window he didn't like. Marc and I sat in the back, exchanging text messages in silence.

Why didn't you warn me? I'd typed once we were on the road. Surely he would've known Arthur was heading our way.

Marc gave me an apologetic look. **Sorry,** he mes-saged back. **I had no idea. When I got to Seattle this morning he was just THERE.**

OMG. Of course I had some sympathy for Marc, but I dug in the knife anyway. **Gee, I couldn't imagine being confronted by Arthur Dagon when you weren't expecting it,** I wrote, rolling my eyes. Exactly my experience not even an hour ago, too. Marc's ears turned red.

What's going on with you and the lumberjack?

I shrugged. I wasn't sure how to answer—or if I even knew the answer. I turned to look out the window at the now-familiar route out of Bayview, watching for glimpses of Pacific between the trees. It was eerily quiet in the jeep, just the white noise of tires on a wet road, the thump of the windshield wipers, and drops of rain pelting the windows. Forest must've been thinking the same thing. I was relieved when he pressed on the sound system and called up a jazz playlist.

When we reached the turnoff for the Blacks' estate, Arthur growled, "This isn't even a road, for fuck's sake. Where are you taking me?" He grabbed the assist handle as the jeep careened over bumps and dips in the gravel.

Forest was polite but assertive. "Domino asked me to show you the boat."

Arthur grumbled, his breathing audible as we turned into the Blacks' winding driveway. I wondered if Forest had texted ahead. It was one thing to surprise Henry and Olive with me in tow, as we'd done last week. It was something else entirely to show up on someone's doorstep with Arthur Dagon. I shot Poppy a message while it was on my mind to warn her mom that Grange Hall was next on our list.

The visit went surprisingly well. Henry was as gracious and affable as he'd been with me. Arthur seemed comfortable to be with people of his own kind—people with money. It dulled his sharp edge. He grunted approval of the *Redemption*, as though he'd expected nothing less.

Georgia was standing under the overhang outside Grange Hall when we parked in the empty lot. Poppy must've warned her what to expect. She trembled with nerves watching Arthur approach—and she curtsied once he was in front of her like he was some kind of royalty. I was glad to be standing behind him so I could suppress a giggle in the elbow of my coat sleeve.

Inside, Arthur stalked to the middle of the hall, his big hands dangling at his sides like a gorilla's. I knew we were doomed when his breathing grew heavier and he began shaking his head. "You can't be fucking serious," he spat.

Marc shrugged when I looked to him for assistance. Georgia's cheeks burned pink, and she kept her eyes on the ground, her hands clasped low in front of her. If she could've shrunk into the ground at that moment, she would have. I stood tall. "This is an excellent space, Arthur. It's big enough for us, with room to spread out. All the electrical has been updated—" Georgia nodded in encouragement, looking relieved at my words "—there's a large kitchen, and the price is reasonable."

He wagged a finger in my face like a hot dog, scarlet streaking his face from the forehead down. "It's nowhere, Domino, nowhere! You can't expect me to drive—" He clutched his left shoulder, sweat beading his forehead. "You can't expect—" His began wheezing, and he grabbed hold of Marc and pitched forward, leaning into him. The sweat dripped down his nose and hit the floor, the splat audible.

Marc swayed under his weight, then steadied. "Arthur," he said firmly. "Arthur!" he repeated loudly when Arthur said nothing, just clawed his fingers into Marc's shoulder, his breath coming in short, heavy bursts.

"Oh my god, I think he's having a heart attack." Georgia brought both hands to her mouth in shock. "Call 911. Call 911!" She fumbled in her pocket for her phone and frantically punched in the numbers.

Forest stepped forward, hoisting Arthur under the

arms and letting him sag to the ground, his eyes closed, face pinched. "Anyone have an aspirin?" Forest asked without looking up. He undid the top two buttons of Arthur's shirt and loosened the area around his neck. I slid my coat off and knelt to position it under Arthur's head. Georgia had moved to the side of the room to speak with an emergency responder.

"Arthur, can you hear me?" Forest asked in a clear, measured voice.

Arthur's face had turned blotchy. His hair was wet with sweat, and stains appeared like upside down kidney beans beneath his chest. But he nodded, grabbing Forest's arm. "The squeezing—" he grunted.

Forest and I exchanged a worried glance. "Should we do CPR or something?" In all my years on sets, there'd always been medical personnel around; I'd never learned first aid.

He tucked two fingers to the side of Arthur's neck and shook his head. "Not yet. He's breathing, and his pulse is strong. That's what we're watching for. Arthur, you with me?"

"Uh," Arthur said, eyes fluttering open and closed. Forest held steady, withstanding Arthur's grip on his left arm and keeping his right hand on Arthur's chest.

"They say how long?" Forest asked when Georgia came to stand near us.

"Two minutes." She fidgeted with her purse straps. "Lucky for us they're at Bob and Ida's. They're okay," she rushed to add when Forest's brow knit with worry. "Bob twisted his ankle. He'll be fine."

Marc stood still as a statue, the color drained from his face, his eyes wide. "Why don't you go over there and take a seat, Marc," I suggested. The last thing we needed was Marc passing out next to Arthur. He nodded without expression and moved like a robot to the side of the room where chairs were stacked in neat rows.

The room fell quiet as we listened to Arthur's strained breathing before the silence was broken by an ambulance siren growing louder as it approached. Georgia looked relieved when the crunch of gravel sounded outside the hall. She rushed to open the doors for the paramedics, who carried a stretcher inside with them.

Once they took over, Forest and I stood, and my body began quivering, my knees weak and my palms sweaty. As the EMTs carried Arthur out, Marc following behind, Forest picked up my coat from the floor and laid it over my shoulders. "It's shock. Totally expected. Let's sit down." He guided me to the chairs and set three of them in a circle, ushering Georgia and me to sit. "Be right back." He disappeared into the kitchen. Georgia and I sat quietly, hands clasped across the chairs in support as we let the realization of what'd happened sink in and I willed the shaking to stop.

Forest reappeared a few minutes later, two steaming cups of tea in his hands. "Got anything stronger?" Georgia joked, taking her cup in both hands to keep it steady.

I let out a nervous laugh that sounded like it'd come from someone else entirely. Forest stood in front of me, holding the cup of tea, as I burst into uncontrollable laughter. Georgia, too, broke into giggles. At Forest's questioning look, I said, "It's— it's...not...funny," which only made me laugh harder. This situation—with Arthur Dagon, and perfectly ironed Marc, and the ridiculously handsome man in front of me I was trying so hard to pretend I wasn't falling for—it was too much.

A smile made the lines around Forest's eyes crinkle. He relaxed a little and set the tea down on a nearby table before taking a seat. "Okay, it's a little funny," he conceded. "But only because he's okay."

"You think so?" Georgia asked, serious now.

He nodded. "The EMTs said they think he'll be fine. That's the good news."

"Uh oh. What's the catch?" I picked up the cup and sipped.

"There's no way they're going to let him fly. At

least not right away. Fortify yourselves, ladies. He'll be here awhile."

I clapped my free hand to my mouth. "Like how long?" My voice was muffled by my fingers.

"Two weeks, maybe? I'm no doctor, but—" He shrugged.

"You sure handled that well," Georgia said.

"Yah, how'd you know what to do?"

"We had to learn CPR, emergency first aid, all that stuff when I was planting. No ambulance can come screaming for you in a hurry out in the bush."

Georgia circled her fingers around her mug. "Well, you're good at it. I don't know how you stayed so calm. I've underestimated you, Forest Russo. You can rescue me anytime."

Me too, I thought but didn't say. We sat quietly for another few minutes finishing our tea. Forest collected the empty cups and took them to the kitchen before we moved for the door.

Outside, Georgia locked up before she leaned in to hug me, then Forest. "Wait'll I tell Poppy," she said, shaking her head. We walked her to her old green Volvo. The rain had stopped, and a patch of blue was visible in the sky above us.

My shaking had subsided by the time we left the Grange Hall grounds. It still felt as though my stomach was flipping over the high bars, though, and I began to realize it was no longer just the shock of Arthur's heart attack. The man sitting next to me, big and strong and quiet in the driver's seat, was doing all kinds of things to my heart, whether I wanted it or not. My head was telling me one thing, but emotion was wrestling for control. With every day that went by, I wanted to be near him more and more. *How can I make this work?* It seemed impossible. Then I remembered Zoe's words: *"The King of Cups represents a balance between intellect and emotions."*

Use your intellect, Domino, I thought. *Figure it out.* I stared out the window, watching as the fading sun lit the remaining clouds in purple, then pink, then golden orange, silhouetting the tree branches like dancers behind a screen.

"You're quiet," Forest said as we neared the turnoff to the hotel. "Doing okay? Shock's an odd thing. Sometimes it can take several hours—"

I rested a hand on his thigh, stopping him midthought. "It's not that."

He stole a sideways look at me, his eyes illuminated by the dashboard lights. "No?"

"I'm falling for you, Forest. I can't stop it. A freight train of emotion barrels into me the minute I'm near you. I know we said we can't. I know we talked about all the reasons why. But I can't remember a single one of them right now."

He angled the jeep into its spot behind the Drift-wood and shut off the engine. He placed his hand over mine, turning to look at me. "You're an actor. Can't you...?" But his words trailed off. It was hopeless. Reflected back in his eyes was the same yearning, the same need, the same intense desire I knew shone in my own.

I leaned across and kissed him, tenderly at first, then with all the pent-up longing pulsing through my body. His lips were soft, his mouth willing. I felt his hands cup the sides of my face, and desire danced in my belly. I wanted to climb over the console and take him in my arms.

He released me, pulling back, his breath heavy like mine. It was the right thing to do. I knew it as well as he did. But it felt like a blanket being torn from the bed on a cold winter morning, taking all the warmth and comfort with it. He squirmed in his seat, adjusting his jeans around his bulging hard-on, and cleared his throat. "I need time to think," he said. After a beat, he added, "You're leaving."

I huffed out an exhale. "Not for two weeks. You said so yourself."

"You're leaving," he said again. "You don't be-long here, Domino. This world—it's quiet. There's no parties to go to, no talk shows to do. Nothing glamorous. At all. It's seagulls and fir trees and ocean on all sides. And it rains. A lot."

Even though I felt physically like I might burst with need, I needed to think, too. Forest was right. My life was 1,200 miles away in LA—which felt like a million miles away in this moment. I'd be on Orcas Island for six weeks while we shot *Shore Thing*. Then there was post-production, and ADR, and press tours and whatever Trudi and I decided to do next. At this point in my career, I had to be willing to go wherever my work took me, whether that was to shoot a movie in Australia or Croatia or even back in Toronto. No matter how much I liked Forest and this magic little island in the Pacific.

We traipsed into the hotel, Forest walking ahead of me and holding open the door to let me through. It was a culture shock after the hushed cabin of the jeep. In the kitchen steam bubbled from a giant pot on the stove, and George and Tommy moved around the space like bees in a hive. "Dinner rush," Forest said, pushing through the swinging door to the dining room, again holding the door for me.

I felt exhausted, I realized as I looked around the bustling dining room. I smiled a greeting at Bluebell and Fern behind the bar but kept walking, hands in my coat pockets, until I reached the elevator.

"Domino?" Forest asked behind me. He stood with his hands balled at his sides, forehead wrinkled with concern.

"I'm fine," I told him as the elevator dinged. I kept my eyes on the floor until the door slid closed. Once I was ensconced in the small space, the tears fell hot and salty down my cheeks.

Despite his size and temperament and the stress that swirled around him like a tornado, I felt responsible for Arthur's heart attack. I'd failed to find what we needed for *Shore Thing*. Not only that, I'd lost my heart to a man I couldn't have. I pressed my fingertips to my lips and remembered the taste of him. For a woman who was meant to have it all, I was falling apart at the seams.

CHAPTER 22

Forest

Five full days passed before I saw Domino again. The hotel was busy. I spent hours in the basement, taking a few chairs down at a time to reupholster them with the new vinyl that'd arrived the day of Arthur's heart attack. I kept myself busy—intentionally so, filling my hours with any number of tasks that didn't require thinking. The sooner my life returned to the way it was, the better.

On Friday Jack had come to fix the roof. We'd lucked out with a dry day to remove the old shingles and nail new ones in place.

Fern and Bluebell delivered updates on Arthur's

health. He was recovering in hospital and, just as predicted, would be cleared to fly in a week's time. That meant one more week of keeping out of Domino's way—and doing my best to patch the hole that'd formed in my heart. She'd been spending time with Marc and Poppy, apparently, doing movie stuff, as Bluebell put it. Whether I'd ruined her chances of convincing her partners to film *Shore Thing* here, I wasn't sure. But I also wasn't sure I could handle her returning to the island for a month and a half. I didn't think my heart could stand it.

The sun shone all week, as if in betrayal of the way I felt inside. I'd forced myself outside every afternoon. Though my depression fought me for an hour before I left each time, once I was out in the fresh air, running the meandering trails in Sombrio Park or hiking the rugged coastline, I was slowly fortified. Every minute of warm sun recharged my body like a battery plugged in.

Fern joined me Saturday morning since no guests were scheduled to check in or out. Bluebell and Tommy could handle anything that came up.

"He's due out of hospital today." Her blonde hair was tucked under a red wool hat. The rocks crunched under our feet as we crossed Gold Beach, so named for the golden sunsets seen on this side of the island.

"Good luck to him."

Fern shoved a hand against my shoulder. "Come on, Forest. He's an asshole, but he's *our* asshole this week. We still need to impress him."

I stopped, took off my sunglasses, and squinted out at the ocean. The glimmering sea was blinding in the morning sun. I closed my eyes and felt the sun on my face, letting it calm the war raging inside between the temptation of Domino and my desire to protect my heart. I could do this. I could appease an asshole if it meant preserving the family business and maybe cracking me apart in the process. When I opened them again, Fern stood next to me, a new awareness behind her gaze.

"You love her."

"Pffft. Try again, sister." At the shore a heron bobbed its head underwater and emerged, a shiny fish in its beak.

She searched my face, eyes reflecting the azure-blue sky. "Interesting," she said. I kicked the rocks uneasily, avoiding eye contact. "You can lie to me, Forest, but you can lie to yourself only so long." She shielded her face with her hand and took a step forward. "Come on. It's nearly lunch." She took off ahead.

I followed on the cobble beach, thinking over those few simple words. I hadn't let myself go there, hadn't let myself consider the biggest feeling of all. Was I in love with Domino West? I'd long ago closed myself off to even the idea. No woman in her right mind could find intimacy with a man like me—one who'd never been able to maintain a relationship. I'd shut that door in my heart, sealed it off to protect myself from the agony of disappointment.

But Domino was different. With Domino I felt seen. Appreciated for who I was. She was her own woman, with her own life and career and money. Yet she still seemed to want me. The attraction between us was stronger than gravity. Who was I kidding? I couldn't ignore any longer that I wanted her. Wished she'd stay here forever.

There it was—the pang of absolute heartbreak at the realization that no matter how I felt about her, or whether or not she loved me, too, our lives were so far apart they felt like different solar systems. I wasn't leaving Orcas Island. Her whole life was in California. We were just two people whose lives had unexpectedly crossed.

I caught up to Fern where the beach ended and the trail led back to the jeep. As we trekked through the forest of maples and firs, I gathered the courage to be honest with my sister. "I love her," I blurted.

She stopped, rested a hand on my shoulder, and smiled. "I'm glad. As much as you pretended, I could see something different was going on," she said. "You know what? It's been good for you. This week you've seemed...centered, somehow. Like the world tilted on its axis, and suddenly you've found peace."

She dropped her hand and scratched her forehead under her hat before we resumed walking. Was that true? I'd been so busy trying to keep busy, trying to ignore the joy beating in my chest every time I thought of her, that I'd been pushing away any awareness of my behavior. I breathed in deeply, filling my lungs with oxygen from the canopy of green above us. An acorn woodpecker flitted between the trees ahead, its red cap stark against its bright white forehead. They were one of my favorite birds to see, with their wide eyes and clownish faces. I loved the thought of them storing acorns all year, stashing them in specially made holes in the trees. One group member was always on alert, guarding the hoard from thieves, the way my brain was protecting my heart from Domino West.

"What do I do now?"

Fern was quiet a moment, our footsteps thudding on the dirt path. "You have only one choice, brother. You have to tell her."

I swallowed over the bundle of nerves that formed in my throat at the thought. Letting someone see me vulnerable wasn't top of my list of hobbies. In a nanosecond I was flooded with doubt. What if she laughed? What if my worst fears were true, and I was nothing more to her than some backwoods hick she'd used to take her mind off Harry Roman? What if I made a fool of myself?

"What's the worst that could happen?" Fern asked as if she'd heard my internal monologue. "You put yourself out there. Big whoop. It's better than the alternative."

"You said I had only one choice. What's the alternative?"

The path narrowed as we came to a set of stairs cut into the dirt and edged with wood. I took the lead, climbing two steps ahead of my sister.

"You regret it for the rest of your life."

Fern's words echoed in my ears as we reached the jeep. I reached for my water bottle and pressed the button to start the engine. My determination grew with each mile we drove. I had a single-minded focus now: find Domino and pour my heart out.

But as I strode through the dining room, an eruption of voices carried from the lobby. I stood in the arched doorway, watching as Domino wheeled an irate-looking Arthur through the front doors. Marc and Poppy followed behind, her lips pinched in a straight line. Whatever time Arthur had spent in the hospital hadn't done much to heal his demeanor.

When Domino looked my way, the emotion reflected back in her eyes was a mix of weariness and exasperation. It couldn't be easy to psych yourself up for one day with Arthur Dagon only to have it turn into fourteen. "What room are you in?" she asked him as she wheeled him toward the elevator. He barely cast a glance at me. That took the cake. If anything bonded you to a person, you'd think it was guiding them through a heart attack. But this guy seemed to have the emotional intelligence of a brick.

"How the fuck do I know," he spat.

Domino looked at me pleadingly. I stepped across the lobby and behind the desk to grab the key card for room 412.

"Thank you," Domino mouthed behind Arthur's chair as he lurched forward to stab the elevator button with his fat middle finger.

"Can I see you later?" I whispered discreetly.

She nodded as she motioned to Marc to help her push Arthur over the gap between the landing and the elevator. "At least the fucking roof's fixed," I heard Arthur grumble before the door slid closed on his cherry-red face, surrounded by the miserable trio of Marc, Poppy, and Domino.

I went to my room for a shower, then returned to the lobby, figuring I'd hang around until Domino could get away. From behind the bar in the dining room, Fern beckoned me in. She gestured to the two big chairs by the fireplace. Domino sat in one, back to me, hair loose around her shoulders, head down and focused on something in her lap. I strode past a few tables of diners to the far end where she sat.

"Hi." She lifted her eyes to mine when I reached her side. She moved to stand, and a magazine dropped from her lap to the floor. "Don't get up," I said. I bent forward at the same time she did to pick it up. I got it first. I took a step back when I saw her face staring back at me from the cover, her eyes as blue as cobalt. I fell into the seat next to her. "Wait, is that... Moonstone Beach?" The rock formations in the background were startlingly familiar.

She nodded, waiting for my reaction. "I didn't have a chance to tell you—"

"Wow. *Vanity Fair*. That's huge, isn't it?" I scanned the cover copy. "The winter of Domino West," I read aloud, then squinted at the byline in disbelief. "Poppy Willoughby? This is her article?" Impressed, I handed it back. "Congratulations."

She held it to her chest, her cheeks pink. A fire crackled in the fireplace, its orange light bouncing off the glossy cover. "You wanted to see me?" she asked.

Anxious energy zinged through me, my stomach flipping over on itself. This was it. Time to crack my heart wide open in front of this woman and tell her how I felt. "Yes. Listen, I..." I eyed her nervously before I glanced quickly at my sister behind the bar.

Fern nodded confidently, smiling, hands tucked in her apron pocket. The unnerving situation was made even all the more unreal when my gaze landed on Domino's image on the cover of *Vanity Fair,* which she held upside down and clutched against her. As if I needed a reminder this wasn't just any woman. This was a global superstar. Doubt trickled from the top of my head and through my chest like a diver hitting the water. *You can do it,* I told myself, drawing in a breath. I leaned forward, elbows on my knees, hands gripped in front of me.

"I know we agreed—"

"You should read this." Suddenly Domino was on her feet, pressing the magazine into my hands.

"I will. But first I—"

"You should read it now." She sat back in the chair, fidgeting with the ends of her hair. *Is she nervous, too?* She'd tucked one foot under her, but the sole of her other sneaker tapped against the floor.

I leaned back in the leather chair, staring down at the magazine in my lap. "O-okay." I couldn't shake the disappointment of being put on hold. Domino nodded at me encouragingly.

"Go on," she said, heel still bouncing. "Page forty-two."

I flipped through the magazine until I landed on a double-page spread of Domino, pictured at Grind

House, standing on a table in a sheer white dress, lit from behind like a Grecian goddess, a golden-brown doughnut in her hand. I sucked in a breath, then began to read.

The star of *Love Letters* and *The Muse* shares some truths about acting, producing, and—yes—*that* breakup

Domino West is in gray sweats, checking emails on her phone in the window of a hotel somewhere in the Pacific Northwest. It's drizzling outside, and Domino is running late. There's a photographer here to shoot her for this piece, waiting in the hallway while she dresses.

"Wouldn't it be nice to just stay here?" she says, finishing a plate of room-service fries.

She does her own makeup for photoshoots—a holdover from years on indie film sets in Canada. She disappears into the bathroom for what seems like half a second, reemerging in a stunning white Alexander McQueen gown.

"Time to go." She tosses her phone in a little black bag and leads the way to the door.

In the hallway a pair of tourists move aside to let us pass. "You look beautiful!" one shouts as the elevator doors begin to close, as if she'd gathered up the courage to shout it at the last minute.

"You do too!" West says.

~

I met West shortly after she arrived on Orcas Island, where she's been for a few weeks scouting a location for an upcoming movie—the first she's coproducing with partner Trudi Karp. She was wearing the kind of perfect vintage Levi's ten other women are, at any time, combing the shops of Melrose Avenue for. West and Karp have worked together almost five years. Karp was there before her star-making turn in *The Muse*, before her very public relationship with Harry Roman, and in the aftermath of it as well.

"I'd be lost without her," West says, chuckling.

Orcas Island has become a refuge for the A-list actress. "LA is great. But things got...chaotic. I love it here. It's peaceful." It really is beautiful, its towering old trees and miles of beaches like something out of a nature documentary.

West grew up in Toronto, the cultural capital of Canada, known for its diverse population, funky neighborhoods, and the Toronto International Film Fest—TIFF for short. That's where West got her start, walking red carpets for Canadian filmmakers David Cronenberg and Sarah Polley. But when starmaking agent Deidre Dunbow told her it was time to make a move, West relocated to LA, where she rents a modest bungalow in Venice Beach.

Her family stayed in Toronto—and have no intention of leaving. "They're lifers." She laughs.

"Of course I was worried about her going into this business," her mom told me by email. "But I've never been worried about whether she had the talent or magic."

Her mom's got it right. Light seems to travel with West wherever she goes. At today's shoot, which takes us from a tiny coffee shop in the town of Bayview to a beautiful—though windy—beach at the edge of the Pacific, West glows from head to toe.

Love Letters turned West into a breakout star—and introduced her to her famous boyfriend of the last eighteen months. During a break at the beach, I ask what it was like to date Harry Roman. "It was like being shot from a cannon," she says. "Kind of overwhelm-ing."

She sees something splash in the waves and leaps in the air. "Otters!" she cries happily. "Oh my god. Do you see them?"

Yes, I tell her. Two of them.

Before we leave the beach, we have one more sighting. Three paparazzi, huddled in black behind a boulder at the far end. I ask if it bothers her.

"Sometimes," she says. "I believe in kind-ness. That's not where they operate from." But West has learned island life suits her well. "Liv-ing out here, for me, has been really good." She smiles, and I sense she's leaving something out. I don't press her.

~

Two nights later, West and I meet at the Drift-wood Inn. We're perched at the bar, and as people file in to eat, I find myself adjusting my position to stop them from staring.

"That's okay," she assures me. "People here are so cool. They don't care."

I bring up the paparazzi again. "Humans are so fucking weird," she says. "Hollywood is a wild place. The lengths people will go to..."

Her thought trails off as she sips a glass of wine. She doesn't say, but I can't help but wonder if she's referring to the way her life was flipped upside down when the news of her recent breakup broke the internet.

I ask about her first turn as a producer. "I'm letting go of how others look at me," she says. "In my last two movies, the producers had a lot of creative control. That can be a battle. My turn." She sets her drink on the bar. "I feel like it's time for me to steer the ship of my career."

Ironically, rumors from the set of *Love Letters* usually involved a supposed feud between West and Roman. "There was never a moment when we didn't get along," she says. "It's weird. We were really there for each other. I trusted him. Until I didn't."

West pauses, struggling to tie a bow on the riddle.

"It was great for my career," she says. "But I'm glad things ended with Harry. It brought me here." She smiles again, like a cat with a secret. "It's been life-changing."

I wait for her to expand. Her cheeks turn a shade of pink I can only achieve with makeup.

"The love of my life is here," she says. "I'm

holding on forever."

I ask if that means she's moving to the Pacific Northwest for good. "I believe in following your heart," she says. "I'm hoping to make an investment here too."

My heart threatened to beat out of my chest. I read the words a second time. They blurred on the page as my eyes welled with tears. I wiped them with the backs of my hands, too embarrassed to meet Domino's gaze. I read on.

West checks her watch. Tomorrow she's due to meet with her producing team. Damon Mann is attached to the film, she tells me. Arthur Dagon is directing. He's recovering from an undisclosed illness here on the island.

"I pinch myself most mornings," she leans over and confides. "Is this all real?"

Right now it's time for us to shoot the last image for this piece. She goes upstairs to change, and, as we head out of the hotel, another guest warns us about paparazzi outside.

"What should I do?" I ask.

She laughs. "Just get in the car," she says, like it's the most obvious thing in the world.

I stared at Domino, mouth open. The magazine fell

closed in my lap. The look she returned was full of warmth, and her eyes, too, were shiny with tears.

"But this says..." I flipped the pages again, searching to find the article, sure I'd misread it or misinterpreted her words or imagined them on the page. But suddenly Domino was beside me, lifting the magazine from my lap and pulling me to my feet. She wrapped her arms around my neck.

"I know what it says."

"But who's the love of—"

She placed her pointer finger against my lips, her eyes dancing with twin flames from the fireplace. "It's you." Her eyes dropped to my lips, her smile turning to something like hunger.

"But I—"

This time she stopped me by pressing her lips against mine. "But nothing, you old grump," she murmured. "Kiss me."

CHAPTER 23

Domino

I hadn't meant to profess my love for Forest in the pages of a magazine. But talking to Poppy felt like talking to an old friend, and once it was out of my mouth, I didn't want to ever put it back in. Besides, there was something poetic about a public declaration of love after the very public breakup with Harry Roman.

Forest sat again in the big leather chair, pulling me into his lap. I kept my arms around his neck and nestled against his ear, enjoying being enveloped in his arms and that familiar scent of pine and Pacific.

He tucked a strand of hair behind my ear, cradling

my chin with his fingers, turning me so we could see each other straight on. "Domino?"

"Mmmm?"

"I love you."

I touched the end of my nose to his, our foreheads pressed together. A smile beamed across my face. Was *this* what love was supposed to feel like? If it was, I never wanted it to end. I wanted to capture this feeling in a bottle and keep it with me for the rest of my life. My tears fell on his cheeks, mixing with his own. I don't know how much time passed; it could have been seconds or it could have been eternity.

"Hey, lovebirds, get a room!" a voice called behind us, followed by a chorus of laughs.

I let go of Forest's neck and wiped the tears from my eyes. Smoothing my bangs, I looked over his shoulder to see Fern, Poppy, Marc, Bluebell, and a small group of other faces that'd grown familiar to me in the past two weeks. A hand went up at the back of the group, drawing my attention, and when I saw it was Angela, cheering her approval, fresh tears fell.

Forest lifted me off his lap, and we stood, facing everyone. He didn't make a move to dry his cheeks, just left our tears there for everyone to see. His willingness to be vulnerable made my heart skip a beat.

Bluebell popped the cork on a bottle of champagne. As a cheer went up, she filled two flutes Fern held, then filled another set in Marc's hands.

Fern presented a glass to each of us and held up her own, clearing her throat to silence the group. "I know what you're all thinking," she said loudly enough her voice carried. "That my brother would never find anyone who'd savor his bad moods the way he does himself." She paused for laughter. "But along came Domino. A literal ray of sunshine that could melt even the coldest icicle."

Fern reached for my hand and held it in hers. "Turns out it's not a bad mood." She giggled. "He just doesn't like anyone. Except Domino." A rumble of laughter went through the small crowd that'd assembled in front of us.

"In all seriousness. Domino, I know you're in the business of happy endings. But this is the beginning of an incredible love story. I'm so thrilled for you both." She clinked her glass against mine and Forest's, then held it up in the air. "To love!" she shouted.

"To love," people called back, raising their glasses in a toast.

Marc stepped forward as the other folks resumed chatting and returning to their tables. Forest's arm was draped over my shoulder. I wrapped mine around his rib cage, cuddling into that safe space between his armpit and chest. "So, Domino," Marc said in a singsong voice, "I guess this means you win."

"I do?"

"Seems even Arthur Dagon is impressed with your man. After the way Forest got him through his—what did Poppy write?—'undisclosed illness,' he's adamant we film *Shore Thing* here."

I squeezed Forest even harder. "He is?" My voice sounded a register higher than normal. "But this afternoon he was such an asshole. I was sure he thought this place was cursed."

"Eh, his bedside manner leaves a lot to be desired. But so does his personality in general." He threw back his head and laughed. "God, that felt good to let out. You shouldn't speak ill of the...ill, or something like that, but I can't help it. That guy's the *real* grump around here."

"Ha! Imagine that, Forest. You're a pussycat next to that guy." I rested a hand on Marc's arm. "But he'll do a great job with the movie. Won't he?"

"Might need to rethink that production space. But yes." Marc nodded and turned toward the bar. "Wouldn't put up with him if not," he called over his shoulder. "Glass is empty! Congratulations, you two."

I twirled under Forest's arm to face him, and he tilted his head to catch me in a tender kiss.

"Domino?"

"Mmm?" I said, cocooned in his warmth again.

"What's this investment you want to make?"

I crooned my neck and pressed my lips to his. "We can talk about that later. Right now I need you to whisk me to your room before I tear off your clothes right here."

Forest made love to me like a man at a river after a week in the desert. As the sun set outside the window, bathing the island in purple and gold, he kissed me from head to toe, moving his mouth over my breasts until I ached with need. When he flickered his tongue delicately across my clit, back and forth, back and forth, every cell in my body lit up like the stars in the night sky. Tension built inside me until I thought I might scream, and then finally, as Forest covered my pussy with his warm mouth, my body exploded with sensation, and I rode the waves of ecstasy until I was sated with oxytocin and afterglow. Afterward, I knelt before him and took him in my mouth, sucking until he pulsed in climax and cried my name.

I'd never felt so vulnerable, so exposed, so wide open to another human—and I was beginning to feel like I never wanted to close myself off again. My heart was more full than I'd imagined possible. Thanks to this man, on this island, in this magical little paradise. I was home. Forest was home. I finally belonged.

Later, after we'd lay naked, the blankets thrown off, exploring each other's bodies with our eyes and hands, we climbed into the shower together. I watched in awe as Forest ran soap over his muscled chest. He was beautiful. He was mine.

He called down to the kitchen and ordered dinner as I slipped into one of his old T-shirts and tied my hair in a bun using a pen I found on the table by the window. A knock sounded on the door, and he padded over to open it in gray sweatpants that should by all measures be the least sexiest thing a man could wear but were just the opposite. Fern raised an eyebrow at his bare chest and my bare legs but marched into the room, pushing a room-service trolley that held a bottle of champagne on ice, two flutes, two plates covered in silver domes, and a set of flickering candles. I stood by the bed, and as she passed me on her way back to the door, she grabbed my hand and squeezed it. "Told him yet?" she asked, then cast a glance at her brother before closing the door behind her.

Forest crossed his arms over his bare chest, feet firmly planted at shoulder width. I smiled, grabbed the trolley, and pushed it to the table. "Come on. It'll get cold," I said cheerfully.

"Told me what?" He wasn't moving.

I moved to him, grabbed hold of his arm and hugged it to my chest, tugging him to the table. "Sit," I told him and pointed at the chair. I crossed my own arms, waiting until he did. I lifted the champagne bottle from the bucket of ice and spun the label to face me. "Piper Heidsieck. That's not local." I laughed, tipping the bubbly golden wine into two glasses. "Fern's really outdone herself. Here."

"Hmph," Forest grunted but unfolded his arms to take his glass.

Under the silver domes I found linguine noodles topped with chicken breast, chopped cashews, mango, and sprigs of fresh basil. Setting both plates on the table, I took the seat across from Forest.

"I'm not eating until you tell me." The grump was back.

I picked up a fork and twirled it around in the noodles as steam rose around it. As I chewed, I held up the pointer finger on my other hand in askance for Forest to wait until I'd finished the bite. His forehead creased. I giggled around my mouthful of pasta.

"So Fern and I were talking this week. While you were hiding from me."

"I don't hide."

I raised an eyebrow. "I want to stay here, Forest. Make a life here." I set the fork down and took a sip of champagne. My fingers lingered around the stem as I set it on the table. "Anyway. I asked Fern what she thinks of taking on a partner."

Forest's food sat untouched in front of him. "She

already has one."

"A third partner, I mean. I love you. I love this place. I want to buy a stake in the hotel."

"No."

"What do you mean, no? We're a team, Forest. A team in love. I'd like to be a team in life, too."

"Look, I don't know what my sister told you, but I'm not using your fame to boost my business. Whatever you think it looks like—" the hurt in his eyes was plain "—the Driftwood is doing just fine. It was fine before you arrived, and it'll be fine after this."

I was pleased when he finally picked up a fork, a feeling that quickly reversed when he stabbed the noodles, sending nuts flying onto the table. I laid a hand on his. "Stop." The look he gave me could have cut the chicken on our plates. "I didn't explain that very well."

He dropped the utensil and crossed his arms again but seemed resigned to letting me speak.

"I know the Driftwood is fine. It's better than fine. It's perfect. I want us to work together to keep it that way. You—" I pointed at him, then my own chest "—me, and Fern. I'll be a silent partner if you want, but I want to be part of it in some way. I realize now I've been trying to belong somewhere my whole life. I've finally found where that is." I swiped a tear away.

"It's here, Forest. With you. *This* is where I belong."

Forest's anger melted like an ice cream on a hot day. He got to his feet, knocking his chair with the backs of his knees, and knelt in front of me, grasping my hands. "I'm so sorry." His eyes burned with remorse. "I'm sorry," he said again. "Can you forgive me?"

"If you'll let me into your life—your *whole* life."

"I will," he promised. "I misunderstood…" He got off his knees and sat in the chair again. Shaking his head, he added, "I do that a lot."

I reached across to touch him. "I believe in you, Forest. I trust you. With my whole heart. I'm not here to question you or doubt you or second guess you. Ever. I promise." When Forest leaned forward, his chest precariously close to the candles, to plant a kiss on my lips, I knew he believed me. Believed in us.

I had to shoo him away when the kiss began to heat up. "Okay," I said, laughing. "Eat, will you? Before it's well and truly cold."

Over linguine and champagne, we discussed the future—ours, the hotel's, and what we hoped this wild little island in the Pacific had in store for us. I told him Fern and I had talked about digitizing reservations and updating the website. About how important—how crucial—social media would be for the business moving forward.

And about how no matter where my career took me for shoots or press or anything else, I'd always come back to Orcas Island. This is where my heart lived now. The place I'd never known I needed.

To read the bonus epilogue for *The Farthest Star*, sign up for Sally's newsletter:
BookHip.com/GNXVTSQ

Get book 2 in the series, *Second Chance Rose*:
geni.us/secondchanceros

ABOUT THE AUTHOR

Sally Glover is the author of the Wildflower books, set in the Pacific Northwest. She lives and writes on Vancouver Island, a wild little paradise on the west coast of Canada.

Website: sallyglover.com
Instagram: @sallygloverwrites
Amazon: @sallygloverwrites
Newsletter: geni.us/sglovernew
Goodreads: goodreads.com/sallygloverwrites
BookBub: bookbub.com/authors/sally-glover